Scotsman in the Stacks

ALANA OXFORD

8N PUBLISHING

First published by 8N Publishing, 2022

This novel is entirely a work of fiction. The names, characters and incidents portrayed in it are the work of the author's imagination. Any resemblance to actual persons, living or dead, events or localities is entirely coincidental.

Alana Oxford asserts the moral right to be identified as the author of this work.

First edition

Cover design by Purpose on Paper
Interior design by Nicole Scarano

Contents

"A very cute, feel-good book with Hallmark movie energy."

-NETGALLEY REVIEWER

"This is a sweet, uplifting romantic comedy that is perfect if you want something light and fun."

-NETGALLEY REVIEWER

"Definitely, a love letter to Michigan."

-NETGALLEY REVIEWER

"Adorable, cute, funny romance that I read in one whole sitting!"

-NETGALLEY REVIEWER

"This will make a great summer read, it was heartfelt and beautiful. And filled with all great characters!"

-NETGALLEY REVIEWER

"A super cute rom-com that had a fun little road trip that had me questioning if I should go to Michigan and if I should be a librarian."

-NETGALLEY REVIEWER

To Karen and Rhys

Yours is the most magical real-life library romance I had the honor to witness

Guide to Scottish Terms Used in This Book

- A & E - Accident and Emergency Department (Emergency Room)
- Aye - yes
- Braw - good, fine
- Caird - card
- Cannae - can't
- Couldnae - couldn't
- Didnae - didn't
- Dinnae - don't
- Dinnae ken - don't know
- Guid - good
- Isnae - isn't
- No' - not
- O' - of
- Och - an expression of surprise or regret
- Tae - to
- Wee - small, little
- Willnae - won't
- Wouldnae - wouldn't

$\mathcal{One}$

NERVOUS? Of course she was nervous. Paige had never proposed to anyone before. Had never even considered it, to be honest. When she'd thought of her engagement to Dylan, she'd assumed it would be traditional. He might not get down on one knee, but she figured he'd at least declare his undying love, present her with a ring, and ask her to be his wife.

She may be a librarian with a penchant for love stories and happy endings, but she didn't think she had unrealistic expectations for a proposal.

Her apartment smelled delicious. She peeked through the glass lid of her slow cooker at the pork tenderloin cooking inside. It had been marinating in apricot glaze and she hoped it would be as good as it smelled.

The truth was, she was tired of waiting for Dylan to get around to it…to the tune of six and a half years tired. No, she hadn't really been counting down from the day he asked her out. She wasn't that ridiculous. But they had been together for more than enough time. She'd dropped plenty of hints, which had been deflected, but she wouldn't be deflected anymore. It was time to officially start their life together. If he was too nervous to do it, she'd just have to defy convention and do it herself.

"It's fine," she murmured to herself as she turned down the burners on the potatoes and green beans. "I'm a modern woman. I can do this."

While the tenderloin finished cooking, she stepped into her modest dining area to make sure everything was ready. She'd purchased a new tablecloth for the occasion, white with scalloped edges and silver embroidered embellishments. It had cost a little more than she'd wanted to spend on a tablecloth, but she figured it would become the special occasion cloth for the rest of their lives. Might as well do it right to begin with.

The clean white walls of her apartment, paired with the white tablecloth, had seemed a little too sterile for her liking. To combat so much winter white, she added a hurricane shade with burgundy pillar candles in the middle of a simple wreath of greenery as the centerpiece.

It looked cozy and elegant to her. A quiet setting for the momentous occasion.

The buzzer rang, signaling that he'd arrived.

Paige smoothed her hair, rubbed her lips together to freshen the lipstick she'd put on a little earlier, and quickly lit the candles.

This was it. The scene was finally set for her engagement. It may not be the way she'd imagined, but at least she wouldn't be waiting any longer.

She pressed the button to let Dylan in. The sound of footsteps on the stairs outside her door marked his progress up to her apartment. She'd already unlocked the door for him.

He gave a light knock before coming in, as was his habit.

She hurried to the door to greet him with a quick kiss.

"How was work?" she asked at the same moment he said, "Sorry I'm late."

She should have noticed that his eyes drooped in tiredness, but she didn't. The jittery feeling coursing through her body didn't leave much room for observation.

"No worries." She smiled in a way that didn't reach her eyes, but Dylan wasn't looking at her face anyway. He was busy getting out of his winter coat and hanging it in the closet. "Dinner took a little longer than I expected, but it's ready now. Why don't you sit down and I'll pour the drinks."

She disappeared into her tiny kitchen and Dylan did as she said, collapsing into his usual chair at the table. He was rubbing his hands over his face when Paige came back to pour the milk.

"You ok?" she asked, once the glasses were full.

Dylan blinked a few times and shook it off.

"Just tired. We've got a tight deadline on this project. They wanted me to stay later, but I told them I needed to at least go take a dinner break. I don't know if I'll go back tonight or just go in super early tomorrow."

That was already a monkey wrench in her evening, but Paige understood. Sort of. Well, she'd learned that Dylan kept crazy hours in his graphic design position for the ad agency. It wasn't worth fussing over. It was just part of the gig. A crappy part, but overall, Dylan enjoyed his job. He made good money, which was an excellent counterbalance to the wimpy part-time pay she brought home from her librarian job. Nobody became a librarian for the money, and Paige was living proof of that.

She set down the pork tenderloin on her nicest serving platter, which had been a fun find at the thrift store. She served the green beans and mashed potatoes in mismatched bowls and sat down with Dylan.

"Everything looks great." Dylan helped himself to a generous portion of the pork.

"Thanks. It smells really good, so we'll see. I haven't tried this recipe before but it looked great in the picture. Mine doesn't quite look like the one in the cookbook, but looks can be deceiving." She was feeling a little rambly. She'd have to cut through the small talk and get to the point or she'd end up babbling like an idiot.

Dylan cut a bite from the meat and held it up on his fork.

"Moment of truth!"

Paige smiled nervously as he popped the fork in his mouth.

"Mmm. Paige. This is really good. You nailed it."

She didn't relax at all. The state of the pork wasn't her biggest concern at the moment.

"Oh good." She took a deep breath. "So, Dylan. I was thinking—"

Paige had thought about proposing but not specifically what she'd say. Now that she was in the moment, she felt at a loss for words. She knew what the heroes usually said in the movies or in romance novels. She even knew, mostly, what Eric had said to her best friend, Kayla, when he proposed a couple years back. It had seemed like she'd just know what to say when the moment came, but apparently she'd been wrong about that.

She tried again.

"I mean, now that you've got this great raise, I was thinking about our future."

It was a song and dance they'd been through before, but she had a completely different ending in mind this time, if she could just figure out how to get to it.

The fluttering in her stomach reminded her of the way she felt on roller coasters, scared and a little bit sick. But excitement was like that. Only a hair's breadth away from fear. The only way to get over it was to get through. She just had to forge ahead and say it.

Dylan looked up, as if seeing her and the special setup at the table for the first time. His eyes widened for a moment, not unlike a deer in headlights, but the look passed in a split second. "That reminds me, I've been thinking about our future too." He set down his fork and grinned nervously. "I think you'll be really happy."

Paige's already hammering heart managed to increase its rhythm. Was Dylan hijacking her proposal to propose himself? He was right. She would be really happy with that!

"Ok." She encouraged him without leading the conversation. She'd tried to lead too many times with poor results.

She could tell he'd started bouncing his knee, so he must be just as nervous as her. That had to be a good sign.

"Well, I was thinking that it's probably time to move our relationship to the next level." He peered down at his plate as if he couldn't quite bear the intensity of her gaze.

She could hardly believe he was finally saying this.

"Yeah?" She nodded encouragement. "I agree." She more than agreed. He knew that very well.

"I know your landlord is raising your rent once your lease is up this summer, so I was thinking…" He took a deep breath and smiled at her.

This had to be it. He was finally, FINALLY, going to propose. She'd dreamt of this moment for literally years. All the anxiety about getting married and starting a family that she'd been grappling with suddenly melted away as she was facing down this magical moment. Her time had finally arrived.

Paige sat up a little straighter and put down the fork she realized she was clutching.

"Paige…what if you gave up this place when your lease runs out and you could move in with me?"

Dylan stared at her with raised eyebrows. His lips were pressed together as he awaited her answer. He didn't seem to be on the verge of saying anything else.

"And?" Paige prompted, thinking perhaps he just needed a little more of a nudge to get there.

He chuckled. "And maybe get a cat or something? That would be fun, wouldn't it?"

Her excitement from just moments before was a million miles away; a cold, frosty memory. The butterflies must have migrated because they were no longer stirring things up in her stomach region. In their place was something more like a lump of charcoal beginning to catch flame. Not the sexy fire of desire. No, this felt like the first spark of arson.

"So you're asking me to move in with you and get a cat?" She had a glint of an edge in her voice that Dylan didn't seem to notice.

He leaned forward, closer to her, his face smoothing into confidence.

"Yeah. You know? We could try things out. Really see if we're compatible for the long haul. Get started with the next phase of our lives."

The explanation was vastly worse than the omission of the question she'd been hoping for.

"See if we're compatible?" The words struck the charcoal in her core and ignited the brittle husk of her feelings for Dylan. "What have we been doing for the past six and a half years then? You know I don't want to move in with you until we're at least engaged. Don't you think it's time to do that?"

Dylan blew out a long breath as if this was new information he hadn't foreseen.

"Come on, Paige. People live together before they get married. That's not a crazy idea. People are different when they live together than when they're just dating. You know that."

Paige's hands were shaking, so she mashed them into her lap.

"It's not like we haven't slept over at each other's apartments a thousand times. There aren't any real surprises here, Dylan, are there? You just don't want to get married, do you? Or, maybe, worse than that, you don't want to marry me."

Dylan closed his eyes for a moment before he tackled responding to that grenade.

"You know I love you, Paige. I don't get why you're acting like moving in is so different from getting married. You know the only women I've ever lived with are my mom and my sister. This is huge. I thought you'd be happy."

Not only did his words hit her, but so did a terrifying realization. It was like her subconscious had come forward and slapped her right across the face and then dumped a bucket of ice cubes over her head. Despite all the years they'd spent together, Dylan did not love her. Maybe he thought he did, but he certainly didn't love her the way her future husband should.

See if we're compatible. The phrase circled around in her brain like a car crash on a carousel. Around and around, again and again, until it turned into a sickening, ugly, blur.

There was nothing Dylan could have said that would hurt worse. Not even if he'd said he'd met someone else and they were running away together once he finished the dinner Paige had served him. After all these years, what had he been doing? Biding his time? Waiting to see if someone better came along? *See if we're compatible?* She'd been waiting, patiently at first, less so in the last couple years, to marry this man, and he didn't know her at all.

Paige stared at Dylan as he looked back like a surly teenager. For the first time in a long time, she saw exactly what was sitting across the table from her. A classic commitment-phobe who would never give her the life she wanted. While he'd been busy waiting and seeing, she'd been dreaming of the babies they'd have and the house they'd buy in the same neighborhood as Kayla and Eric. It had all been a fantasy. A stupid fiction she'd created for her life rather than seeing the truth right in front of her.

Dylan did not love her the way she'd loved him and she had no more patience for him.

Her colliding emotions were so strong she could feel them about to burst her body. While she might have thought a primal scream was about to erupt, even her own body surprised her. It wasn't the sound of rage that came out, rather, she started laughing.

To her own ears, the sound was hollow and mirthless, but from his reaction, that wasn't the impression Dylan got at all.

His features smoothed and he sat back in his seat, comfortable, and started to laugh too. Did he actually think she was happy with his worthless concession? Too little. Too late.

They laughed and laughed together until tears streamed down Paige's face. They weren't happy tears, but Dylan was too inattentive to tell the difference.

In the moment, she was mostly angry with him, but also supremely disappointed in herself for being such a fool. How could she have been so duped? So weak? So desperate to enjoy a happy marriage, like her own parents, and start a family alongside Kayla, that she refused to see that her chosen mate wasn't interested in those things?

It was a classic error and she'd never felt like such an idiot in her entire life.

The laughter was well and truly over now, and she was just openly sobbing.

Dylan leaned forward in his seat again, his face going serious.

"Hey, are you ok?"

She grabbed her napkin and smashed it to her face.

"No," she managed to say, shaking her head emphatically. "I want you to leave."

Words she thought she'd never say. Not to Dylan, of all people.

"Leave? Paige. What's wrong?" He got out of his chair and came around to kneel next to her.

Of course, now he'd kneel next to her. Not the way she'd imagined he might.

She shook her head again, too emotional to put anything into words at the moment.

"Hey. I know it's scary. It's a big step. If you're not ready that's ok. I just thought that's what you wanted. If it isn't, we can wait." He tried to take her hand, but she pulled it away.

She wanted to laugh ruefully, but the sound that came out was more like a choke.

"What I want is to get married and start a family. I don't need to live with you to see if we're compatible. I know right now we're not and I'm not wasting any more of my time on you. Please leave."

Dylan had the audacity to look stung. Really? Like she hadn't been showing him jewelry ads and talking about their lives together. That wasn't exactly the conversation of someone who wanted to move in together and see where things might go.

"So, what? I ask you to move in with me and now we're breaking up?" Dylan stood up and backed away from Paige like she was contagious.

"Yes." Paige said. "If you don't know by now that you want to stay together forever, moving in isn't going to fix that. Go find what you're actually looking for. I can tell it isn't me."

Paige's voice trailed off into sobs again, but luckily she'd been able to make her point before going unintelligible.

With nothing more to say, Dylan turned away and left Paige's apartment. He'd just proven her point. She wasn't what he wanted, otherwise he would have stayed to talk things out. He really had been biding his time waiting for someone better to show up. That was the thing that seared into her heart. She hadn't been enough for Dylan. And now, she was farther from her goal than ever.

At twenty-nine years old, she was single, her biological clock ticking, and she didn't know any single men under seventy years old. The library wasn't exactly a hotbed of eligible young men.

She may as well embrace the stereotype. Once she stopped crying and cleaned up the largely untouched dinner, she should head straight to the humane society and adopt a cat lady starter pack. Probably three cats would be good to begin. Then she'd have to grow out her straight brown hair so she could start wearing it in a bun. She already wore glasses and cardigans so her librarian spinster persona was nearly complete.

She would have laughed again if she didn't feel so sorry for herself. After all those years, she was left with nothing and she didn't know what to do.

Two

JUNE - TODAY

PAIGE'S happy place was standing in front of the new bookshelf. It was especially wonderful in that quiet hour before the library opened. With no patrons to help, no prying eyes peeking at her selections, she could just bask in the possibilities offered in each lovely volume.

She was in the mood for literary comfort food and the available books that morning did not disappoint. There were so many beautiful summer romcoms, the covers with color palettes like rainbow sherbet. She picked up *The Summer We Met*, *Rogue of My Heart*, and *Love at Loch Ness*. They promised to sweep her up in plenty of swoon-worthy adventures to warm her frustrated heart.

God knows her own love life had turned into a lonely disaster, so she had to live vicariously through the happy couples in the books. When those heroines had a commitment-phobic boyfriend, he'd come around after the black period with a grand romantic gesture. Or, if that wasn't the case, she'd dump the emotional freeloader and the real man of her dreams was right around the corner.

Neither of those things had happened for Paige. In fact, in the six months since her breakup with Dylan, her black period became even blacker when her landlord gave notice of an uncomfortably high rent increase coming soon. As if that wasn't upsetting enough, she hadn't so much as seen an attractive, single man. The fact that she only went to work and to her married best friend Kayla's house was beside the point.

Clearly, drowning her sorrows in fiction was her best option.

She turned over *Love at Loch Ness* to read the back. It'd be perfect for Kayla.

"Which one you got there?"

Paige turned, surprised that her quiet opening ritual was cut short by her boss, Christie's voice.

"This one." Paige held up the book so Christie could see the cover. "My best friend has been a Nessie fan for as long as I've known her. I thought she might enjoy a Loch Ness romance while she's waiting out the last weeks of her pregnancy."

Christie nodded in understanding. "That's a great cover. I like the cartoon Nessie between the man and woman. Looks like a fun read."

"I mean, who doesn't want to see the Loch Ness monster and fall in love at the same time?"

"You're not wrong," Christie laughed before her face went serious and she changed the subject.

"Hey, while I caught you in a quiet moment, I wanted to give you a heads up on something."

Even though Christie was a great boss, her comment hit Paige with a little apprehension. She hoped she hadn't done anything wrong.

"Sure. What's up?" Paige cradled the books in her arms and did her best to sound breezy and casual.

"I don't know if Yolanda's said anything to you or not, but she's going to be retiring at the end of the summer. Now that her son and his wife are having a baby, she wants to move to be closer to them and be a full time grandma. In the meantime, we're going to be transitioning some of her bigger projects to other staff and I'd like you to take over the book discussion group."

Paige gripped the books tighter in her arms as she absorbed the news.

"Wow, she's retiring? She's been talking about becoming a

grandma non-stop so that'll be wonderful for her. And I'd be happy to do the book discussions. It sounds like a lot of fun."

"Well—" Christie hesitated a little, the serious expression on her face bringing Paige back to earth. "The thing is, the book discussion has been dwindling. It's been in a decline for a while now. There's a core group of regulars, but they're getting pretty old. I'm worried if we don't revitalize the group, it's going to fade away. I think having you take over will be a nice break from the way we've always done it and give us a chance to try some fresh ideas.

I'd like to have you co-run it with Yolanda next Saturday so the regulars can have both of you there before the full hand off."

Paige was already scheduled to work next Saturday, so it was no problem schedule-wise. She knew the book was something to do with sailing, which wasn't particularly her cup of tea, but it was a relatively short book. She could get it read in a week.

It was a lot to take in, but just the kind of challenge Paige was looking for. How to revive a book discussion group? It would take some brainstorming, but she knew she could do it.

"No problem. I can do that!" She was already mentally sifting through what she could do to contribute to the discussion with Yolanda, but there was one other thing on her mind.

"Do you know, by any chance, if you're going to post Yolanda's position?"

Public libraries were notorious for either not filling vacant full-time positions, or turning them into two, or even one, part-time position. The reality of being a single woman without any romantic prospects had forced her to reevaluate her priorities. Part-time work was fine when she thought she'd be engaged and leaving her apartment to move in with Dylan. Now she had even more difficult choices to make, like whether she could comfortably afford the impending rent hike or if she'd have to move somewhere cheaper. With Yolanda retiring, there was a tiny inkling that at least something might be looking up for Paige.

Christie cocked her head as she considered her answer, causing Paige's heart to beat faster in anticipation.

"I have to meet with John to discuss it. I want to fill it, but we'll have to see how it goes."

Paige desperately hoped John, the library director, would be on the same page as Christie.

"Anyway," Christie nodded her head toward the front door. "Some of the regulars are already chomping at the bit. I'll let you get to it."

Conscious of the waiting patrons watching her every move, Paige put away the books she'd selected and started getting the department ready to open.

By the time the doors were opened, Paige had everything ready to go and her mind buzzed with excitement about taking over the book discussion. She was already searching online to see what other libraries were doing, when she was interrupted by a familiar voice.

"Hey, it's Librarian Paige. I haven't seen you around for a while. Thought you got fired!"

Paige's heart sank as she looked up from the reference desk computer and saw one of her overly-friendly regulars, Norman Gorsfield, standing in front of her. After five years of reference librarianship, she'd tried her hardest to hone her peripheral vision to the point that annoying regulars couldn't sneak up on her, but sometimes, she just got too caught up in actually doing her work to notice.

Paunchy and balding, complexion like bread dough, he stood grinning like he'd just come up with the funniest line the world of comedy had ever heard. He couldn't be a day under seventy and the way he always swept his gaze over her, from bosom to eyes, when he talked made her skin crawl. He looked a little underdressed today as well. Although the forecast predicted a 90 degree June day (a little too hot for early summer in Michigan), he only wore a loose fitting tank top and nylon running shorts. The embarrassingly short kind. As in, everyone who looked at them felt embarrassed, but not the person wearing them. The distinct lack of perspiration on him was both a blessing and an indication that he hadn't just jogged up to the library. He probably could have put on something that covered a bit more flesh, but that was Norm for you.

Paige pulled her white cotton cardigan closed around her chest and smiled weakly in response to Norm's stale and all too familiar "joke."

"Oh, I've been here. Just busy." She kept her eyes on her computer screen. She was ever hopeful that if she didn't bother with eye contact, Norm would get the hint and leave her alone. Unfortunately, it had never happened yet.

"Every time I see you, you're so busy!" he huffed with exasperation.

"Yep. That's because I'm at work. Working." She punctuated her comment with a small smile to indicate that she wasn't being rude, but she wasn't in the mood to chat either. Customer service was a fine line between keeping the patron happy and trying to maintain personal boundaries too. Paige often struggled with the latter and patrons like Norm were expert at taking advantage of it.

Instead of taking a hint and moving along to conduct his own business, Norm launched into a rundown of a true crime mini-series he'd been watching that Paige "would just love."

Paige felt her blood pressure rising as she tried to figure out a way to shut him down so she could work on ideas for the book discussion. Impressing Christie with a stellar plan for improving the discussions could literally improve her life situation. Listening to Norm praise a show for its depictions of human depravity and cruelty, would not.

While Paige waited for Norm to tire of talking at her, she noticed a sweep of motion from the corner of her eye. A middle-aged woman with flowing gray hair and an equally flowing earth-toned skirt was leading a group into the library. The rest of them looked to be around Paige's age. One of them was a petite young woman with black hair cut into a dramatic geometric bob. She was wearing a tight cherry-red halter top and wide-legged white pants. Her style was intimidating but lovely.

The rest of the people in the little group were men. One of them was a tall, thin man with deep brown skin. His head was shaved bald and it looked really good on him. He was wearing a simple white t-shirt and a pair of black track pants with a white stripe on the leg.

In contrast, the man next to him had a head of wavy black hair that hung to his shoulders. He was wearing black rimmed glasses, a pastel green button-down shirt and suspenders with his tight black pants.

The last man made Paige sit up straighter, suddenly conscious of good posture and possible fly-away hairs.

This man had the most beautiful auburn hair. It hung to mid-cheek length and her heart beat a little quicker when he lifted a hand to push it back from his face. He had a light, well-trimmed goatee. Of the three men, he had the most muscular arms and chest, shown to good effect in a snug navy t-shirt and black jeans.

The group walked right behind Norm and into the non-fiction section where they disappeared into the stacks. Pity they didn't need any help. Any one of that group would have been welcome to linger at the desk and have a conversation with her…especially that redhead. Why was it only the likes of Norm who actually did?

Norm finally finished his preamble and wandered over to the computer area where she knew he'd easily get sucked into the wormhole of the internet for a couple hours. At least it would give her a reprieve from his chatter.

She hoped to at least catch a glimpse of the redhead again before he and his group left, but she didn't. Oh well. What did it matter? It's not like she was going to find love at the library anyway. She needed to come up with a viable plan for meeting worthwhile men, but first she had a book discussion to rescue and hopefully, a promotion to land.

Three

AT THE END of her shift, Paige pushed the heavy staff door open and blinked into the dazzling June sunshine. After a long, dark winter, and a cold, gray spring, Paige relished the moment to soak the rays into her skin and breathe in the warm air. Three in the afternoon was so much nicer when sunset wasn't looming within the hour. Bright, sunny days didn't stick around nearly long enough in Michigan so you had to make the most of them when you could.

Paige jumped into her car with a bulging tote bag of books. This time, most of the books weren't for her. She had a very important delivery to make before heading home.

While she drove, she decided to make a quick call to her parents to check in with them. Her dad had taken an early retirement package from Ford Motor Company and they'd moved to Florida a year ago "so we can enjoy it before we get too old." While Paige missed having her parents around every day, she was happy they had the opportunity to soak up the sun all year, plus, it gave her a nice place to visit whenever she needed a break from the long Michigan winters.

"Hi honey!" The cheerful, booming voice of her dad made her smile instantly. "We're just about to head to Liz and Stuart's for poker and an early dinner. How are you doing?"

"That sounds fun. I won't keep you long. I just wanted to let you know there might be a full time position opening at the library soon. Yolanda is retiring."

"That's wonderful, dear! Which one is Yolanda, again?"

Paige smiled. Her dad did his best to keep up with her library stories but sometimes the details got a little fuzzy. "She's the one whose son is going to have a baby. Her first grandchild."

"Good for her. Sounds like the perfect time to retire and enjoy that grandbaby."

"Who has a grandbaby?" Paige could hear her mother in the background.

"Here." There was a beep from her parents' side of the line. "I put it on speaker so your mom can hear too."

"Oh, is it Paige? Hi honey!"

"Hi Mom." She quickly filled her mom in on the possible job opening and her hopes to get it.

"Wouldn't that be wonderful? You're such a great librarian, I bet you'll be top of their list. I'll tell the ladies in my prayer group about it and we'll all be praying it works out."

"Thanks Mom." She could use any and all types of intervention she could get. Paige hadn't told her parents about the impending rent increase because she hadn't wanted to worry them. They were already crushed for her about the Dylan situation, but if they knew she was worried about how she'd afford her apartment, they'd probably send her a wad of cash and that's not what she wanted. She was old enough to make her own way in life, and that's what she intended to do. Even if it meant moving to a smaller, cheaper, apartment.

"Well, I'm nearly to Kayla and Eric's. I'm dropping off some books for her."

"That's so sweet of you. Tell Kayla we say hi! She must be getting anxious for that little one to get here. Did she find out what she's having?"

Paige had met Kayla in high school and they'd been best friends ever since. They'd spent so much time at each other's family's houses over the years that it was like they had two sets of parents.

"No, they want to be surprised when the baby's born."

"I don't know how the women these days have the patience for that. We wanted to find out as soon as possible when we had you. Didn't we, dear?"

"Yes we did." Paige's dad agreed. "Couldn't wait to find out."

Paige smiled at the idea of her parents as a young couple awaiting their only child. They were so cute. "I'll give her an extra hug for both of you. I'm pulling into the driveway now, so I better go. Have fun at dinner!"

"We will! Love you!" her parents called in unison. "Hope the promotion works out!" her dad added before they hung up.

Paige thought about how lucky she was to have supportive parents as she parked her car. Even from across the country, they could still make her feel like everything would turn out for the best. She only hoped they were right.

In a minute, she stood outside Kayla's house, knocking on the front door.

"I'm coming!" Paige heard Kayla's voice calling from inside. "Just takes me a bit to get there."

Paige shifted the tote bag strap on her shoulder, since it was really digging in under the weight of the books.

It was only a moment later when a heavily pregnant Kayla opened the door. Her long, black hair was pulled back in a ponytail. She was wearing her glasses instead of her preferred contacts, silently warning that she was tired or already having a rough day. She also had on an adorable knee-length maternity skirt in rainbow stripes and a flowy peach colored tank top. Paige noted, with a grin, that Kayla was also barefoot.

"Barefoot and pregnant, huh?" Paige teased.

"Please, have you seen my cankles? I'm not stuffing these sausage feet into shoes or sandals if I can help it. And, what is it outside? 120 degrees?" She fanned her hand at her face, which was looking a little pink. "You're lucky I didn't answer the door naked. This weather is way too hot for pregnant women."

Paige laughed and pulled Kayla in as close as she could with the enormous baby belly in between them.

"Well, you look beautiful. No one can tell you're anything other than radiantly pregnant."

Kayla scoffed and blew away a stray strand of hair that had escaped from her ponytail.

"I love you, but you're such a liar sometimes," Kayla teased.

"Hi Paige!" Kayla's husband Eric was nothing more than a disembodied voice coming down the hall, along with the sound of clanking dishes. He was a very good man like that, even more so now that Kayla was pregnant. It was almost as if he thought she'd break if she did too much. It was adorable, and Paige had no doubt he'd be just as attentive when the baby arrived. Kayla was truly lucky.

"Hi Eric! I'm just here to bring your wife some books."

"Thank God!" Eric called back. "I think she goes through two or three a day lately."

"He's right," Kayla agreed, ushering Paige into the living room to sit down and get comfy on the couch. "There's not much else you can do when you're this pregnant. Netflix and books are my favorite activities. Besides, it's not like there's going to be much time for that anymore after little one shows up."

"What's he doing home already?" Paige plunked her heavy bag on the floor and nestled into the sage green overstuffed reclining couch that she absolutely coveted. Like so many other Michiganders, Eric worked in the automotive industry, in the advanced polymers technology department. It sounded like a lot of math and science to her, so she just trusted it was a good job and they didn't talk about it. It wasn't a holiday, so she was surprised he wasn't at work at 3:30pm on a weekday.

"He worked a half day in the office and then came home early to go to my prenatal appointment with me."

"That makes sense. How'd it go?"

Kayla shrugged. "The new standard. Got probed by the doctor. Peed in a cup, which is no small feat when you have a belly like this to reach around. It was a rip-roaring good time."

Paige laughed, trying to remember the last time she'd had to pee into a cup. Maybe a UTI test when she was in college. It hadn't been a very dignified experience then, and she could only imagine trying to do it with a large watermelon belly. She reached into her bag and began to pull out the contents for Kayla.

"Glad the doctor went well. Here are the books you wanted, and a few others I thought you might enjoy." She handed the books one-by-one to Kayla so she could see her reaction. That was the best part of picking out books for someone, seeing their face light up when they held just the right one. Librarian matchmaking at its finest.

"*Your Birthing Options*. Yes! The ladies in my prenatal water aerobics class said this is a really good one. *The Beginners Guide to Breastfeeding*. God, sounds so scary but I heard it's a good one too. *Sleeping Through the Night: How to Start Your Baby on the Path to Good Sleep from Night One*. Not sure how legit this one is, but figured I might as well try. And, *Birth Without Fear - Harness Your Inner Womanity to Experience the Birth You Want*. Perfect. Thank you Paige. God, it's good to have my own personal librarian."

"But that's not all!" Paige clutched her tote bag like it was Santa's toy sack. "These are the ones you didn't ask for." She pulled out a short stack of paperbacks and handed them over to Kayla.

"*Love at Loch Ness*?" Kayla laughed at the title of the first book in the stack, but there was no mistaking that twinkle in her eye.

"If you have all this time to kill pre-baby, you might as well be enjoying a few romcoms. I thought of you the second I saw it on the new book shelf. Mythical beasts bringing people together for a love connection? Yes, please!"

Kayla flipped the book over and eagerly read the back cover aloud.

"Tessa Green just knows that Nessie exists and she's going to prove it. She brings a team of divers from her New England hometown and sets off for a sabbatical at Loch Ness. She's determined to find real evidence of the beloved creature, but first she'll have to get past Fergus MacDougall. He's salty, not a fan of Americans, and certainly not a fan of folks looking to disturb the local legend. But as they clash over dive time and boat regulations, they dredge up more than evidence of a sea monster. Could their shared love of Nessie turn into love for each other as well?"

Kayla clutched the book to her chest.

"Ooh, you know me so well. I'm going to have to start this tonight. Did you read it already?"

"I thought I'd let you read it first. But I'm absolutely going to read it when you're done."

Paige leaned back on the couch, totally comfortable. She kicked off her flats and put her feet up on the coffee table, as only a best friend is allowed to do.

"Nailed it!" Paige said, congratulating herself on a job well done.

"Of course you did." Kayla slumped back into the couch too, but kept the Loch Ness book in one hand, resting the other hand atop her round belly. "You're the best librarian there is."

"Good enough to score a promotion, you suppose?"

If she hadn't been pregnant and tired, Kayla would have sat up and squeezed Paige's arm. Since she was both of those things, she just lolled her head over to look at Paige.

"Seriously? There's a promotion available? Spill it."

Paige filled Kayla in on Yolanda's pending retirement.

"Of course you'll get it. This is you we're talking about. The best employee they have." Kayla was in full-on supportive friend mode. "Not only do you deliver books to your heavily pregnant best friend, you plan the best programs, have the friendliest smile of any librarian ever, and you genuinely care about people. Even those annoying ones who come in and bug you all the time. They're fun to complain about, but I know you have a heart for them too. There's no other choice for that position. Tell me who I have to talk to and I'll make it happen myself."

"I hope so. They just have to decide to fill it first. I'll lose what's left of my mind if I don't get it. It wasn't so dire when I thought Dylan and I had a future, but now I really need to rely on myself here. It's kind of scary."

Kayla snorted and shook her head.

"You don't need Dylan. You're more than capable of making it on your own. You've been doing just fine, thank you very much. Clearly, he was only holding you back. I mean, look at the facts. Now he's gone and you're up for a promotion that hasn't been available in all the years you were with him. Coincidence? I think not."

Paige smirked. "I hardly think breaking up with Dylan was the catalyst for Yolanda deciding to retire."

Kayla shrugged. "Maybe not directly, no, but you know, there's something to the power of positive thinking. You make a positive change and positive energy follows."

Paige glanced at Kayla in all her pregnant beauty. It was true what people said about some women absolutely glowing in their pregnancy. Kayla was one of them. She had the love of a wonderful husband, a bright cozy home, and was soon to have a perfect little baby to expand their family. That was positive energy. Not breaking up with the man you'd envisioned marrying. She didn't want to get stuck in the sad old adage of "wasting her good years," but she had to be realistic. Wasn't it easier to find a mate before turning thirty? College was a ripe picking ground for meeting similarly minded people. What was left now? Bars? She really wasn't a drinker. "Dating" apps that seemed to actually be sex apps. That wasn't what she was looking for. What was she going to do if she didn't want to end up alone in a one bedroom apartment forever?

"What's this?" Kayla fluttered her hand at Paige's face. "Brooding. I see you brooding."

She couldn't hide anything from Kayla. They knew each other too well.

Paige sighed. "Yeah, I am. You know. I just wanted to be planning my wedding right now. Not worrying about how I'm going to get by on my piddly salary if the promotion doesn't come through. I didn't want to be making it alone at this stage in the game, and I'm still mad that I didn't realize sooner that Dylan was a classic commitment-phobe. If I'd just walked away when I started seeing warning signs, I could have found someone who wanted the same future as me. That's all."

"Oh, Paige." Kayla sat up straight and grabbed Paige's hand.

"You're not alone at all. You know me and Eric are here for you no matter what."

Paige's heart swelled as her eyes got a little misty. "Thank you. I love you guys, you know that, but I don't expect you to start paying my rent."

"Seriously, Paige. You know if it came down to it, we would definitely spot you some money. Or, heck, a live-in nanny probably wouldn't be a bad thing once this baby gets here. I hear mother's helpers are game-changers."

Paige laughed, mostly to try to squash the tears, but she knew her friend meant it sincerely. Kayla and Eric wouldn't hesitate to put her up for any length of time if Paige needed it, but she couldn't encroach on a growing family like that. This was their time. She'd be there to help them however she could, of course, but she knew they needed space to be a family without a spare librarian on the couch.

"Besides that," Kayla continued, "you have to stop beating yourself up over this. Dylan was the one with hang-ups. He knew you wanted to get married and get on with your life and he was too selfish to walk away and let you pursue that. He was lucky to have you as long as he did. I know it hurts, but you're going to be fine. Better than fine. Your Mr. Right is right around the corner. I can feel it."

"Yeah?" Paige asked half-heartedly.

"Absolutely. I'm pregnant. My senses are heightened. I'm in tune with these things now."

Paige couldn't help but laugh.

"What else does Madame Kayla see? Can you see how I'm going to get this promotion?"

"You've already done the hard work of being a phenomenal librarian. The job is as good as yours."

"Well, I hope Christie's as confident about all this as you are."

"She is," Kayla said with conviction. "She told you about it for a reason. She's not an idiot."

No, Christie wasn't an idiot. In fact, she was a very fair and easy boss to work for. Still, nearly every other part-time librarian within a fifty mile radius would be desperate to snag that job. She appreciated Kayla's surety, even if she couldn't share it completely herself.

"I hope you're right," Paige said.

"I am." Kayla wasn't at all bothered by her friend's insecurities.

Eric appeared in the entrance to the living room, a little wet strip along the belly area of his shirt giving away the fact that he'd just been washing up.

"You ladies want a drink or anything? Staying for dinner, Paige? I'm going to grill some hamburgers and corn."

Paige glanced at the clock. It was nearing 4:00pm. She could tell Kayla was tired and she didn't want to mooch dinner.

"Thanks Eric, but I better take off. I have a hot date with Netflix."

Kayla yawned. "Sorry I'm so boring today. This little person kept me up half the night somersaulting through my abdominal cavity. It's too late to take a nap now, but you've brought me this irresistible book, I might just have to peek at the first few pages."

Paige stood, slipping her feet back into her shoes and gathering up her bag.

"You know that's a dangerous game," Paige warned. "Just a few pages always turns into just the first chapter…just one more chapter… until you're in way too deep."

Kayla chuckled. "True, but it's Nessie! I can't just leave it languishing until morning."

Eric smiled. "I don't know. She may not be good at staying asleep all night, but she's gotten amazingly good at nodding off instantly."

"It's true." Kayla nodded. "I've never fallen asleep so fast in my life, but then I have to wake up all night to pee, or sometimes it feels like baby has stretched up into my lungs, or baby starts kicking up a storm for an hour and who can sleep while someone's tap-dancing on your internal organs?"

It sounded crazy when Kayla put it that way, but it also gave her a deep twinge of longing. She would have so loved to be going through all this right alongside Kayla. If only.

"Don't get up." Paige leaned down to hug Kayla again. "I'll see myself out."

"Thanks for the books," Kayla called, making no move to get up. "You really are the best."

"I know." Paige agreed and gave Eric a quick hug too as she passed him on her way to the door.

She was infinitely grateful that her best friend lived a short twenty minute drive from her apartment, but their lifestyles felt like lifetimes away. When she got home, after being in Kayla and Eric's cozy nest, her little apartment felt so undergrad.

She looked around the one-bedroom apartment that she'd called home for the past five years. She would never call herself a decorator, but she'd made the place her own over those years. Her living room had a modest sized TV, flanked by a pair of large bookshelves. She'd decorated the tops of them with framed photos and art prints, but every available bit of shelf space was taken with books. She loved those books and really, really, didn't want to pack them up and move. Well, she should rephrase that. If she was getting married and moving into an adorable little bungalow like Kayla and Eric's, she'd be more than happy to move. Carting them across town to a cheaper, sadder, apartment? That was just wrong.

She dropped her purse on the little table near the door, plopped into her non-reclining secondhand couch and turned on the TV. Her Netflix account greeted her with a long list of suggested shows: *Unexpectedly Single*—a reality show about middle aged divorcees living together in some Hollywood mansion vying for the attention of an attractive millionaire. That was a hard pass. *Second Chances*—another reality show about former couples who wanted to give it another go. Nope. "Move on ladies! You can do better!" she yelled at the screen before flicking to the next suggestion, *Medieval in Manhattan*. Ah! That looked promising. She watched the trailer and discovered it was a time travel romance with a literal knight in shining armor who found his way into the life of a modern day woman. She was a high powered executive for a fashion company. When he showed up, looking very confused, in the lobby, the heroine didn't bat an eye, thinking he was there for a photo shoot.

If only romance could be that simple. The little group that had come into the library popped into her mind. She imagined that she'd gotten up and offered to show them around. Why hadn't she done that? She wasn't exactly soaking up the nightlife looking for guys and the only single men she usually saw in the library were men like Norm. She might be working, but she could still be more proactive about the limited opportunities she had, couldn't she?

It was probably too much to ask though. After all, she had met Dylan at the university library. Could she really meet another potential partner in a library? The odds didn't seem good, but what else could she hope for?

Four

PAIGE HURRIED to the reference desk to relieve Yolanda for her lunch break.

"I'm so happy to see you!" Yolanda jumped up as soon as Paige came around the corner.

A response like that could only mean one thing.

"Full moon today?" Paige asked with no enthusiasm.

"It sure seems like it." Yolanda confirmed her fears. "The guy on computer 10 has had trouble writing and uploading his resume all morning. He doesn't know anything about computers and it's been so busy I haven't been able to give him much attention. He'll probably be up in a few minutes for more help. Before him, a mom with a baby came up to ask a question and the baby just opened her mouth and spit up all over the desk. The poor mom was so embarrassed, but I had Jim come out and clean and disinfect the desk. And I see resume guy heading up here now, so I'm outta here. Good luck!"

Yolanda hurried around the desk and made a beeline for the staff area. Paige could guess Yolanda wasn't regretting her decision to retire after a morning like that.

"Excuse me." Resume Guy walked up, eyes shifting around

making him look uneasy. "The other lady was helping me with my resume. Is she still here?"

"Sorry." Paige flashed a bright customer service smile. "You're stuck with me now. How can I help you?"

It was a full moon day for sure. After she'd spent a few twenty minute intervals helping Resume Guy format and upload his resume to a few different job sites, a sharp-eyed, birdlike woman had asked Paige to consult her "Google database" to look up the email address of her "friend" because she'd forgotten it. It hadn't gone well when Paige informed the woman no such database existed.

When Paige got a moment to sit at the reference desk, she thought she'd be able to breathe for a minute, but the ringing phone disabused her of that notion quickly.

"Adult reference, this is Paige speaking, how may I help you?"

"Hi there, Paige. I'm Maxwell. I need you to look something up for me. I'd do it myself, only I seem to have misplaced my glasses and I can't read this tiny screen on my phone."

"Of course. What do you need?" Paige poised her fingers over her keyboard, ready to type in the search and get on with her day.

"I'm looking for books about sex over fifty."

Paige had been in libraries long enough to know better than to react to unexpected requests, even when they came in over the phone. Never let them see you squirm. It was a tactic that had served her well over the years. Inside she was hoping this wasn't just another perv who was trying to get his jollies by making her uncomfortable.

"Ok, let me take a look in the catalog and see what I can find here." She typed in the search, all the while hoping there wouldn't be many results and she could get this over with quickly. Her heart sank when she saw there was, indeed, a hefty selection of sex books for the over-fifty crowd. From the looks of it, the authors had a sense of humor besides.

"All right, sir, we have a few different options here. Were you looking for a specific title?"

"No, nothing specific. Just tell me everything you've got."

Paige wasn't particularly keen to rattle off the titles, but that was how the job went sometimes.

"Ok, there's *Steamy Over Sixty — A Guide to the Ultimate Sexual Positions for You and Your Partner, Keeping It Up — Staying Sexually Active and Defeating Erectile Dysfunction the Natural Way, Frisky After Fifty — How to Keep Your Libido From Outlasting Your Performance, The Long Game — Hot Sex for All Phases of Your Life—*"

The whole thing became weirder when she felt the presence of another patron at the desk beside her. She didn't dare look up and make eye contact with them. What had they heard? Maybe they'd get embarrassed and walk away. She sure wished she could do that.

"Hold on, hold on, you're reading them too fast." Maxwell sounded annoyed, as if he was the one being taken advantage of in this situation. "Could you read them again, slower this time? And a little louder. You're a bit hard to hear."

Paige sighed. Was this guy putting her on or did he seriously need her to re-read all these outrageous sex book titles to him? She decided to err on the side of decency. Besides, she had someone in person who was overwhelmingly more likely to have a serious question, or at least, something non-sexual to ask her.

"I'm sorry sir, it's really busy here at the moment, I'm afraid I'm going to have to let you go. I've got your number here on the caller ID, I'll give you call back when I get a chance. Take care."

"But you—" Paige didn't wait to see what Maxwell Sex Books wanted to argue about. In an uncharacteristic move, she hung up the phone and turned to face the waiting patron, who had probably just heard too much.

To her utter mortification, the patron was the red-haired man she'd seen come in with the group the other day! Up close, he was even more striking. He looked at her with twinkling blue eyes. His pale skin was perfectly set off by that gorgeous auburn hair. His simple black t-shirt fit snugly over his toned delts, biceps, and broad shoulders.

The day was suddenly looking a lot better. Except that he'd just heard her reading a litany of sex book titles into the phone like she was working at a mythical after-hours library for the lonely and lecherous.

And why was she staring at the bemused smirk on his full lips as she thought all this?

"Excuse me, miss, is this where I pick up ma library caird?"

What new heaven was this? The way he pronounced his words made her ears perk to attention and her heart pound in excitement. Not only was this fine specimen much younger than retirement age, attractive, but foreign as well? A trifecta of appeal!

The phone started ringing again, forcing her to come back to reality and tear her eyes away from the stranger. She glanced at the caller ID: Kresner, Maxwell. Oh no. No more Max. She wasn't going to answer that again.

She turned back to Hot Foreign Guy.

"You were here the other day, weren't you?" The words popped out of her mouth before she could even process the implication of what she was saying.

Hot Foreign Guy looked surprised for a moment, then his face broke into a smile.

"I was, aye. I dinnae remember seeing you though. I wouldnae forget that."

Hold up now. A distant memory flickered to life in Paige's brain. She knew what was going on here. He was totally flirting with her! Paige needed to dust off her dormant dating skills, but not too much though. She needed to remember she was at work and drawing a paycheck for being professional.

She glanced at the still ringing phone for a moment to compose herself.

"You need tae get that?" He gestured toward the phone, his eyes big, blue, and beguiling.

"Uh, no. Unfortunately, I think you overheard that last conversation I was having. It's a call back. Not going there again. I'm all yours."

I'm all yours? Who was the lecherous one now?

Paige knew she was blushing. She furiously wished she wasn't, which embarrassed her more, making her blush all the harder. It was a vicious cycle that only ended with her looking like a cooked lobster.

Hot Foreign Guy's lips morphed into a crooked half-smile. They were perfectly formed lips. Looked like they'd be a dream to kiss—

"I was no' eavesdropping, but…" He made this adorable little shrug that made her notice how very well his shirt fit around his shoulders and upper arms.

Paige laughed, a little shrill, feeling self-conscious. He wasn't eavesdropping and she wasn't spontaneously having fantasies of kissing those lips that spoke words so lyrically. Thank goodness he couldn't read her mind.

"Yeah, I think we both heard a little too much there."

They stared at each other for a couple beats, as if they didn't know whether to dive in about her weird sex book conversation or move on with professional business. Hot Foreign Guy made the decision for her.

"Right, well, I'm needing a library caird. Is this the right place?"

A library care? She cared, all right. She'd also love to assemble some sort of care package to welcome him to the reference desk. Not filled with creepy sex books.

Suddenly, her brain snapped to attention. A library card! Of course. Good thing she recovered before she embarrassed him for the gorgeous way he spoke. If only she was good enough with accents to know what it was. Something from the UK, she was sure, but where? Ireland? Scotland? England? It didn't matter to her. She just wanted to hear more of it.

"Ah, um, no. I'm sorry." She willed her brain to function properly. She was a professional, after all. Not some moron behind a desk. She had to talk to the likes of Norm all the time and she kept it together for him. Now there was someone she actually wouldn't mind having a lengthy conversation with, she had to keep her "ums" and "ahs" at bay.

She cleared her throat and tried again.

"Actually, you have to go to the checkout desk for that." She gestured across the way to circulation. "They'll just need to see your ID with your current address or a piece of mail, like a utility bill that shows your address."

He screwed up his face in an adorable example of dismay.

"Right then, cheers. I'm only here for eight weeks. I dinnae have a permanent address."

Just eight measly weeks? Her heart plummeted. Pity that the likes of this guy would never be seen again, but Norm and his ilk would continue to be as regular as book deliveries to a library. Life was supremely unfair.

"I'm not the expert on those things," she admitted, "but they may be able to give you a temporary card while you're in town."

"I hope so," he lilted in his delicious accent. "It'll be a long, boring summer without some good books to read."

He was hot and a book lover. Fate twisted the knife a little deeper. Did it really have to tease her like this? Not only that, but the way he pronounced 'books' made her go all gooey inside. He said it like the 'oo' in moose and it was absolutely endearing to Paige. She wanted to listen to him talk for hours. Days. Whichever she could get.

"We do have plenty of good books here."

Paige felt her face heating up again. Apparently, she'd lost her ability to competently talk to attractive men since the whole Dylan thing. It had been so long since she'd wanted to flirt with someone new. Maybe she didn't know how to do it right anymore. Maybe what she remembered as right was now considered completely wrong. She hadn't even thought about that. Not only had Dylan wasted her prime dating years, could he have made her outdated to the opposite sex? But more importantly, why was she trying to mentally date this guy? Perhaps the over fifty sex books had put her into the wrong frame of mind to cope with this guy's obvious charms.

The corners of Hot Foreign Guy's lips quirked up, obviously amused by the colorful display Paige's face was putting on for him…again.

She tried to redeem the situation.

"Well, if they can't do anything for you, please come back over here. I'm sure I can work out something for you. After all, I wouldn't be a very good librarian if I couldn't keep you in books!"

'I wouldn't be a very good librarian if I couldn't keep you in books?'

Nope. That wasn't going to salvage anything, but now she didn't seem to be able to stop talking.

"What kind of books do you like?"

At least that was intelligible.

"Those titles you were mentioning on the phone just now sounded interesting."

Paige stared at Hot Foreign Guy in shock for a moment, before she caught the glint of mischief in his eye. Instead of feeling embarrassed again, she felt like someone was in on one of the ridiculous workplace hazards she dealt with from time to time.

"Oh no, not you too!" She shook her head in mock disappointment and he cracked a real smile, revealing a set of endearingly imperfect teeth. Not braces straight like her own, but not awful either. Natural. Cute. Was she really calling a man's teeth 'cute?'

"I'm just joking." His face went all serious. "I should no' have said anything."

Paige chuckled. "No, you're fine. That was definitely a bizarre phone call. You made the perfect excuse to end it. I'm not sure where that conversation was heading and I'm glad I didn't have to find out."

"Well then, happy to be o' service." He ran a hand over his hair and turned to look at the desk she'd indicated might give him a library card.

"I'll see if those ladies can get me a caird and I'll let you know how it goes."

"Good luck!" She twisted her index and middle fingers on both hands and held them up to indicate that she really meant it, or to indicate that she was a little weird. However he chose to interpret it.

"Thanks." He tapped his finger on the desk and turned to try his luck at circulation.

While Paige mentally berated herself for acting like an idiot, she also kept her eyes on him as he walked away. His black jeans clung to his hips and thighs in all the best ways. How was she supposed to get her pulse under control with that to look at? Undoubtedly, he had a girlfriend or even a wife, but Paige didn't mind appreciating the view while she had it.

She thought she sensed someone else coming up to the desk so she tore her eyes from Hot Foreign Guy and turned back to her job. She actually jumped back in her seat when she found Norm leaning over the top of her computer to get his saggy face all the closer to hers.

"Did you get a chance to watch that mini-series I told you about last time?" He'd definitely had garlic recently. Paige made a quick note to inhale as infrequently as possible to get through this interaction.

"No!" she exclaimed, heart racing from the shock of being too close to Norm after being not close enough to the previous patron. It was more effective than a cold shower.

Completely unaware of her discomfort, Norm shook his head slowly.

"I can't believe how busy you are." He didn't back up one bit. "You really need to relax more. It isn't healthy to stay so busy. But it looks like you have a minute now. You can look it up on your computer and see what I'm talking about."

Paige was crashing back to reality as she positioned her fingers over the keyboard, ready to play this little game with Norm for the thousandth time. But before things could play out too much, someone quietly slid behind Norm to wait their turn for help.

She had never been more grateful for a line to form.

"Uh, sorry." She leaned around Norm to wave her new favorite patron forward. "I have to finish helping this gentleman here."

Norm glanced at the young man behind him before groaning. "Maybe I'll just write the title down for you and drop it off before I leave."

"Great idea." Anything that didn't involve going down the rabbit hole with Norm was fantastic.

Norm shuffled to the computer area where he could stay forever, for all Paige cared.

"So, what's the verdict?" She leaned forward on her desk, not worried about being closer to this guy.

Hot Foreign Guy held up his empty hands. "No' good, I fear. I'm doing an artist residency in Ann Arbor this summer and dinnae have any proof o' address. They were very kind about it, but unable to get me a caird."

How the ladies up at the circ desk had had the strength to deny this man anything was beyond her.

Then her mind caught on what he'd said.

"Artist residency? That sounds amazing! What do you do?"

He looked down, suddenly resembling a bashful young boy.

"Ah, well. It's no' as impressive as it sounds. I work on a tour boat with my uncle. I like to use my hands, so I got into carving and woodworking. There's a rich shipbuilding history in my hometown of Glasgow, but that's mostly in the past now. I use my art to connect to the heritage of my community."

Paige was openly gaping at him now, but with no trace of embarrassment. Not only did she know what his delicious accent was now, Scottish, but she could feel the whole story lurking beneath his words. A diminishing industry turned to artwork. What a message. She wished she could see some of his work. Whatever it was, it sounded fascinating and powerful.

"That sounds even more impressive! You must be very good to end up in another country for a residency. Congratulations!"

He shook his head, looking down to avoid her earnest gaze.

"It's no' as difficult as you'd think. I just needed a change, you know? I researched artists' residencies abroad and sent out some applications. This one happened to work out. I'm no' sure why, but I'm very happy to be here."

Humble. Paige could appreciate that.

"Well, I'm sure the people who saw your application believe you're very talented. That's wonderful. And it's just this summer?"

"Only eight weeks. Long enough tae get comfy here, but no' tae feel it's permanent. It'll be interesting. Although—" He looked around with a half frown on his face. "Might be less interesting since I cannae check out any books, but I'll live. You have other things going on here, surely."

"We do." A sneaky idea popped into Paige's mind. "As a matter of fact, I'm doing a book discussion next Saturday on a book you might enjoy, *Dreams of the Sea* by Douglas Crown. It's the story of a man who has only one dream, to sail across the Atlantic on his own. It's inspired by the life of Edward Allcard, the first person to successfully make such a journey, in both directions, on his own. It's a really inspiring book and the discussion is a low-key group. Since you work on a boat, I bet you'd have all sorts of great insights to share if you'd care to join us."

When Christie had asked her to help Yolanda with the upcoming discussion, she hadn't been too excited to read a sailing book. Suddenly, it was starting to feel a little like fate. Or maybe she'd been reading too many romcoms lately.

She pulled out a program brochure from the holder on her desk, flipped to the relevant page, and handed it to him.

He looked her in the eye, one eyebrow quirked up in what she hoped was amusement, as he took the brochure from her hand. She realized she was basically asking this guy out, even if it was only to her program. Maybe she should reign it in and back away from this hard-sell approach she'd never used before.

She tucked a stray lock of her brown hair behind her ear and looked down at her desk, embarrassed by her over-enthusiasm.

"I mean, I'm sure you're plenty busy with your residency and getting to know Ann Arbor. But, you know, if you happen to have some spare time on a Saturday."

He tore his eyes from her face and read through the description on the paper. She took a deep breath to slow her pulse while he wasn't looking.

"You're the one leading the program?" He peered at her again.

"Yes. Well, me and the other librarian I'm going to be taking over for."

"I've no' read the book, but it does sound interesting. I suppose I could pick it up in a bookshop. Is there one around here?"

An idea, albeit a stupid one, was forming in her mind at that very moment. Paige prided herself on being a rational person. Someone who played by the rules. Someone who generally didn't do foolhardy things, but this stranger was having a very uncharacteristic effect on her.

"Oh," she tutted. "We can't have that."

She looked toward her computer, as if there was an answer to be found there, but really, she just needed to take a quick break from looking at him before her face put on a color change show again.

"Well." She glanced back up at him. *Sweet Lord, how can his eyes be that blue?* "This is an unorthodox solution, but if you find something you'd like to check out, I'd be happy to put it on my personal account for you. You have to promise to return everything on time though!"

What am I saying? Inside, Paige couldn't believe she had even suggested such a thing out loud. Getting too involved with a patron, especially a complete stranger, was a terrible idea. She knew better. Why had those foolish words come out of her mouth?

His eyes widened in surprise, then sparkled with warmth. Her impulsive suggestion may have been worth it for that alone. "That's kind of you. I'd appreciate that."

His wide smile was definitely worth it. Even if he checked out the ten most expensive books in the library and never came back again, she wouldn't regret her offer.

"Of course. We can't have you languishing away for two months with no books! Is there anything specific I can help you find today?"

"This discussion book is first on my list." He pointed to the listing in the program for emphasis. "I'm no' a fast reader, but I should get it read in a week. Can you help me find it?"

"Absolutely!" Paige may have had a little more enthusiasm in her reply than necessary, but Hot Foreign Guy seemed to enjoy it, so she didn't mind. She got to her feet and walked around the desk to join him.

Norm shot her a sour look from the computer area, but she didn't even turn her head in his direction. For once, she had a patron who was worth all her attention.

"By the way—" He held his hand out to her. "I'm James MacKinnon."

Her hand practically leapt into his of its own volition. His fingers closed around hers and squeezed, just a little bit, but it was enough to make her feel all swoony on the inside. The handshake didn't last long, but the warmth of his hand lingered on her palm. A thought popped into her head of how nice it might be to just hold his hand. Let the pad of her thumb gently caress his…

She clasped her hands behind her back, digging her thumbnail into her palm a little in an effort to get herself under control. It was like she'd never spoken to an attractive man before in her life.

"I'm Paige." She was careful not to give out her last name. He may be exquisitely good looking, she may be acting like an idiot, but she still had enough wits to withhold something. Even stalkers and serial killers could be hot, after all.

"Paige." He repeated her name, sounding like music from his mouth. "It's a pleasure to meet you."

"A pleasure to meet you too, James. A book-loving artist from Scotland. Definitely an unexpected surprise around here."

He laughed good-naturedly, although quietly, since they were in a library.

She turned toward the stacks to their right. "This is the fiction section. We have designated sections for general fiction, romance, sci-fi, westerns, and mystery. If it isn't obvious which of those sections it might be in, be sure to ask one of the librarians."

He looked at her and nodded seriously. "*One* of the librarians?" He quirked an eyebrow up. "Here I was thinking you would be my personal librarian, since you're gracious enough to share your caird wi' me."

It took all of Paige's willpower to keep from dissolving on the floor in a puddle. She was sure her face was aflame again. That wasn't all she wanted to share with him. In an attempt to cover the blush, she laughed.

"Not to brag, but I am the best."

"I have no doubt." His eyes sparkled with amusement and (dare she think it?) interest.

Her eyes flitted to those strong biceps. She noticed that his left arm had a sleeve tattoo peeking out from underneath his shirt. It was an intricate tapestry of Celtic knotwork in deep black ink. It came down to just above his elbow, and she couldn't tear her eyes from it.

He noticed her noticing and grinned. James pulled his sleeve up to his shoulder so she could get a better look.

"It's called a Glasgow knot. I got this beauty when I was nineteen. Just a skinny kid. I wanted to be tough but pay tribute to my roots. I've never regretted it."

"No, it's too magnificent to regret."

"I see that twinkle in your eye. You're getting the urge to do it yourself. Or do you already have any?"

She leaned closer to admire the artistry of it, feeling the warmth of his skin in the air around her face. "Unfortunately not. I could never settle on anything I'd want to be stuck with permanently, but yours is beautiful." She caught herself. "Or should I say manly? Does one get a tattoo to be beautiful? I'm hopeless."

"Beautiful is the perfect compliment. Thank you. They did great work on this."

She wanted to trace her finger over the intricate pattern of the knots, and feel the smooth skin of his upper arm. Instead, she squeezed her hands even tighter behind her back.

"They really did. How long did it take?"

"I had to go back for a few days to get it all finished. The artist was very conscientious and neither of us could stand to do it for too many hours at a time."

"That's more dedication than I would have. I'd probably just get something small, or maybe a good literary quote. So many to choose from."

"You know what they say." James rolled his sleeve back down. "Tattoos are addictive."

"I have heard that, yes. Do you have more?"

James's eyes twinkled and he smiled a mischievous grin. Paige realized what she'd asked. Obviously, if he had more, they were concealed somewhere under his clothes...and now she was thinking about his naked body.

Enough. She was at work, she must remember. She wanted to get a promotion. Flirting on the job probably wasn't the way to do that.

"Never mind that question." She tore her gaze from him and looked at the rows of multicolored book spines instead. "Let's get you the discussion book." Her eyes scanned the shelves for the author's last name as she focused on breathing normally and slowing the pounding of her heartbeat.

"It's my only one, so far." He didn't ignore the question. "But I may have to get one here to remember the experience."

Paige tried very hard not to think about where he might put a commemorative tattoo for his artist residency. She mumbled a non-verbal response and then tried to move back into librarian mode.

"Here we go!" She pulled the book off the shelf. "Last copy. It's your lucky day."

James took the book from Paige and gazed into her eyes.

"It certainly is." He looked down quickly, as though he realized that could be taken in a more flirtatious way.

Paige could hear her heart pounding furiously in her ears. It wasn't only her face that felt flooded with warmth. How could this even be happening? He really was flirting with her.

She tucked her hair behind her ear and turned away from the intensity of those clear, blue, eyes.

"What else would you like to see of the library?"

"Show me everything."

She could have told him the same thing. Instead, she reconnected with the professional part of her brain and led him around the entire library. When she got him to the computer area, Norm looked up from his computer.

"Oh, Paige, are you almost done with this guy yet? I need your help with something."

Her heart plummeted. Wasn't there anything she could do to get away from that leech?

James seemed to immediately sense how Paige felt about the situation.

"If you dinnae mind, Paige is helping me find my way round the library at the moment. I'll no' keep her long." He winked at Norm to soften the blow.

"Well, there's this website I—" Norm persisted, but James wasn't having it.

James held up his hands. "I'll no' keep her long."

Norm opened his mouth as if to argue, took a better look at James's muscles and seemed to rethink it.

Internally, Paige was jumping up and down. James must be enjoying this at least half as much as she was. Otherwise, he would have been fine with leaving her to Norm and getting on with his day. Things just kept getting better and better.

Happy for a real excuse to get away from Norm, Paige walked toward the reference desk, James right beside her.

"Oh my God, thank you." She leaned in and whispered so no one else could hear her being unprofessional. "That guy is here all the time and I can't stand him."

"I got the feeling, the way you tensed right up as soon as he spoke to you. Is he a problem?"

"He's just gross, you know? He could be my grandpa, but that doesn't stop him from trying to chat me up." She cringed saying it out loud.

James looked over his shoulder in Norm's direction again.

"He cannae be making you uncomfortable like that." His voice had a harder edge to it, as did the set of his jaw.

Paige was touched that James seemed genuinely concerned for her, but realization dawned on her that she shouldn't be bashing other patrons to James, no matter how annoyingly inappropriate and relentless that patron happened to be. She had to pull herself together.

"Well—" She spread her arms out. "That's the library. I'll let you browse and you can bring me whatever you find and I'll check it out for you myself."

James looked a little crestfallen before he replied.

"If you dinnae mind, can I trouble you a little longer, Miss Paige?"

The way he said her name made her knees absolutely weak.

"Of course. What else do you need?" He didn't need to ask her twice.

He gestured toward the fiction section. "Who better to recommend a good book than a librarian? Would you help me make a good choice?"

He flashed her a cheeky grin. Oh, he was good. He was flirting, no doubt about that, but he was also keeping her away from Norm. For that alone, she could fall in love with this man.

"Thank you," she mouthed.

He winked and they disappeared into the stacks, well out of sight of Norm, even if he came up to the desk looking for her.

"Do you seriously need a recommendation or are you just being awesome?"

"I willnae be able to read more than the one book this week, so I suppose I'm just being awesome." He grinned.

"Where have you been all my life?"

"Glasgow."

He grinned like a naughty schoolboy and nudged her with his shoulder. She felt her nerve endings spark to life with just that little touch. It was suddenly feeling a little warm to be wearing a cardigan.

"Seriously though—" James settled into a serious expression. "I'm happy tae be of service, now that I'm here. Does he bother you often?"

Paige dramatically rubbed her hand over her face. "He's just the tip of the iceberg that is public service. Oh, I could tell you some stories."

James's eyes widened and he cocked his head like a quizzical puppy.

"Could you? I might like to hear them."

Her heart was definitely racing now. Things had shifted quickly from another slog with Norm to a fun time with James. This wasn't the sort of thing that happened at her library. Could the full moon finally be having a good influence?

"You might? Hmmm. I don't know. There are some stories that definitely aren't for the faint of heart." She cast an appraising gaze over him, as if trying to assess whether he could handle hearing about the things she'd been through over the years.

He leaned in and whispered, an intimacy that she didn't mind one bit.

"Try me."

She was tempted, so very tempted, to do exactly that.

"Well—" She cleared her throat, as it all of a sudden felt dry. "Everyone thinks libraries are these quiet, quaint places to work where all we do is sit around reading all day. That couldn't be farther from the truth."

"Now that you mention it—" James rubbed his chin, "I cannae say I've ever seen a librarian reading."

She raised her eyebrows and pointed at him.

"You see? You're starting to get it already."

Before James could respond, an elderly woman with a cane appeared at the end of the aisle.

"Excuse me," she said. "Do you work here?"

"I do, yes." Paige turned her full attention to the petite woman. She was dressed smartly in a long pink skirt and a matching shell top. Her white hair was coiffed in a neat bun.

"Could you help me, please, Miss? I brought this list of books I want, but I forgot my glasses and I can't tell what I've written here." She chuckled at her own expense. "Don't ever get old, Dearie."

"Of course, let me see what you've got there." Paige reached for the list and took a look at it. She did like her job when she was actually being helpful. It was just being a captive audience to leering old men and rude people that got her down.

She turned back to James quickly. "Just bring me any books you want. Back to work for me."

"Thanks for your help," James called after Paige as she walked away with the woman. Her feet felt heavier as she walked away from James, but that was pure silliness. A man that hot couldn't possibly be single. And if he was, there must be something seriously wrong with him. Perhaps another commitment-phobe like Dylan. James was so lovely though. She kept replaying his tantalizing accent over in her mind. The way he said, 'book,' 'Paige,' and 'Glasgow,' were especially intoxicating. Ah, but there was no use getting carried away. He said it himself. He was just a temporary visitor in her part of the world. He would get on a plane in a few weeks' time and be back in Scotland, which might as well be another planet. If she was very lucky, he might come back a few times to check out more books before he left. Maybe they could flirt a little more and then Paige wouldn't have to feel so hopeless about her romantic prospects. It figures that the first good looking guy to walk through the library doors and show any interest would be one that lived halfway across the world.

Paige helped the lady find some of the books on her list. The others weren't on the shelves. She led the woman back to the reference desk to place holds on the remaining titles. A quick glance at the computer area revealed Norm deeply engrossed watching some video with a pair of library headphones over his ears. She breathed a quick sigh of relief. He was occupied now and wouldn't be needing her to 'help' with anything after all. James had saved her from two Norm encounters in the span of a few minutes. Perhaps letting him check out books on her card wasn't as foolish as she'd feared. At least he'd earned it.

After she'd helped the woman, Paige leaned back in her chair, feeling confident that she'd survived the worst of her shift. James hadn't come up to check anything out so she was sure he was still in the building somewhere. The idea made a sparkly little shiver go down her spine.

As she'd hoped, the rest of her shift went smoothly. There was only an hour left before the library would close for the night. Norm stayed glued to his computer screen and the people who did come up to the desk had legitimate requests.

At last, it came time to start her closing duties. This was a favorite activity if someone like Norm was in the building. She had lots of things to walk around and check at the end of the night. She was a moving target and could usually orchestrate her movements so that she could stay away when Norm, or others like him, were looking around to say goodbye before they left.

She began her walk-through, straightening shelves, checking the meeting rooms and the stacks for stragglers. She found herself keeping a careful eye out for James. He hadn't decided to forgo checking out the book, had he? Not that he had to check it out. He was free to leave. To walk out of her life forever, as if their encounter hadn't woken up a little piece of herself that she feared might be dead, or worse, obsolete. Still, she was a bit surprised by the jolt of relief that surged through her when she discovered James in a far back corner of the fiction section. The library had armchairs scattered around so patrons could find a cozy little nook to settle in and read. James had done exactly that. He had a pair of earbuds in and looked wholly engrossed in the discussion book Paige had given him. Maybe he really would show up for the program. She could hope.

There was something magical about seeing someone fully absorbed in the world of a book. She could tell he had no idea she was standing at the end of the row. His eyes were zeroed in on the words on the page. Nothing else existed for him. Since it was closing, she was compelled to disturb him. Even though she wasn't eager to break the spell for him, she did want to clear up and go home.

She walked toward him, wondering how close she'd have to get for him to notice her. As it turned out, she had to rest her fingertips lightly on his shoulder to pull him from his trance. It was just a little touch, but he felt warm and firm. He startled and looked up.

"Oh! Sorry. I didnae notice you there. Good book!" He stuck his finger between the pages, so he wouldn't lose his place.

"Ready to check out? I'd be happy to let you read, but we're closing in ten minutes."

His eyes widened. "I guess I got sucked into this thing. Yes, please. I promise tae take good care of it. I wouldnae want to be responsible for ruining a librarian's perfect return record!"

Paige smirked.

"What's that for?" James gestured toward her face. "There's a story there. I can see it."

Her smirk widened into a grin. "Should I tell you a little librarian secret?"

"You have tae now. You cannae say something like that and then back away from it."

"Good point. Come on, I'll tell you while we walk back to my desk."

James stood up and followed close enough that Paige could feel the heat from his arm next to hers, even though they didn't touch.

"Right. We're walking. What's the story, Paige?"

She leaned in so he'd catch her whisper. If it also meant that her upper arm pressed into his a little, so be it.

"Librarians never turn their books in on time because we don't have late fees."

James's jaw dropped as if he was properly shocked and he turned his face toward hers. Those blue eyes! They were literally sparkling with vitality. He was so close. So very much in her personal space, but it didn't put her off at all. Her nerves were alive, pulsing with energy. Her brain was firing on all cylinders. It was like she'd just been sitting around, withering under the burden of people like Norm, waiting for a lively, interested, decent individual to come along and remind her what was good about humanity. Well, maybe that was going a bit far, but she didn't care. That's how she felt.

She sucked in a breath and turned away before she found her face any closer to his than it already was.

"Tell me it isnae true!" James said in mock horror. "I've only just met you and you're already shattering all my deeply held beliefs about librarians."

"Oh, it's true. And if that's too hard to believe, maybe I shouldn't tell you any more librarian secrets. I wouldn't want to be the reason librarians fall in your estimation."

"On the contrary!" He put his book on the counter when they reached her desk. He stopped in front while she continued around behind to bring up her own patron record.

"I dinnae think I've appreciated librarians more than I do right now."

She smiled and reached for the book so she could check it out. Out of the corner of her eye, she saw Norm walk behind James on his way out of the building. He was facing her, willing her to look up so he could interrupt, but she made a big show of flipping to the barcode on the book and getting it to scan.

James had spared her another Norm encounter. Paige felt like queen of the world!

"Here you go, sir." She smiled and handed the book over to James. "That'll be due back in three weeks, give or take."

"I'll have it back to you at the discussion," he promised, all seriousness. He pressed the book to his broad chest, as if placing it on his heart. "Thanks for doing this for me. It's kind of you. I'll no' do anything to make you regret it."

"You're very welcome," she said. "It was nice to meet you."

"Very nice to meet you, too. I'll see you next time. Have a lovely evening."

She wanted to tell him she already had.

Five

WHEN PAIGE PULLED into the parking lot of her apartment building, she was still flying high from flirting with James. The stereo in her car was cranked up loud and she belted out the song like a driver's seat diva.

By the time she got into her apartment, she felt like she was soaring through the stars with all the force and energy of a rocket ship. No trace of closing shift exhaustion. She could stay awake all night if she had to. Maybe she would.

She popped a frozen dinner in the microwave and called Kayla. It was after nine o'clock but she couldn't go to bed without telling her best friend about this.

"Hey," Kayla answered. "How was work today?"

Paige felt her excitement bursting against her ribcage. She couldn't contain it any longer.

"I met someone!" she squealed.

"Wait. What?" There was a shuffling sound as though Kayla had dropped something or was moving in to hear better.

Paige realized she may have been a tad overenthusiastic and misleading. "Well, I didn't meet someone, meet someone, but this gorgeous Scottish guy came into the library today and he was chatty and so dreamy."

"Tell me every single detail."

Paige grinned and the whole story tumbled out. The accent, the blue eyes, the sleeve tattoo, all of it.

"That's awesome! He sounds gorgeous. And that definitely sounds promising." Kayla sounded impressed and happy for her friend.

"It would—" Paige paused a moment, coming back down to earth. "But it's not meant to be."

"What the heck are you talking about? He saved you from Norm. He's coming to your book discussion. He sounds like living sex appeal. Don't go sabotaging yourself already!"

Paige sighed. "It's not me. It's life. Don't forget the part where he actually lives in Scotland. That's a heck of a long distance commute for anyone. And he's only here for eight weeks anyway. To be honest, I don't even know if he's at the beginning of those weeks or somewhere in the middle."

"Paige, stop." Kayla was already developing a mom voice and she didn't even have the kid yet. "It sounds like he was interested. I guess you'll have a better idea when he comes to the book discussion."

"If," Paige corrected her, discouragement taking a firmer hold of her. "Just because he seemed into it tonight doesn't mean he'll actually show."

"You said he was sitting in the chair reading the book. That's a pretty substantial clue as far as I'm concerned."

"It seems like it, yes. It's crazy. On the one hand, I'm really excited, but on the other, I'm trying to be realistic. This isn't a romance novel."

"Oh, but what if it was!" Kayla enthused. "What would it be called? *The Scottish Rogue*?"

Paige scoffed. "No! *The Literate Scottish Gentleman*, perhaps."

"No way. Where's the fun in that? *Molded by the Scottish Sculptor*. That's better."

"*Banged by the Woodworker*." Paige laughed.

"Why Paige—" Kayla feigned indignation. "What a saucy minx you are!"

They both bubbled over in laughter. It felt good to laugh with Kayla and imagine outrageously bawdy scenarios with James. She may never see him again, but at least he'd given her something to fuel her imagination for a while.

"Seriously though, what are you going to do now?" Kayla asked.

"What am I going to do? Well, I need to figure out how to get this book discussion going so I can nab the promotion."

Kayla sighed. "I meant about the guy. The pregnant wife has to remind you how to date? Look him up. Get his number. Ask him out. Move this thing along, Paige!"

Paige was glad Kayla couldn't see her exasperated face. "He was cute and fun, yes, but come on, Kayla. I already wasted most of my twenties on Dylan and we both know what that got me. I don't have time for short term, casual fun. I have to think smart and put my time into something that can have a future."

"You know what I mean." Kayla had a gentler tone now. "Look him up, at least. You're the librarian. I don't have to tell you how to find information. You can still have fun looking."

That was true. Paige had been surprised by how many people came to the library trying to get information on other people. She tried not to think about what their motives were when they came in and asked her to find an address or phone number for a "friend" of theirs. Paige never asked why they didn't have contact information for their "friends" but set about doing the best she could to find something. Generally, that kind of information was public, however unsettling that might be.

"I don't want to stalk him!" Paige exclaimed.

"Right. And I bet you don't want to find a picture of him to enjoy either."

Paige had been too busy thinking about the real deal to consider there might be pictures of him online to whet her appetite. Surely an artist would have a website. Or a social media account at the very least. Maybe she could see some of his work too.

"I don't think so." Paige considered everything, her mind going into overtime concocting scenarios and situations. "What if he has a dating profile and he's everything I want except that he lives on the other side of an ocean? I don't know if I can handle disappointment like that. I've already had a big enough let down with one relationship. I don't need to start one knowing it's doomed to fail."

The disappointment and anger at herself for being duped by Dylan was still very fresh in her mind. She'd been too caught up in her imagination to see what was there in front of her. She already knew James couldn't commit because he was only passing through. Better to release this fantasy before she could let it get the better of her.

Kayla sighed. "Sorry. I guess you're right. You just sounded so excited. You know I just want you to be happy like me and Eric."

Paige softened. "I know that. And I was excited. Talking to you now made me realize it's just a fantasy. Nothing I should get invested in."

"Still, this is the first man you've shown any interest in since Dylan. That's a good sign, right? You're definitely ready to get out there."

Where "out there" was, Paige wasn't exactly sure. Good looking single guys weren't exactly beating a path to the library every day. She'd met Dylan in college, which was literally a pool of single people with at least the common goal of getting an education. Now, her world was so much smaller. With her best friend married and pregnant, it wasn't like she was going to drag Kayla out to bars or clubs. Those weren't her scene anyway.

Oh well. It had only taken a few years for a guy like James to show up at the library. Maybe in another five or ten, there'd be a single guy who was actually charming and local. She could hardly wait.

"If you'd seen him, you'd understand why I was so excited. Plus, the accent. It's like he walked off the pages of our favorite Brit Lit. But that's ok. I'm under control now. Thanks for listening."

"I'll listen to your good-looking guy stories anytime. Maybe I'll have to come to this book discussion and check him out for myself. I was excited before, but you got me with Brit Lit."

Paige laughed. "Please do! If I can get a good turnout of new blood, my boss will be really impressed. You can bring Eric. Bring your sister-in-law. Bring everyone you know! Please!"

Kayla laughed softly. "You know I love you, but I don't know if I can read the book. Didn't sound like my sort of thing. Didn't you say it was something about sailing?"

"Don't even read it." Paige was really warming to the idea of Kayla showing up for the program. If she could just get people in the seats, the rest would follow. She was sure of it. "Isn't that how personal book groups work? No one reads the book and everyone just sits around sipping wine for a couple hours?"

"Are you serving wine? That would turn your discussions around. Not that I can have any at the moment."

Paige had considered it. There were book discussions at other libraries that met in local coffee shops or bars, but she didn't want to copy exactly what other libraries were doing. She wanted her discussions to stand out for other reasons. She just wasn't sure what those reasons might be.

"No. No wine. There will be refreshments though. Hmmm, now that you mention it, I could do a Desserts and Discussions theme, couldn't I?"

"Now you're talking!" Kayla agreed enthusiastically.

It was too late to advertise it properly for next week's discussion, but Paige thought the idea might have some merit. Maybe she could partner with local bakeries and ice cream shops and take turns featuring their desserts each month at the discussion. Who didn't like a free dessert?

She got up and grabbed a notebook to jot down her idea before she forgot about it.

"Thanks, Kayla."

"Not sure what I did, but you're welcome. Seriously though, if you have dessert at this next one, I'll read a synopsis of the book and I'll be there. I dare anyone to get mad at a pregnant lady for not reading the book."

"You're really milking the pregnancy thing, aren't you?" Paige teased.

"Hey, some women love every second of being pregnant. I am not one of them. The first trimester morning sickness was so bad I was sure I'd die. I feel like I weigh as much as a T-Rex. I've got heartburn like you wouldn't believe, and I have to get up to pee all night. The best thing I've got going right now is sweet treats and the fact that I'm expected to gain weight. I'm taking whatever positives I can get!"

Paige wasn't about to go up against that. Besides, she was just hoping to get as many people to the discussion as possible. If bribing Kayla with dessert would fill another seat in the program, she'd do it.

When Paige got off the phone, she pulled her now lukewarm Lean Cuisine out of the microwave and peeled off the cellophane. What a day it had been! Paige's brain was on overload. Naturally, James seemed to be taking up the most bandwidth at the moment, as impractical as that was. She looked around her little apartment. Maybe she should spend more time thinking about the reality of increasing rent and stagnant salary. James couldn't help her with that, no matter how friendly, flirty, or gorgeous his accent. He'd been a fun diversion for one day, but she didn't need to waste her energy on another man she wouldn't be able to have. She'd learned her lesson the hard way and she wouldn't make that mistake again.

ON SATURDAY MORNING, Paige pulled into the staff area of the library parking lot. If the weather was any indication, it should be a good day for a book discussion. The sun was out, but partially obscured by passing clouds. So it wasn't so glorious out that people would skip the library for a backyard cookout. Hopefully.

Regardless of what the weather did, she knew the steadfast handful of regulars would be there. She only hoped she could break through the stagnation and get some fresh readers involved. Maybe a real miracle would occur and James would surprise her by showing up again. Just thinking it made her heart skip a beat. She'd have to get a handle on that quick or else she'd be really disappointed when he didn't show up.

She dropped her purse at her desk and headed into the program room to help Yolanda set up.

"Hi. What have you got there?" Yolanda nodded at the big brown bag Paige was carrying.

"I thought it would be fun to reward our attendees with doughnuts. I'll get these set up and take some pictures for the social media accounts. Show people what they're missing and maybe it'll help inspire some new people to sign up."

"That would be nice. It's a good core group that comes every month. I'll really miss them. You'll have a great time here."

"I'm definitely excited for it."

Paige started unpacking her doughnuts. Next she'd grab the coffee maker out of the kitchen and get that going too. Who didn't love coffee and doughnuts?

Paige and Yolanda finished getting everything set up and ran through a few logistical points about how they'd run the event. Finally, there was nothing left to do but wait for the patrons to show up. Paige tried not to hope too hard that James would come. She knew all too well that it wasn't worth it to live in a fantasy land.

Fifteen minutes before the program was supposed to begin, she was arranging napkins on the snack table when she heard Yolanda go into librarian mode.

"Well hello. Are you here for the book discussion?"

"Aye. Am I too early?"

Paige quit fiddling with napkins and turned to face the door.

James was actually standing there, holding his copy of the book in one hand. Or was it just an apparition? No, it was definitely him. In the delectable flesh. Was it possible his eyes were even bluer than when they'd met? This time, he was wearing a forest green short sleeved button up shirt and snug black jeans. The shirt accentuated the red in his auburn hair, which was just as full and beautiful as before. She bet James never had a bad hair day.

She hadn't seen him again since they'd met and he might actually look even cuter than she remembered. Relief and excitement flooded her in equal measure that he'd really come back to see her. That is, that he'd come for the program. The fact that she'd picked out a cute sundress in seafoam green with her cutest white lacy cardigan and gold strappy sandals was simply because the weather was so nice. Definitely not for his benefit. Even though she couldn't be imagining that his gaze traveled quickly up and down her body, culminating in a shy smile.

"No, you're right on time. The others will be here shortly. Make yourself at home." Yolanda greeted him professionally, as she should, while Paige was too pleasantly surprised for that.

"James! You came!" She resisted the powerful urge to give him a welcome hug. The running line in her head had become: *You're at work. You're at work. You're at work.*

"Aye. Of course. I wouldnae miss it. This is my first event as a local."

The words hit their mark in Paige's rapidly beating heart. First event. Could it mean that he was at the very beginning of his artist residency? Paige's rational mind grappled with the hopeful part that was currently running wild. Hadn't she already decided a summer fling wasn't worth the wasted time? She needed to find a guy who had the potential for a future, not just an accent she could listen to for days on end, and gorgeous blue eyes, and a sleeve tattoo she really wanted to touch.

"Oh, are you a friend of Paige's?" Yolanda asked. It was a perfectly reasonable question given Paige's reaction, but it made Paige blush.

"Oh, aye," James said without missing a beat. "Well, I've only just met her but she's a lovely person."

"She certainly is." Yolanda smiled and Paige blushed even more furiously.

"Have a doughnut?" Paige asked thrusting a paper plate in James's direction.

He grinned, no doubt amused by her tendency to blush every time he saw her.

"Thank you." He took the plate and she stepped aside to let him get his snack.

"I'm sorry I didnae have a chance to come in again." James put a glazed doughnut on his plate and grabbed a cup for the coffee. "I had an orientation and welcome dinner for the residency and then I've been busy in the studio. Eight weeks seems like a luxury to spend on art until you start working. There's so much to do before the gallery showing."

Paige struggled to contain her smile. He thought she was lovely and he was at the beginning of his eight weeks. If luck was with her, she'd be able to listen to him talk a few more times before he went back home. That's definitely all she wanted to do with him. Yep.

"I have no idea how an artist residency works," Paige admitted, forcing her thoughts back into friendly territory. "Are you expected to furnish pieces for a whole showing at the end?"

James shook his head and took a sip of his coffee.

"I dinnae have to make everything. There's a small group o' us doing the art. I'm just no' used to creating on a deadline like this. It's a wee bit daunting is all."

"It does sound intense, but I'm sure you'll do a fantastic job. I just have a feeling about you."

She'd never stop blushing at this rate. *I just have a feeling about you.* What a thing to say to a handsome stranger!

James gave her a sly glance and the corners of his mouth twitched up like he was holding in an enormous grin.

"Thanks for your confidence. I appreciate it."

"Anyway—" She tried to move things into less flirty territory, "I'm extra honored you took the time out from your art to come to the discussion."

"It sounded fun. I've never been to one to be honest. I did mention it to a few people at the studio, but they're no' exactly what you'd call bookish. I'll have to try harder next time."

That was sweet of him to try to drum up support. Why did he have to be so nice?

"I'm also really glad you brought the book back." She mimed wiping her brow in relief that she wouldn't have to cover the cost of a stolen book.

James let loose with a bright peal of laughter at that.

"I bet you are." He put a hand over his heart. "I think it's a sin to steal books from a librarian. You'll no' catch me doing that."

Paige chuckled. "I believe you."

James caught her eye and held her gaze for a long beat. She ran her suddenly sweaty hands over the sides of her skirt and then clasped them in front of her. She was very aware that Yolanda was in the room with them and she found herself wishing they were alone.

She cleared her throat, which seemed to have gone dry all of a sudden. "Hey, what do you think of this? I was going to rebrand it as a

Desserts and Discussion group. I'd bring in desserts to sample and then we talk about the book. Do you think people would like that?"

"I dinnae think you can go wrong with desserts. Are you going to tie in the books with the desserts somehow? You've got doughnuts today. You could say they're life rings to go with the sea theme."

Paige cocked her head quizzically. "Life rings? You mean life preservers."

"You dinnae call them life rings here?"

"Not that I've ever heard."

"Well now. You learn something new every day."

"If you hang around the right people." Paige grinned. "Anyway, that's a good way to tie the doughnuts in with the theme. I never thought of that."

"Sure you did." James winked.

"Yeah." Paige laughed. "I mean, that's exactly why I did it."

"Aye, now you've got it."

"Welcome, welcome!" Yolanda called out, startling Paige.

"Hello! Hey, it looks like we have some newcomers this time." A gray haired man smiled as he escorted an equally gray haired woman into the room. Paige had seen them in the library before. They always seemed like a really sweet couple.

"Yes we do," Yolanda said. "This is Paige, she's one of our librarians here, and her friend…I'm sorry I forgot your name."

"James."

"Excellent. Good to see some new faces here. I'm Jim and this is my wife, Nancy. We've been coming to this group for many years now. It's a great group of people."

"Hi! Welcome guys." Paige greeted them.

Nancy's eyes shifted between James and the refreshments.

"Well, well, well," she said. "We've got new people and treats this time. How exciting."

"Yes, help yourselves," Paige said. "I thought we could try out something new. Desserts and Discussion."

"Sounds delicious," Jim agreed, heading straight over to grab a plate.

After that, a few more people came in, including Kayla and Eric. Paige hadn't really expected Kayla to come, let alone Eric. So she was already responsible for increasing the program numbers by three, and she was only co-running the program this time. Not too bad!

Kayla quickly noticed James and then made big eyes at Paige, conspicuously jerking her head in James's direction.

Paige put her finger to her lips in stereotypical librarian style and then stole a surreptitious glance back to see if James was noticing any of this.

James had his book open in one hand while he held the last bite of doughnut with the other. Satisfied that he wasn't watching, Kayla mouthed OMG in a comical exaggeration. She leaned in to whisper in Paige's ear.

"That's the hot Scot right? Good for you!" She squeezed Paige's elbow as a subtle sign of encouragement.

Paige let go of her professional demeanor for a moment to share an excited smile with her best friend.

"I'm sitting to his left, so help yourselves and take a seat."

Eric gave Paige a supportive pat on the upper arm while Kayla made her way to the desserts.

"You know what? I picked up the book one night after Kayla fell asleep and it was really good. Figured if I was going to read it, might as well help you out too. Good luck on the promotion."

Paige reached out and squeezed his arm. "Thank you. I'm so glad you enjoyed the book. It warms my librarian heart." She really was lucky to have these two in her life.

By the time everyone was in and settled, Paige looked around the room and tallied the number of participants. It was eleven if she counted herself and Yolanda. She'd take it. After all, she was hoping to build the program up. It didn't need to happen overnight. Three new faces below the age of sixty was a fantastic start.

After most of the doughnuts were gone, Yolanda kicked things off. She explained to the group that she was retiring, which prompted congratulatory sentiments from the regulars. She went on to say that Paige would be the new head of the program and Paige's heart was warmed as everyone congratulated her and offered their support. She really was inheriting a great group.

"I know Paige and I both came up with questions for you guys today, so I think I'll let her kick things off, if that's ok."

The group nodded their assent and Paige picked up her copy of the book and smiled.

"Ok," she said. "Let's get started."

Everyone tidied up their crumbs and pushed their plates away, ready to dive into the book.

"Since we have some new faces here today and I need to get to know everyone, why don't we go around the table and do a quick introduction and say something you liked or hated about the book. I'll start. I'm Paige, your new discussion leader. I would not normally pick up a book like this for myself. Sailing the Atlantic is definitely not a topic I know much about, and I wasn't sure how interesting the book would be, but wow. It was really well-written and I found it fascinating to see what goes into sailing alone. Talk about amazing, right?"

The room mumbled in agreement and then Paige turned to James. "How about you?"

"Me then? Right." James sat up a little straighter in his chair and looked at the little group seated around him. "I'm James and you may guess I'm no' from around here."

A smattering of amused chuckles rumbled around the table as all eyes turned to the source of the lovely accent.

"I'm in town for the summer and Miss Paige here told me about your lovely book group, so here I am. I'm from across the Atlantic in Scotland myself, but I've no' crossed it in a boat like our main character here. Actually, I was pulled in from the forward at the beginning where it says his friends and family thought he was a bit daft for wanting to go. I could relate to his drive to do something his family didnae understand. Mine were no' very keen on my coming here this summer, but I couldnae let it go."

He looked to the next person and Paige felt a ray of empathy swelling in her chest. His family didn't support him coming for the artist residency? She didn't even know him and she was awestruck by the talent he must possess to land something she assumed would be very competitive. It took guts to try for something like that in the first place, let alone if your friends and family didn't support you along the way. But she didn't have time to ruminate on it much longer, the next attendee started speaking.

"Welcome James, I'm Judy. I didn't quite catch everything you said, but your accent is absolutely lovely." Judy was in her late sixties and had conspicuously dyed red hair and dark eye makeup that had probably been her signature look since her twenties.

James bobbed his head in a self-conscious nod.

"I'm here with my husband Phil." The white haired man next to her gave a little wave. "I thought the book would be boring because I don't know anything about sailing, but like you said James, it was more emotional than I expected. Talking about his relationship with the folks back home who hadn't supported him the way he expected. I found that fascinating."

Everyone went around the room until both regular couples, Judy and Phil, Jim and Nancy, and the feisty pair of widowed sisters, Sandy and Carol, knew the newcomers, James, Kayla, and Eric.

Paige wanted to run the discussion as diplomatically as possible, but she was also dying to know more about James.

"I did a little more research into the life of Edward Allcard, who was the inspiration for this book, and I realized that he and James here have something in common. Allcard had an apprenticeship in Glasgow building ships and James is also from Glasgow. I thought that was a cool coincidence."

"I've always wanted to see Scotland," Sandy mused. "Well, ever since I read those *Outlander* books. I've been reading them since the first one came out. Do you think they portray Scotland accurately?" She turned to James to see what he thought.

"I've no' read them," James admitted.

Sandy shrugged. "I suppose not. They are marketed as women's fiction, but they're good stories nevertheless. At least that's what I think."

"Let's get back to this book—" Sandy's sister, Carol, interrupted her. "It's a real triumph of the human spirit book isn't it? Imagine having a dream like that, to sail the Atlantic by yourself. Most people who think about those things never do them, but this guy did. Against the odds, he made it happen. I like books like this. It's good to think that there are people with big dreams out there and that they accomplish them."

Paige thought a person like that was sitting right in their midst. James wanted to be an artist so bad that he had crossed an ocean to do it. She wished she could talk more about him than the book.

"Is anyone here into sailing?" Eric piped up, looking around the room.

"We have a pontoon boat up north at our cottage," Jim said. "That's about the closest we've come to an interest in sailing."

"My uncle David owns a company that does boat tours on the Clyde," James admitted. "I've worked alongside him for ages."

"What's the Clyde?" Judy asked.

"The river that runs through Glasgow."

"I guess I should have figured that out." Judy chuckled at herself. "That sounds like a fun job."

"My grandfather had a bicycle shop," Phil chimed in. "My dad took over when my grandfather passed. He wanted me to take it over, but bikes just weren't my thing. I worked there when I was a teenager, but anyone could see animals were my passion. I was always catching snakes in the garden, constructing bird houses, bringing home stray cats. My parents weren't surprised when I wanted to go to veterinary school. Still, it was sad when it was time to close up the old bike shop."

James's eyes shone with interest.

"Aye. I ken what you mean. My family plans on me taking over from my uncle. I dinnae think it's what I want to do, to be honest."

Phil nodded. "It can be a tricky thing, but in the end, you only get one life."

Phil's wife, Judy, patted his hand. "And Phil's done a lot of good for the animals he's seen over the years. It sort of ties in with the book. Sometimes, other people's expectations for you just aren't right, no matter what they say. When you put your energy into your own desires, you can make incredible things happen."

"Like sailing the Atlantic by yourself." Carol thumped the top of her book for emphasis.

James's eyes burned with an intensity that Paige wanted to explore but she glanced at her list of prepared questions for the book and continued on with that.

Before she knew it, the hour had passed and she could easily say the discussion had been a success. The conversation had flowed beautifully and everyone had been charmed by James. The men of the group had gone over to shake his hand before they left and the ladies expressed their hope that he'd join them again in the future if he could.

"So, what's the next book going to be?" Sandy asked before anyone had left the room.

"Well, if he's going to be back—" Carol pointed at James. "I think it'd be fun to do a book about Scotland. It'd be sort of like our own travel adventure with a native guide. If you'd be up for it, of course."

To Paige's delight, he said he would.

"We can definitely do that." Paige had already picked out a book for the next discussion but this was much better. Not only would she get a chance to see James again, but the group was taking ownership of the program. Surely that was a good sign. Maybe if the library wasn't so focused on leading, the program growth might become more organic? It was worth a shot.

Paige grabbed a library laptop and pulled up the catalog. Together, the group brainstormed a good book for the next month. James had suggested a few Scottish authors and they found that the library had a copy of a short story collection by one of them.

"Short stories. I might even have time to get through some of those before the baby gets here. Maybe I'll be back." Kayla patted her belly as she considered returning to the group.

"I hope you do." Carol smiled warmly. "It was very nice having you and your husband here. Always good to have new friends in the group."

So it was decided. The next month's program would be a dip into Scotland. Paige could hardly wait.

While Yolanda mingled with her regulars to say her goodbyes, James, Eric, and Kayla helped Paige clean up.

"Thank you so much for coming!" Paige started. "You really made this a great discussion. I'll be putting up a couple pictures on our social media pages. I think seeing that the discussion isn't just for retirees will help draw in a new crowd of readers."

"Good, I hope it does. Turns out, it was actually fun, even if I didn't read the whole book. You did a great job." Kayla gave Paige a big hug.

"You really did," James was quick to agree. "You had thoughtful questions and were really good at keeping the discussion on track. I'm impressed."

Kayla exchanged a glance with Paige and stepped over to shake hands with James.

"Now that we've shared our innermost thoughts on this book, I can tell you I'm actually Paige's best friend. Known her for years. It's nice to meet you."

"Ahh." James clasped Kayla's hand warmly. "I thought there was a familiarity between you. I've only known her for a few days, but I can already see she's an extraordinary person. Very kind, helpful, good at her job, and has excellent taste in friends."

Kayla was putty in his hands.

"All true," Kayla agreed, slowly withdrawing her hand from the handshake. "So, Paige tells me you're an artist?"

James's eyes widened in a bemused expression. He shot a mischievous grin at Paige. She felt like a kid caught with her hand in the candy jar.

"Did she, now?" James said.

Eric shook his head and busied himself with piling the chairs back on their storage rack. He knew better than to get involved with Kayla's schemes.

"Well," said Kayla, "it's not every day a handsome Scottish guy walks into the library. An artist at that! That's definitely newsworthy. What do you make?"

"I dinnae ken about that, but thank you. Aye, I am an artist. I do mainly woodworking and I like to carve ships and other nautical themes. The industry isnae what it used to be. Times change, o' course, but it's still in the blood of a lot o' Glaswegians. I dinnae want that story to be lost and art felt like the most natural way for me to express that."

"Sounds very special. Maybe we could see your work sometime?" Kayla asked. Paige made a 'cut it out' face at Kayla, but she didn't seem to notice.

"I'd like that very much." James trained his gaze on Paige. "I only hope it won't disappoint."

"You've got to have some flaws somewhere, but if you're here doing an artist residency, I have the sneaking suspicion that your artistic abilities aren't one of them." Kayla turned to clean up the refreshment table.

James joined Eric in putting up the chairs and Paige pushed the tables back into the formation they were normally stored in.

With everything in order, Paige had work to get back to, even though she'd prefer to stay with her friends and James.

"Thanks so much for everything guys," Paige said. "Especially giving up some time on your Saturday to talk books with me. It really means a lot."

Kayla and Eric took turns giving Paige hugs.

"I never thought I was the book discussion type," Eric admitted. "But it was fun."

"We'll let you get back to work," Kayla said. "It was a good time. Almost as good as binging Netflix, eating ice cream on the couch, and waiting for this little one to show up."

Paige knew that was high praise indeed.

"You." Kayla pointed at James. "I hope we'll see you again."

James smiled, eyes twinkling with interest. "Me too." He held his hand out to shake with Kayla and Eric again before they left. "Wonderful to meet you."

Kayla hurried Eric out the door, as much as a waddling eight month pregnant woman can hurry.

Paige certainly didn't mind being left alone with James in the quiet room. After the little glimpse into his mind that she'd gotten from the discussion, she wished they could just disappear for awhile and get to know one another better. As friends, of course. Definitely just friends.

"So, what do you really think? Now that everyone's gone, you can tell me the truth. Are you ok with everyone nominating you to be our official guide to all things Scotland next time?"

James ran a hand through his hair and smiled shyly.

"I'm glad everyone seems so keen to learn about Scotland. It's my home. I'm proud o' it. I dinnae mind helping the group learn more. Nice people. I hope I didnae hijack your program though."

"No, no. This is wonderful. If these people are so interested, maybe it'll be infectious and we'll get an even bigger group next time." She looked down, feeling a little vulnerable. "I really owe you for this."

"Hey!" James's eyes brightened with a new idea. "Are you here until close today?"

The tone in his voice made her nerves buzz with anticipation. "I am."

"Is there any chance you might…" James looked down, hesitating for a moment.

"Yes?" Paige's traitorous mouth spat out the word, in a hopeful tone, before she could stop herself.

She wouldn't find out because someone stuck their head in the door. "Ah, Paige. I wondered if anyone was in here. I've been waiting at the desk for nearly five minutes and no one's there. Can you help me?"

Paige's heart plummeted from the soaring heights to the murky depths. It wasn't Norm, thankfully, but it was another of the regulars, Sylvia. Sylvia came in so often, she felt overly comfortable at the library. That in and of itself wasn't such a bad thing, except that Sylvia had felt bold enough to just stroll into the staff area a few times when she didn't get helped quickly enough. The library director had had to speak to Sylvia about respecting the boundaries between the staff and public areas, but it never seemed to sink in for very long.

Normally, she'd be annoyed that Sylvia had waltzed in and disrupted her. This time, it was probably for the best. Paige was learning she couldn't trust herself around those clear blue eyes. Paired with the delicious way James pronounced things, she was embarrassingly bewitched by him. She had to get a grip on herself or she'd rush headlong into more hurt that she absolutely did not need.

"I'm just closing up here after the book discussion." Paige gestured around the empty room, her pulse returning to normal.

"Ok," Sylvia said. "Then I'll just pop into the restroom. Meet me at computer seventeen when you're done."

Sylvia disappeared as suddenly as she'd arrived.

"You certainly are popular around here," James remarked.

"It's a busy place."

The moment broken, Paige and James walked out of the room and Paige locked it up.

"Well," James paused beside Paige at the locked door. "I guess I'll be heading back to the studio. Lots to do, but this has been lovely." His eyes got serious. "Maybe you'd like to meet me for coffee, or dinner sometime?"

Oh boy. There it was. Sylvia hadn't been as much of a wet blanket as she'd hoped, but she had interrupted Paige enough to get herself under control again. She never thought she'd be grateful to Sylvia for anything, least of all for forcing her to be rational about a really hot guy.

Inside, the irrational part of Paige was laughing, and dancing, and pumping her fists shouting, 'Yes! Yes! Yes!' But a tiny little piece of her remembered she would be turning thirty very soon. On the threshold of her thirties, she needed to be clearheaded and practical. What was a summer fling going to do for her? She'd be right back where she started, single, sadder, and a couple months older. As much chemistry as she felt around this guy, it just wasn't meant to be. She'd read the books. Star-crossed lovers didn't work out well. It was time to make wiser choices.

"That sounds lovely…" She tried to figure out how to do this in a friendly manner.

The light in James's eyes dimmed. "Ah. There's a 'but' coming. I should have asked if you were seeing anyone before I went and put my foot in it." He looked away, clearly uncomfortable that he'd misread her flirtation.

"It's not that. This is probably TMI, but I'm looking for something serious right now. I got out of a long term relationship earlier this year because the guy wasn't ready to commit, but that's where I'm at right now. If you were here longer than eight weeks, I would be delighted to go out with you, believe me. But something so temporary, I just can't handle that. I'm sorry."

She felt genuinely terrible for having to let him down. To be honest, she felt terrible for letting herself down, but it was the right thing to do. She knew it. Sometimes the right thing wasn't the easy thing. Better to nip this in the bud before it continued any further.

"I understand. That makes a lot o' sense. I'm sorry. Hope I havenae made things weird now."

Paige shook her head, feeling a strong desire to set him at ease.

"Oh no. Being asked out by a nice, good-looking guy is probably the least weird thing that's happened to me at the library. I'm very flattered you asked. If anything, I'm the one making things weird with the whole 'I'm only looking for a serious relationship' thing. Argh." She covered her face in embarrassment. "I'm hopeless."

"You're no' hopeless." James reached out like he was going to gently pull her hands from her face, then stopped himself. "You're a woman who knows what you want. That's admirable. Maybe we could be friends while I'm here. So far, I've only met the other artists and they're no' from around here either. We're the ones who are hopeless trying to figure out what to do here when we're no' at the studio."

Paige put her hands down, feeling a lot less self-conscious about turning down his invitation.

"They have you come all this way and don't even tell you what's around? That's terrible!"

"Art people. They're no' librarians." He grinned, clearly feeling better now that they'd gotten past the awkwardness.

"Right. Well, I'll let you get back to work. I'll see you around." He gave a little wave, which Paige returned. He wandered off toward the front door and she went off to meet Sylvia at the computers.

She felt a little bad that she hadn't made a hot date with James, but at least she knew she hadn't become irrelevant to the opposite sex. She had that going for her.

Seven

DRIVING HOME FROM WORK, her Elvis ringtone went off, indicating that Kayla was calling.

"What's up?" Paige answered.

"You're done with work, right? Why don't you come over to our place for dinner. We've got a lot to unpack from that book discussion. Plus, Eric's been grilling again and he made way too much."

"Sounds good. I'll stop at the store and bring some more dessert and iced tea."

"You're a saint! We're running low on iced tea. Baby thanks you."

After Kayla had gotten through the morning-sickness phase of her pregnancy, she'd been hit with a craving for iced tea. Paige tried to remember to bring a bottle with her whenever she visited Kayla. It was a simple enough thing and it made Kayla happy.

Paige pulled into the Kroger that was on the way, to pick up the dessert and iced tea she'd promised. Since the weather was so nice, she decided on the perfect summer dessert: a pint of strawberries, an angel food cake, and whipped cream. She put her selections in the cart and joined the line for the self-checkout. While she waited, she zoned out, thinking about how well the discussion had gone and congratulating herself for handling things maturely with James.

She was so tuned into her thoughts that she jumped when she felt a tap on her shoulder.

"The librarian in the wild. Eating cake and iced tea for dinner, just like the rest o' us."

Paige had certainly not expected to run into James at the grocery store, but she couldn't help the instant smile that appeared on her face at the cadence of that accent and the sparkle in his eyes.

"James!" she exclaimed. "How nice to run into you." Then she laughed. "I'm just picking these up and heading over to have dinner with Kayla and Eric."

"Right. I'm just picking up some things too. This isnae my dinner at all." He held up a mini-apple pie, a bottle of Vernors Ginger Ale, a bag of Better Made potato chips, and a pre-packaged sub sandwich for her inspection. "They had a local sticker on the shelf, so I figured I'd try them while I'm here."

Paige looked over his armload of items and felt struck with sadness. She'd had those subs before. The lettuce was usually so old and thin it was translucent. The tomatoes were more pink than red and made the bread soggy. If you were lucky, there was more than one slice of meat to tide you over. The whole thing was just an unsatisfying mess.

She imagined James heading back to some sort of lonely room to eat and then discovering what was really between those two halves of bun. She had no idea what kind of accommodations artist residencies provided. Did he even have a kitchen to prepare meals in? What if he was in a dorm room or a hotel or something equally dismal? It'd been so nice of him to actually come to her discussion, and return the book, as he said he would. She couldn't let him suffer like that, could she? That's not how friends treated each other.

"The chips and the Vernors are Michigan staples, but…" She pulled a face at the sub package. "If you're looking for Michigan foods, you'd be better off stopping at a Tubby's sub shop. There's one not too far from here."

"Thanks for the tip." James looked behind him, noticing the line of people who were also waiting for the self-check machine. He turned back to Paige and shrugged. "Guess I'll have to face the consequences at the moment. Don't want to get in the back of this queue."

"There's a check-out open." A man behind James bluntly pointed out the fact that while Paige and James were jawing away, they were holding up the line.

"Sorry." Paige apologized to the man and flashed an 'oops' face at James.

As she scanned and bagged her four items, she wondered what she should do next. Would it be weird to wait until James was done and walk out with him? Should she just take her things and go? Take her things, give James a wave, and then go?

Paige took her receipt, popped it into the bag with her items and turned to see where James had ended up. He was just getting to a self-check of his own. With just a couple of items himself, it wasn't going to take him long.

The impatient man was quick to take Paige's spot at her check-out so she slowly pulled her receipt out of her bag to examine it. Did she really get the sale price on the iced tea she'd chosen? While she was carefully checking those prices, James caught up to her. Dilemma solved.

As they walked toward the exit, an idea began formulating in Paige's head. A terrible, foolish, irresponsible idea. It was also terribly appealing. Her palms got sweaty and a warmth began to radiate from her core as another out-of-character idea came to her. James seemed to be good at eliciting that response from her. She wouldn't say anything though. She could keep it to herself.

"Hey, I was thinking…" The words popped out even as she was telling herself not to do it. "Do you want to come with me for dinner? Eric's been grilling and made way too much food. He's good with the grill. I can promise it'll be even better than a Tubby's sub."

Her heart thudded in her chest like the footfalls of patrons rushing to the computer area at opening time. Why had she said that? She had just told him earlier that she preferred not to go out with him and here she was, only a matter of hours later, asking him to go out with her. She knew Kayla wouldn't mind, but she suddenly worried that James might think she was toying with him. That was definitely not her intention.

"As friends, I mean," she hastened to add before he could say anything. "Just a group of friends hanging out for dinner. It's not a date or anything."

She was digging herself deeper. "I'll just shut up now."

James chuckled at her awkwardness.

"That's a generous, and delicious sounding offer, but I dinnae want to impose."

Was he trying to let her down easy or was he really just that polite? She'd gotten herself this far, might as well keep going.

"It's no trouble at all. Kayla and Eric loved you. They won't mind. Here, I'll call Kayla now, just to be sure."

She pulled out her phone, dialed Kayla, and pressed the phone to her ear before James could object further. Why was she pushing this so hard? Maybe her blood sugar was too low and that's why she was acting so strange. That had to be it. She needed to hurry up and eat some dinner or God knows what other ill-advised things she'd start doing.

"What's up?" Kayla answered.

"Hi Kayla, new plan. I ran into James at Kroger just now. He'd been fooled by one of those sad subs in the deli case so I asked if he wanted to join us. Would that be ok?"

Kayla's excited squeal reached through the phone and straight into Paige's ear canal. "Yes! Yes! Yes! Bring him! Good for you, Paige!"

Paige was certain James had heard every high pitched word. Well, at least she wasn't the only one who'd gone bonkers about James. In a friendly way…of course.

"Great. Thanks. I think James just heard all of that too, so I guess we'll be over in a bit."

"Tell him how much you—" Paige ended the call before he could hear Kayla say anything that might be instantly regrettable.

She turned to James, sure that she was slightly red-cheeked. Again. "Well, I'm sure you just heard that you're more than welcome. If you want to come, of course. You might not. Apparently, we're both a little…" She tried to search for a word that might convey how she was not usually so impulsive and mixed-signally and that Kayla didn't think Paige was a desperate cause that needed to be celebrated for just showing interest in a guy. Friendly, interest. Naturally.

"A little…excited. To get to know new people."

James grinned at her, amusement sparkling in his eyes. "Do they no' get many visitors?"

Paige laughed, as much at herself as at James's question. "Not visiting from Scotland, no. We all just want you to have a good experience here."

"Well, I cannae refuse a kind offer like that. But I feel like I should bring something." He held up his bag and frowned at it. "It isnae polite to show up unexpectedly and empty-handed."

"You're fine." She tried to assure him. "You're my guest. The dessert and iced tea can be from both of us."

He looked a little skeptical, but didn't argue.

Paige held her keys in her hand and looked around the parking lot. Now what was she going to do? Ask a mostly unknown, but cute man into her car, precisely in the manner women are instructed never to do? Tell him to follow her? Either way, he was about to find out what car she drove. It was a little late for safety first now.

"Ok." She figured they were in it together anyway. "How do you want to do this? You're welcome to ride with me, or, if you don't want to leave your car here, you can follow. I'm over there." She gestured off to the left, wondering how James was going to play it.

"I'd feel like an arse rolling up with a bag of food I cannae share. I should have listened to you and ditched the sub."

Paige could respect that. If roles were reversed, she'd definitely feel weird showing up to dinner with a bag of her own food. The pop and chips were fine, but the sub would just get grosser if he left it in the car.

"You want to swing by your place and drop it off first?"

"Is there time? I wouldnae want to make you late."

"Plenty of time. They don't live far from here. Plus, I've known her forever. She'll still love me no matter when I get there."

"I'm only about fifteen minutes from here myself. That way." He pointed in the opposite direction of Kayla's house, but that wasn't a big deal.

"You want me to follow you there, you can drop off the food, and I'll drive to Kayla and Eric's?"

"If we were in Scotland, I wouldnae inconvenience you like this but…" He looked down at the ground and shuffled his feet a little uncomfortably. "I'm still getting used to driving on the wrong side o' the road."

She hadn't thought about that. She'd be terrified if someone plunked her down in Scotland and expected her to drive a car on the opposite side of the street.

"Oh my gosh, don't worry about that at all. I don't mind driving. Really."

James relaxed and gazed out over the parking lot filled with cars.

"Mine's a hire car. A silver Nissan. I parked over there." He gestured to the right.

"I've got a bright red Ford Fusion." She pointed to the left. "You can't miss it. See ya at your place!"

She found his car and followed him easily enough. Poor James. He hugged the right lane and hovered about five miles below the speed limit. Cars were passing them left and right. She was grateful no one honked or gave them the finger as they zoomed past.

Finally she followed him into the driveway of a small property that fronted the Huron River. Even though she'd lived in the area her whole life, she'd never really noticed this particular place. It was set off from the road and the land had a huge oak tree in the front of the house. It looked like it might be a duplex.

He hopped out of his car with his grocery bag and came around to her.

"You wanna come in while I put this away? I might freshen up a wee bit since we're going out."

The look on his face was so open and maybe even a little hopeful, that she found herself persuaded. Not only that, but she was curious to see what kind of accommodations he'd have from the residency and if there were any little personal items she might find to give her a better idea of who he was.

"Sure." She pulled her keys out of the ignition and stepped out.

"Mine's around the back on the right." He led her around the side of the house to the full river view. People were taking advantage of the warm June day. Paige spotted a family canoeing and a handful of kayakers dotting the river.

"This is a fantastic view!" Paige gazed across the river. Gallup Park stretched along the back of the opposite side and she saw the train tracks beyond that. The tree line was full and lovely and the sky was a brilliant summer blue. She inhaled a deep breath of river air. "What a perfect place to house an artist. This must be pretty inspiring to wake up to."

"Aye." James unlocked his door and turned to admire the scenery with Paige for a moment. "Reminds me a wee bit o' home. I do love to be on the river."

He walked into the apartment and Paige followed him in. She was surprised to find herself in a tiny space that looked like a studio apartment within the house. There was a brown leather couch along the wall to her left. Beside the couch stood an end table with a blue glass lamp on it. A flatscreen television was mounted on the opposite wall, with a double bed below it. She couldn't help her mind flitting to an image of him sleeping in that bed…shirtless with a pair of cotton boxers. She'd be able to get a really good look at his tattoo with his shirt off. She turned her back on the bed before it could influence her any more than that.

On the far side of the room, on the left, was the small kitchen. Straddling the kitchen and living room area was a bistro table with two chairs.

"No tour necessary," James joked. "Bathroom's off the kitchen to the right. That's it."

For a temporary home, it was a cozy enough little space, but Paige wouldn't want to live in a place so small for long. Her rent issues popped into her mind and for a moment, she imagined moving into a place like this to save money…except without a soothing waterfront view. She pushed the thought from her mind with the hope that her next book discussion would seal the promotion, and her current living situation.

"What's in the rest of the house?" Paige turned in a circle trying to settle the small size of this room with the looks of the house from the outside.

"The Ann Arbor Art Council owns it," James explained, putting his sub and pop in the fridge. "There are four units here. The other three artists this summer are in the others."

"That's pretty cool." Paige wandered to the end of the couch where she noticed a little picture frame on the end table. "Is that who you came to the library with that first time?"

She bent down to examine the picture. There was a woman with hair the color of James's leaning her head toward the shoulder of a tall, robust man with a beard. In the background she could see a wide river and a silver arched bridge that reminded her of the St. Louis Arch. The woman was looking at the man, rather than the camera. Her auburn hair streamed out behind her, proving that the picture was taken on a windy day. Her mouth was open and her eyes were crinkled like she was laughing into the wind. The man's eyes were squeezed shut but his mouth was a huge grin. She wondered if this must be James's parents.

"Aye." He walked over to stand beside her and she stood up straight. "They're all different types o' folks interested in different mediums. They're a bit intimidating to be honest."

He picked up the photo and handed it to Paige for a better look.

"That's my ma and Uncle David."

"The uncle with the boat tour business?"

"Aye. You were paying attention, weren't you?" He nudged her shoulder with his playfully, and Paige enjoyed the warmth even that little touch produced.

She laughed a little self-consciously. "Yeah, I was. Your life sounds so interesting to me."

James shrugged modestly. "I'm just a guy getting by."

Paige kept soaking in the details of the photo.

"That's a cool bridge. It's kind of like the St. Louis Arch we have in

Missouri. Futuristic looking. And your mom looks like an adventurous lady." From just that picture, Paige got the impression she was a strong woman with a big personality.

"That's the Squinty Bridge. Goes across the Clyde and aye, she is. Stubborn too. There's no stopping her once she's made up her mind." He stared at the picture for a few moments, a cloud coming over his expression for a beat before he blinked it away and reached for the photo to put it back on the table.

"Do you have any other pictures from home?" Paige found that she was dying to see more than this little peek into where James had come from. "I know you're from Glasgow, but I'm ashamed to admit that doesn't bring up any pictures in my head. When I think of Scotland, I think of mostly Nessie and kilts. That's hopelessly American of me. I'm sorry."

"It's no' bad to be what you are." He pulled his phone out of his pocket. "I didnae have a clue what Michigan would be like." He started scrolling through his camera roll and Paige tried not to look over his shoulder in case there was something embarrassing or intimate in it that she shouldn't be seeing. But she couldn't help wondering, who were the people whose faces were flashing by? How had they impacted his life? She wanted to know everything about him and she couldn't find out fast enough.

"Here you go." James stopped scrolling and held out his phone for her to see clearly. "That's me in front of the Armadillo."

"Armadillo? Do you have those in Scotland?"

"This one isnae an animal. It's a building, see?"

Paige looked at the photo of James's smiling face in the foreground and the distinctive building in the background, across a body of water, which she now guessed was the River Clyde. It reminded her of photos she'd seen of the Sydney Opera House, the iconic peaks of the building on the other side of the water.

"It really does look like an armadillo. Is it an opera house?"

"It's an event space," he explained. "No' as posh as an opera house. It has concerts and trade shows, mostly. Things like that. Here, let me find you another picture you might like."

He scrolled through a little more and stopped at a picture of him holding a swath of heavy rope on a boat painted with 'MacKinnon Tours' on the side.

"Your uncle's boat!" She exclaimed, eagerly soaking up the image of James's flexed muscles hard at work.

"Aye. There she is. The place I spend most o' my time at home."

Paige glanced at his face but couldn't quite read the emotion on it. He turned off the phone and put it back in his pocket.

"Well now, we should be getting along to Kayla and Eric's. Shouldn't keep a pregnant woman waiting for dinner."

Paige laughed. "Oh, she'll be happy to start eating without us. I've known her too long to worry about formality."

"So, you've been friends with Kayla since you were kids?"

James and Paige moved toward the door and back out into the sunny early evening.

"Since high school. I was a bridesmaid in her wedding a couple years ago. Now, she's pregnant with their first kid. She and Eric are such an adorable, fairytale kind of couple. They just complement each other, you know? They've definitely set the bar high for what I want in a relationship."

She didn't know why she'd mentioned her relationship goals to James. A tingle went up her spine at the implication. No. She had to put that away and try to reconnect with the reasonable part of herself. Surely, it was still in there somewhere. He was only temporary. She had to keep that in mind. Just like Dylan, James wasn't going to be 'the one' either. Just an interesting new pal, who she was apparently spilling her relationship goals to.

They came around toward the car and James made a beeline straight for the driver's side.

"Oh." Paige stopped short. "I thought you wanted me to drive."

James startled and then hung his head sheepishly. "Och! Sorry. My instincts are all wrong here. That's passenger side back home."

She unlocked the car door and he hopped into the correct side and she slid into the driver's seat. His presence filled the whole car with a charged energy that made Paige feel alive.

"So—" James buckled his seat belt. "Give me an example of how Kayla and Eric are your ideal relationship?"

She backed out of the driveway and tried to keep her attention on driving safely to Kayla and Eric's house. A friendly answer. That's all she needed to give.

"Well…" She stalled, trying to find a way to put it into words. "I like that they're very attentive to each other. They fill in for each other's weaknesses. For example, Kayla gets tired easily at this point in her pregnancy and Eric just takes over the things she used to do for the household when she needs to rest. He notices the details. But she does the same for him. When he's had a difficult day at work, she'll take over the chores he usually does. People say there should be give and take in relationships. Kayla and Eric really do that."

James nodded. "I get it. My Uncle David and Auntie Cait are like that. Both hard workers but they roll up their sleeves and work alongside each other to get the job done. They've made a good home together."

"Do you have any brothers or sisters?"

"Just me. But I'm close to my cousins. David and Cait have three daughters: Kirsty, Nicola, and Fiona. We grew up like siblings. The oldest two are married now. I'm closest in age to Nicola, but Fiona and I are the only two not married. How about you?"

Paige shook her head. "Nope. I'm an only child too, but my cousins don't live around here. I sort of adopted Kayla as my honorary sister after we met."

"It was nice of her and Eric to come to your discussion. They do seem like a braw couple."

"Braw?" Paige repeated the unfamiliar word.

"Aye. They're a braw couple, just like you're a braw librarian. Good. Fine. Braw."

"Braw." Paige said it again. "I like it. I love talking with you. I learn so many new things."

He kept his face straight ahead, but she could see that he turned his eyes toward her and curled his lips in a grin.

"I love talking with you as well." He fell silent for a moment, but his hands were fidgety.

"So, how does someone from Glasgow end up in Michigan? I don't feel like it's a state anyone tends to think of abroad. New York and California, yeah. Michigan, no."

"You're no' wrong. Things were getting, eh, a wee bit… heavy for me at home. I found myself wantin' to get away for a while, so I decided to see what was out there for an artist. The residency in Ann Arbor popped up online and I figured I'd apply. I applied for a few others too, I should say. This is the one that worked out."

Things were getting heavy at home? Paige wondered if he meant taking over his uncle's business, but didn't know if she should press. She didn't want to ignore it either, in case he did want to talk.

"I'm sorry you wanted to get away. You mentioned that you don't really want to take over the boat business. I can't imagine that's an easy situation for you."

James blew out a long breath.

"No. It's no' easy at all."

When he drifted into silence, Paige knew he wasn't interested in unburdening himself about that, so she steered the conversation back to less angsty territory.

"I'm really impressed you got selected for the residency. That is so cool to me."

"Right, well that didn't take much." James reached out and tapped Paige's shoulder playfully. It sent a sizzly jolt through her that she had to pretend wasn't happening. How did he keep doing this to her? In all the time she'd been with Dylan, she didn't remember feeling this kind of electricity in his touch. Even when they first started dating, and definitely not at the end. Is this what they meant by 'chemistry' when she read about magnetic attraction in books? She'd always chalked it up to a fanciful literary device. An exaggeration of what attraction really felt like, but here she was, buzzing and sizzling with the best of her literary heroines.

Paige tried to laugh at his joke, but it was more of a nervous release of energy than a real laugh. She hoped he couldn't sense the tension in her. Oh, what had she done?

"So…" She choked the word out in a somewhat froggy voice. She cleared her throat and attempted to calm down and make normal conversation. "How long have you been in Michigan so far?"

"Just ending my first week. I've wanted to stop by the library, but first there was the jet lag to adjust to, then I had to get started on producing some art, then there's the whole driving thing. It terrifies me to drive here, so you've no idea how glad I am that you offered to do it."

"You're very welcome. I was just thinking it'd be easier for me to drive to a place I know. I hadn't even considered that everything is weird and backwards here for you on the roads."

"It's no' a good way to drive. And there's so much traffic here."

"They don't call Detroit the Motor City for nothing." She turned to look at James for a second. "We're the car capitol of the US. Maybe like how you said Glasgow has shipbuilding in its people? We have the car industry in ours. But still. Don't they give you lessons or anything before putting you behind the wheel here?"

"Nothing."

"They just plop you in a foreign country and expect you to under-stand the road signs and rules you haven't encountered before?"

"That's it, exactly."

"I'd be too scared to leave my room, if I were you."

"I've had the same feeling. And your public transportation is shite. My options are to take my life in my hands and drive to the studio space, or slack off and get sent back to Scotland."

"No pressure though, right?"

He laughed softly. "Right. Absolutely none."

Paige couldn't imagine what it would be like to do what James was doing. Sure, it sounded glamorous to fly across the ocean and spend the summer there, but when she thought of the practicalities, it was pretty scary.

"I can't believe you came this far by yourself. I think you're a lot braver than me." She knew it was a different world to be a man traveling alone than a woman, but it must still be a stressful experience. So much could go wrong during travel and she didn't want to think what it'd be like without at least a friend to consult with.

"You could do it if you wanted to. It's just me, but that's exactly what I needed right now."

Again, Paige felt that there was a bigger story under the surface. He was dancing around it though. She filed it away to ask about another time. If there was another time, of course.

"So, you really don't know anyone here."

"I've met a few people affiliated with the residency program, o' course. They're nice enough but we all keep our own odd hours. They all went to university for art related degrees, but I didnae. Besides, they aren't nearly as pleasant as a certain librarian I've had the good fortune to meet."

A smile crept over her face as that humming energy turned up in her again. He was getting really good at doing that to her in just this short span of time.

"Have you gotten a chance to be a tourist and see anything fun? Do they have any plans for you to sightsee at all?"

"No' a thing."

"What?" Paige risked another quick look at James.

He held up his hands in an expression of defeat.

"Well, you already know I'm no' going to drive far."

"Oh no." Paige turned her attention back to the road. "You're not spending a summer in Michigan and not seeing anything. What's the point of being here if you don't get to enjoy some of what makes it unique?" She felt another ill-advised idea coming on.

"I'm no'?" James grinned.

"When exactly do you go back?"

"Early August."

"Ok." Paige figured in her head how much time he had and what he should absolutely see. It was only early June. There would be Fourth of July holiday time he could take advantage of. At least, she assumed he'd be able to, not having any idea how an artist residency actually worked. A road trip to see the Mackinac Bridge might be a nice idea.

Maybe squeeze in Sleeping Bear Dunes. Her mind was racing with memories of her favorite family vacations and the sights and sounds of her state that were vastly underappreciated by the wider world. She sort of felt like an ambassador forging Michigan-Scotland relations for the greater good. She liked the feeling.

"What are you thinking?" James asked. "I can see that massive librarian brain working like mad."

"I'm thinking of all the best places you need to see before you leave. There's so much to see in Michigan. Beaches, forests, touristy little towns, the Mighty Mac. You've got to see it all!"

"I'd love to." James leaned back in his seat and fiddled with the latch on the center console. "Do you know anyone who might be willing to act as tour guide?"

Paige slowed the car and flicked on the turn signal. The conversation was veering into dangerous territory again. He had said 'tour guide' though. That was a neutral term. Besides, it was sort of like being a librarian. Just on the road. With a good looking single man.

"I have a pretty good idea of someone who might be interested." She glanced at James out of the corner of her eye and turned down the street to Kayla and Eric's house.

"I hope we're thinking of the same person." His face was amused, but he wasn't leering at her or anything.

"I think the odds are good," she said, wondering who the hell she was and what had happened to her normal self.

"Could the library spare you for tourism purposes?"

The images his question conjured were making her blush. The tour her brain was assembling at that very moment provided a lovely backdrop for strolling hand in hand along the beach of Lake Huron, stealing a kiss under the shadow of the mighty Mackinac Bridge, running her hand along the knot work of his tattoo while they lay on a blanket together under the stars. She shook them off with a shiver and babbled about the library.

"Well, I'm actually only part time. Full time jobs in libraries are almost like a mythical beast. The plus side is that I do get to enjoy a fair amount of flexibility. The downside is no medical benefits through work and, of course, less money."

"All jobs have their pros and cons. You know mine isnae always a joy either. It was fine when I was growing up, but now I'm a man. I've my own interests. I dinnae want to be ungrateful, but it makes Ma and Uncle Davie mad if I say anything. It's what he's always done and he thinks it should be the same for me. I just wanted to get away for a while and see what's out there. I was suffocating."

I was suffocating. His words pierced her heart and echoed around in her head. She just wanted to pull the car over and wrap him up in a giant hug.

James sighed, but shook it off quickly.

"Enough o' that. I have it on good authority that even librarians have their share o' troubles."

"More than their fair share," Paige agreed, even though her mind was turning over what he'd said about his job and the pressure from his uncle, and apparently, his mom too. She was beginning to scratch the surface of who he was and it sounded like there was a lot more to his story she'd love to hear.

"I've also heard you'd enlighten me on the subject."

Paige pulled her car into Kayla and Eric's driveway and cut the engine. "What?" She'd been so busy trying to imagine what his life was like that she'd forgotten what he was referring to.

"Your scandalous library tales?"

"Ah." She shifted back into pleasant conversation mode and out of the meatier fare they'd been getting to. "I will. But I can't tell you all my secrets that easily. Patience, James. You'll have to be patient."

She opened her door and stepped out of the car, wondering who the heck she was turning into.

Eight

NERVES KICKED in once Paige was standing on the porch with James. It was one thing that they'd had a chance to meet at the library, but this was real life now. She'd stood on this same spot with Dylan on so many occasions. She'd been so sure they were going to get married and live happily ever after just like Kayla and Eric, yet, here she was with James…feeling things she shouldn't be feeling.

Before the foolhardiness of her actions could start to suffocate her, Kayla opened the door.

"Paige!" she exclaimed. "So glad you decided to come, and how wonderful to see you again so soon, James!"

"Thank you for having me." James extended his hand, which Kayla was quick to take.

"Come in, come in." Kayla backed out of the way to allow her guests room to enter.

James gestured for Paige to go first. Kayla clasped her in a tight hug as soon as Paige cleared the threshold. "Good for you! Go out and get it," Kayla whispered in Paige's ear. Paige hoped James hadn't overheard.

"We brought you some things." Paige pulled away and reached

toward James. She'd given him the bag to carry so he wouldn't feel empty-handed.

"Dessert and iced tea." He held the bag out to Kayla. "Paige said that's what baby-to-be wanted us to bring."

Kayla smiled and rubbed her growing belly. "That's right. Baby is a big fan of dessert and iced tea. I don't know why. It's delicious, so I don't complain."

Everyone stood around for a beat, a little awkwardly, until Kayla took over as hostess.

"Well, come on in and make yourselves comfortable. Eric is just finishing setting the table."

Kayla took the bag of dessert into the kitchen. Paige led James into the dining room, where Eric was setting down the last spoon at one of the place settings.

"Hi. Nice to see you again, man." Eric reached across the table to shake hands with James.

"Thanks for having me on such short notice. You've all saved me from a terribly boring dinner alone in my apartment."

Kayla tilted her head in that unconscious way people tend to do when they're observing something that makes them melt inside—a baby, a puppy, an appreciative Scotsman.

"Don't get ahead of yourself," Eric warned with good humor. "You just got here. No telling how epically boring we might be."

Everyone chuckled good-naturedly. It didn't feel awkward anymore.

Paige could see that this wasn't the normal dinner situation here. Kayla had dressed things up a bit with a cheery yellow and orange linen tablecloth, the nice glasses, and even a small turquoise vase with a large, pink peony as a centerpiece.

Paige caught Kayla's eye, nodded toward the table, and raised an eyebrow.

Kayla flashed a quick smile and shrugged.

Paige didn't know what Kayla thought this was. To be honest, she didn't know herself. Did it matter? Maybe Paige should just chill out and enjoy the company.

"Where would you like to sit?" James asked, perfectly sweet and kind.

"Oh, here is fine." She gestured to the closest chair at the table.

James pulled the chair out for her. Paige wracked her brain to think if anyone, in the history of her life, had ever done such a thing for her before. Maybe her dad when she was a little girl, but she couldn't think of a guy, friend or love interest, who had actually done that for her. It was a thoughtful little detail. A seemingly minor thing that actually meant a lot.

The gesture hadn't gone unnoticed. Eric did the same for Kayla and planted a peck on her cheek before she sat down.

"I didn't even put the food on the table yet," she said.

"Let me," Eric insisted.

"May I help with anything?" James offered, having just pulled out his own chair.

"Sure. I'll grab some ice cubes, would you mind pouring the iced tea?"

"No' at all," James agreed and disappeared into the kitchen with Eric.

Paige and Kayla stared at each other, their wide eyes indicating they were witnessing something they desperately needed to discuss in great detail.

Kayla leaned in quick and whispered across the table to Paige. "Is he a man or a dream?"

"So far, a dream," Paige answered. "But tone it down, will you? We agreed to be friends."

"Friends. Right." Kayla rolled her eyes like Paige had said the most ridiculous thing she'd ever heard, but Paige didn't get a chance to refute her.

The guys came back and got to work pouring drinks and getting the food out. It didn't take them long before a tasty spread filled the nicely decorated table. This time, Eric had grilled chicken breasts, potatoes, and zucchini. It all looked so good. Paige didn't realize how hungry she was until she was hit with the sight and smell of it.

"I know this is goofy," Kayla said, "but you have to indulge the pregnant lady." She picked up her glass of iced tea. "Before we dig in, I want to propose a toast. To new friends and quality time spent together with those we care about."

Eric picked up his glass too. "And to my lovely wife who bought me that awesome grill last year on our anniversary."

James had no trouble getting into the spirit either. "To kind-hearted librarians and their generous friends." He looked at Paige over the top of his glass, eyes sparkling a decadent blue that made her feel tingly all over.

She had hoped to sit it out, but she couldn't after that. Paige raised her glass and said the first thing that tumbled out. "To new adventures."

Everyone clinked glasses and the meal got underway.

"So, James..." Eric filled his plate and got straight to business. "How long are you planning to stay in Michigan?"

James explained what he'd already told Paige about his residency.

"I have to ask," Kayla said. "How did you end up with such impeccable manners? Is it just because you're not American?"

Eric shot Kayla an "oh please" face, but if she noticed, she just ignored it.

James chuckled. "That's nice o' you to say. It's my mother's doing. It was just the two of us when I was growing up. She always said no one would be able to say her son wasnae a gentleman."

Paige filed away this new bit of information. No wonder James and his uncle were so wrapped up together. He must have been a father figure for James. That would add an extra layer of obligation to his feelings about staying in the boat tour business.

"Well—" Kayla's voice snapped Paige out of her reverie. "She should be very proud."

James smiled bashfully at his plate for a moment before changing the subject.

"You have a lovely home. How long have you been here?"

Conversation flowed pleasantly throughout the meal. Once everyone was finished eating, the men, once again, took the lead on clearing up and putting everything away.

"Come join us on the patio when you're done," Kayla suggested, slyly taking an opportunity to steal a few moments out of earshot. As soon as the door closed behind her, she pounced.

"What are you talking about with this friends business? Haven't you kissed him yet?"

"What? No! This is only the third time I've been around him! Besides, he's only here this summer. That's just asking for heartbreak, don't you think? Friends is good enough."

Kayla pinched the bridge of her nose like Paige's answer was causing her physical pain. "Listen to you. He's wonderful. He doesn't have to go back to Scotland."

Paige sighed. "That's a lovely dream, but real people don't have a whirlwind summer romance and uproot their whole lives because of it."

"Honey," Kayla said gently, "I can only tell you what I see, and I'm seeing a light, happy side of you tonight that I haven't seen in a long time. You're relaxed, you're having fun. Heck, you're glowing as much as me and you're not even pregnant! And you're not the only one. I've been watching James steal glances at you. There's something there."

Paige rolled her eyes and Kayla nudged her with her shoulder.

"I mean it!" Kayla said. "And, of course, James is great. I mean, the looks and that accent alone are enough to turn heads, but he's so genuine and kind. Listen to me, Paige. He's the whole package kind of man."

She didn't need Kayla to tell her James was great. That was obvious. But that didn't mean she could seriously start a relationship with him. Dylan hadn't been able to commit to her after six years. The odds of Paige and James managing to stay together after eight weeks were worse than finding a new celebrity book on the shelf of a public library.

"Yeah, it sure looks that way now, but I've thought that before and was completely wrong. I guess I'm not the best at picking the right guy."

Kayla put an arm around Paige's shoulders and pulled her close.

"Hey, what happened with Dylan was not your fault at all. We'll never know what his hang ups were, but it had nothing to do with you. You better not be beating yourself up about that. It wasn't you, Paige. You know that."

Paige leaned her head on Kayla's shoulder, happy to receive a little pep talk from her friend. Sure, her head knew that Dylan's unwillingness to commit was his problem, but her heart told her something different. If he'd felt overwhelmed with love, he would have been afraid to lose her. Paige couldn't help but think that somewhere, in the back of his mind, he'd been holding out for someone better than her. She would never tell anyone that, but it was a thought that embedded itself firmly in her bruised heart.

She was spared having to say anything more about it because Eric and James came out to join them.

Kayla and Eric only had a postage stamp backyard, but they both enjoyed gardening and had transformed the small space into a peaceful retreat. Rather than maintaining a lawn, they'd made the area into a garden. Gigantic peony blooms toppled the stalks they hung from and perfumed the air with their heady sweetness. Their lovely pinkness was set off by a border of bright white daisies. In the back, they'd planted a thick row of lemon yellow day lilies. Fuzzy little bumblebees buzzed in and out of the flowers. It was the perfect summer retreat.

James came around to stand beside Paige as he took in the view of the small yard.

"This is beautiful," he said simply.

"Thank you." Kayla leaned her head on Eric's shoulder as he put his arm around her waist. "We enjoy unwinding on the patio here, after a long day."

"That'll do the trick," James agreed, taking a deep breath of the floral air.

If he enjoyed Kayla and Eric's little garden this much, he would absolutely adore the tour through Michigan she wanted to give him.

"Have you traveled much before?" Eric asked.

"No' much," James said. "Just around the UK and an occasional trip to Paris to visit the art galleries, but that's about it. This is my first time in the US. Cannae say I'd ever expected to come here."

"Do you miss Scotland?" Eric was just full of questions.

"It's very different here," James admitted. "It's been a wee bit tough to adjust to some things. Driving, for example, but other things are great. Like massive steaks. Everyone is so friendly and helpful in the stores and restaurants. But the best so far is the fine folks I'm meeting, so things are looking up."

Paige's heart swelled. She'd done the right thing inviting him to dinner. Basic decency dictated that reaching out to welcome a stranger in a strange land was proper.

"What are your friends like back home?" Eric pressed. "Is there a special girl?"

If Paige had been taking a drink at that moment, she would have choked. A girl? She found herself holding her breath in anticipation of his answer.

James smiled, his eyes clouding over, envisioning the people and places he'd left far behind.

"I've got my mates, you know? You unwind out here, we usually unwind down the pub. Most of us have known each other since we were bairns. There's a girl I'd been seeing before I came here. Same story. We've known each other since we were kids."

Paige bristled involuntarily at this tidbit. Of course there was a girl. How would there not be a girl back home? Someone this handsome and charming wasn't roaming the earth as a lonely soul. Women were probably falling over themselves to be near him wherever he went. She was right to keep things friendly. Good decision.

"Anything serious?" Eric asked. Kayla discreetly elbowed him in the side, but he was unfazed.

James rubbed the back of his neck with one hand before he answered.

"I wouldnae say that. We called it quits a little before I applied to the residency. The relationship wasnae really going anywhere. We wanted different things."

"Mmm." Eric mumbled in assent and quickly waggled his

eyebrows at Paige before downing a swig of his drink. He was as bad as Kayla trying to set her up with James.

Kayla glanced at Paige, but she didn't look back.

"Do you have any plans to enjoy the summer while you're here?" Kayla gently tried to nudge the conversation into more neutral territory.

"Paige and I talked about it a bit on the way here. It sounds like she has a great idea o' what I need to see."

"I do." Paige pushed through her jumbled thoughts to focus on travel. "Michigan has a lot to offer. Most of it's an easy day trip from here, but there are plenty of great weekend trips too."

"And you're more than welcome to spend as much time with us as you'd like," Kayla added. "You're one of us now."

"Thank you," James said. "It's an honor to be included with such wonderful people."

"Speaking of wonderful people, you two brought a strawberry shortcake that needs to be eaten." Kayla untangled herself from Eric and headed toward the kitchen to serve it up.

The rest of the evening passed comfortably. They enjoyed the sweet dessert on the patio. Once dusk rolled in and the bugs started to come out, Eric suggested they go inside and see if James was familiar with any of their favorite party games. They laughed uproariously playing their own version of Balderdash. Everyone learned quite a few new words and shared a lot of laughs in the process.

It was nearing 1:00am by the time Paige and James rolled back to his apartment.

"Well, here you are, sir," Paige announced when she pulled into the front driveway.

"Thank you so much for inviting me out. I had a fantastic time."

"You're welcome," Paige said. "I'm glad I ran into you at Kroger. I had a really great time too."

"Can I give you a hug?" James asked.

"Of course."

James did a quick assessment of the inside of the car, undid his seatbelt and tried to figure out where best to place his hands. The center console was far too bulky to allow for much more than bumping their arms together so Paige laughed and undid her seat belt.

"Let's get out and do a proper hug."

"Good idea."

Paige left the car idling in park and jumped out. James walked around the front of the car and pulled her into a firm but comfortable hug. Paige could have melted against his chest. It was a really good hug. His fingers pressed into her back with firm pressure, but not in a too hard way. His breath quickened, moving lightly across her ear and she was filled with that warm, dazzling, energy once again.

She'd purposely turned her face toward his shoulder, rather than his neck, but the heat in her core was making her wonder why she'd done such a silly thing.

The hug lingered until even Paige knew it had to end. She reluctantly pulled away, missing his warmth as soon as she did so.

Standing close, but no longer touching, she looked into his eyes, his face illuminated by the bright glow of a full moon.

Paige took a small step back and tucked her hair behind her ear.

James blinked a few times, like he was coming back down to earth himself.

"You working later today?"

The evening had been so surreal, Paige struggled to remember what day it was and what she was supposed to be doing with her life.

"What is it now? Sunday? Yep. I'll be on the desk."

"Is it ok if I stop in to visit?"

"Absolutely."

He absently licked his lips, making them glisten deliciously in the moonlight. Paige's heart pounded furiously in her chest.

She took another tiny step back.

"I'd better get going." Her voice was low and thick with something that was decidedly not sleepiness.

"Ok then, Paige." James took a step backward too. "Be careful getting home and I'll see you later. Thanks again for a wonderful night."

Paige stayed while James fumbled through his wallet for his key.

He looked up once he'd gotten it and gave her a little wave before disappearing around the side of the house to his entrance.

Paige let out a deep sigh, noticing how his scent lingered on her shirt from the hug. She knew she was getting too close and way too connected to this handsome stranger, but standing in the night, hearing the flow of the Huron as it passed by James's house, she had to admit that this definitely felt like something special.

Nine

PAIGE HADN'T SLEPT VERY WELL. Her thoughts had kept flashing across her mind like flipping pages in a book. There was so much to think about. Every glance from James. Every word he'd said. Why it was such a bad idea to encourage any more contact between them. Those eyes. Those beautifully intoxicating eyes.

She hopped out of the shower and squeezed her wet hair with a towel. The cool water had helped to pull her firmly into the land of the awake and living. She glanced in the mirror for a quick assessment of her looks. Luckily, there were no dark rings under her eyes to indicate her lack of sleep. That was all she could ask for.

Once she got dried off, she headed back to her bedroom to get dressed for work. As she pulled a summery orange, yellow, and blue floral dress from her closet, she heard a new text ping on her phone.

She slipped the dress over her head and smoothed it down over her body. Slowly turning from side to side in front of her mirror, she assessed the look. Cute and summery. She pulled a light cotton sweater, cream colored, out of her closet to cover her arms in case the air conditioning was too much.

She slipped her feet into a pair of adorable and comfortable white flats and then picked up her phone.

So, did you kiss him last night?

Kayla

Stop it! I told you we're just going to be friends.

Paige

You've already had him over to my place. That's pretty intimate.

Kayla

Stop! I ran into him at the grocery store and his dinner was so pathetic. What else could I have done?

Paige

Said 'have a nice night' and come on over to our place alone. Ha ha. Just kidding. He's way too hot for that.

Kayla

Watch out. You'll make Eric jealous if you keep talking like that.

Paige

I think Eric has a bro crush on him, actually.

Kayla

What?!?

Paige

I kid you not. This morning, Eric woke up and the first thing he said to me was, 'Do you think James would want to go golfing with me sometime?'

Kayla

He did not!

Paige

Honest to God, he did. It's pretty cute.

Kayla

That is pretty cute.

Paige

I'll tell him you already called dibs. He'll be so heartbroken.

Kayla

Stop it. Shouldn't you be focused on baby stuff instead of my new FRIEND?

Paige

Keep kidding yourself. Anyway, it's tedious being this pregnant. Did you know an unborn baby can actually kick you in the cervix? It's as unpleasant as it sounds. Maybe worse.

Kayla

On that note, I gotta finish getting ready for work.

Paige

Is James going to be there??

Kayla

He may have said he'd stop in.

Paige

I knew it! Ok. I'll talk to you later. Kiss James when you get the chance.

Kayla

Kayla

Paige

Paige tossed the phone on her bed and then popped back into the bathroom to blow dry her hair at least a little before work. She knew Kayla only had her happiness in mind, but sometimes, the less charitable parts of her wondered. Just because Kayla had found Eric and things were going well for them, maybe Kayla didn't remember how lucky she was. Not everyone found a guy like Eric and made a happy home forever. Maybe Paige was one of those women who just ended up being single for life. She didn't want to play into the tired spinster librarian stereotype, but what could she do about it?

She brushed her teeth, grabbed her stuff, and headed back to the library for another day of unpredictable customer relations.

Normally, Paige's heart would sink a little when the beautiful stillness of the empty library was about to be broken, but this time, she was ready for it. Whoever was going to walk through those doors, even if it was Norm and Sylvia together, she could handle it. It would only be a matter of time before James would be in the library too.

The crowd of computer users shuffled in first, as always. She smiled cheerfully at them and greeted them with 'good afternoons' as they filed past to stake their claims to their favorite computers.

There was a familiar face in the bunch, although not the one she was looking forward to. This one belonged to a thirty-something guy who was built like a quarterback. He came in frequently to look at online dating sites all day. There wasn't a female library employee he hadn't tried to ask out at some point, Paige included.

"Morning, Paige!" He stopped at her desk with a large grin rather than rushing straight to his computer of choice.

"Hi Travis." She let her smile dampen a little.

"Working hard or hardly working?" He winked.

"Just getting started." She pulled a file folder out of the desk and plopped it next to her keyboard.

"Sounds good!" He made a little wave before heading off to his computer. He hadn't decided to linger. Not a bad first interaction for the day.

She settled into her chair, while she could, confident that it would be like any other Sunday: insanely busy.

She kept the folder on her desk, mostly for show, and logged into her shopping cart. She hadn't completed her book purchases for the month and she was just as eager to see all those lovely new books as the patrons would be. For a bibliophile, there was nothing like opening those big boxes of new books, twenty to thirty at a time. She loved to lift them out, one by one, run her fingers over the smooth, cool, edges of pages and breathe in that papery inky smell that only new books possess. She enjoyed being the first person in the library to see those particular books and she hoped the patrons would love them too. Sometimes, when the desk shift was slow, she'd look up books she'd ordered recently to see if they were checked out or not. It was always a thrill to see they were out. That meant she was doing her job correctly and picking out material that resonated with her community.

As anticipated, it was foolhardy for her to try to order anything on a Sunday. The library was only open noon to five and the patrons made the most of it. She was hammered with computer questions, book requests, and telephone calls. There was barely time to sit, let alone work on anything.

Just as her stomach was starting to growl for a three o'clock snack, she looked up and saw James strolling toward her desk with a Tubby's bag in one hand and a fountain drink cup in the other. He also had a messenger bag slung over his shoulder, making him look preppy in a cute way.

"Hi." He greeted her with a smile. "I ken I'm a bad boy and you're no' allowed to eat in here, but I had a feeling you'd have the three o'clock munchies, if you're anything like me."

He handed the bag over the desk as discreetly as he could.

He brought her lunch! How thoughtful. And not only that, he'd remembered her recommendation about Tubby's.

"Thank you, James. That's so sweet!"

He clasped his hands and rested his forearms on the ledge of the desk in front of her.

"Since you had chicken last night, I figured you'd enjoy a turkey and cheese sandwich and a packet of crisps. I knew for a fact you'd drink iced tea."

"All perfect choices."

"You havenae eaten yet, have you?"

"I haven't and I'm starting to get hungry. I was just thinking about taking my break. I only get half an hour, but would you care to join me?"

That last part slipped out before Paige could consider what she was saying.

"I'd like that very much."

Paige phoned the children's department to let them know they'd have to cover her break. She'd have to do the same for them when she returned.

It was supposed to be a beautiful June day, just in the low 80s, so she was already thinking they could sit outside at the picnic table by the staff door. The view wasn't spectacular there, only overlooking the staff parking lot, but there were some trees beyond that and a clear sky above. It'd be nice to enjoy the fresh air, and a normal temperature. She shivered and pulled her thin sweater tighter around her body.

"Come on." She stood up and beckoned him to follow her toward the 'employees only' door. "Now you'll get to see the magical place known as the 'staff area.'" Paige led James through the back to get to the picnic table. She noticed how his gaze darted around, taking everything in.

"I've no' been in the back of a library before."

"It's not as organized as everything out front." She indicated the desks piled with stacks of books and papers. "Our organizational skills are all for show. Back here, you see what we're really like."

"I cannae believe it!" James teased. "I thought everything would be labeled and color coded."

They got settled outside and Paige took a deep breath of the warm air. Someone in one of the nearby neighborhoods must have recently mowed their lawn and the sweet scent of freshly cut grass was absolutely delightful.

She opened the Tubby's bag to discover it held two sandwiches and two bags of chips.

"Hey—" She turned to James who'd sat at the square table on the perpendicular side. "How did you know I'd invite you to join me?"

"Just a gamble that paid off, I guess." He squinted into the sun and smiled at her.

"What'd you get?" she asked, pulling out the first sandwich.

"Same as yours. Seemed only fair since I wasnae sure what your favorite might be."

"Turkey was a good call." She handed him the sandwich. "This is what I usually get. If not this, the chicken parmesan. Yummy."

James tapped his head. "Got it."

"Oh," she said, after dividing up the sandwiches and chips. "Do you need a drink? We have a vending machine in the lounge."

"I'm good." James reached into his messenger bag and pulled out the Vernors from last night. "Thought I'd try this ginger beer."

"Ginger beer? I'm not sure what that is but I'm pretty sure that's not the same thing as Vernors."

James cocked an eyebrow and looked at the can.

"It says ginger ale. It's no' the same thing but in American English?"

Paige shrugged. "I don't think so. I've never heard of ginger beer though."

James twisted open the lid. "I guess we'll find out." He sniffed the drink and gave Paige a 'here goes nothing' face and took a swig. His mouth puckered up and his eyes went all squinty as he swallowed it down.

Paige stifled a giggle. "I get the feeling it's not what you were expecting."

James shook his head and set the bottle firmly on the table. "No. I wasnae expecting that." He pointed an accusing finger at the can. "That is pure sweetness. Where's the ginger?"

"Careful now," Paige cautioned. "Vernors is a Michigan icon, and if you think that's sweet, you should try Faygo pop. That's another of our Michigan treasures. I'll have to get you a Rock & Rye, or a Red Pop before you leave."

"Maybe I'll take you up on that vending machine."

"Would you like my iced tea?" She held out her cup to him. "I'll switch with you. It's been awhile since I've had a Vernors. Now that you've tried and hated it, I could go for a refresher."

James handed her the bottle. "Be my guest."

Paige knew that she'd upped the intimacy a little by offering to take the bottle he'd drank from. Maybe she was more in need of dating than she realized, as she raised the bottle to her lips and felt all tingly because his lips had just been around the same plastic opening. Yeah. She was getting pathetic. And weird.

Paige tucked into her sandwich before her stomach could start gurgling again. Normally, she might be a little self-conscious to bite into a sub in front of a new acquaintance, especially one who was so damn cute, but she didn't have time for the luxury of nerves.

James cleansed his palate with a bite of his sandwich and a sip of iced tea. "You know, you keep saying you're going to tell me these unbelievable library stories, but I've no' heard one yet."

Paige chewed a bite of her sandwich thoughtfully, trying to wrack her brain for a good story to start with.

"There are so many, it's hard to know where to begin."

"The first one that comes to mind will be fine."

Paige took another sip of the Vernors while she narrowed down the first couple stories off the top of her head.

"Ooh, I've got one for you. This one time, I was sitting at the reference desk and a woman walked in with a cat on a leash. She strolled right up to the desk like there was nothing unusual about what she was doing."

"A cat? No way!"

"Oh yes. It was a scary one too. It stood up and put its front paws on the desk and stared right at me. I was half afraid it was going to jump up and scratch me. I had to tell her she couldn't have a cat in the library, and you know what she said to me?"

"Hard to say."

"She said it was a service animal and she was, in fact, allowed to have it in the library."

"You're no' making this up?"

"I couldn't come up with it if I tried. I ended up getting my boss because I had no idea what to do. Turned out, she didn't know either. She ended up having to bring it up at the management meeting. In the meantime, the cat made the decision for us. It started hissing at other patrons so we had to ask them to leave because they were disruptive."

"I would no' expect a person to bring a cat into the library. That's a wee bit eccentric."

"That's putting it nicely," Paige said. "That reminds me of another good animal story. The children's department had a local zoo come in for a program. They brought this baby alligator and it was standing on the floor in our program room. Then it did what all animals are really good at."

James's eyebrows were raised. "Go on," he prompted.

"It peed on the floor. Then, when our director, John, came in later, he asked how things were going. We said, 'other than the alligator pee, good.' He thought we meant 'bug juice.'"

"Bug juice? I think I'm missing the punchline."

"It's a camp thing. When kids go camping, bug juice is usually a sweet, powdered drink mixed with water. It's cheap and easy to make. Doesn't require refrigeration. I don't actually know where the name came from."

"I didnae realize the library was so full of animals."

"It's definitely a wild place," Paige said, making even herself groan.

"Maybe stick to the book discussions rather than jokes," James teased.

"Speaking of that," Paige said, "I think everyone loved you more than me, so we may not be able to let you go back to Scotland."

She didn't know why she'd said that, but even thinking about it gave her a little zing.

"You dinnae ken how tempting that is. Sometimes you just need more time away. But it's nice that they seemed so interested in Scotland. I'll have to be sure I dinnae disappoint them next time."

More time away? Kayla said he didn't have to go back to Scotland, but she was just teasing. And James was only exaggerating. Who didn't do that when they were faced with a hard situation? He kept dropping his enigmatic hints that something was going on back home that made him uncomfortable. She remembered his reluctance to get into it in the car. They were still on a time crunch for her break so she decided to let it pass, again.

"I bet everyone would be impressed if you showed up in a kilt. I mean, I would be. Just saying."

What in the actual heck was the matter with her?

She imagined what a hot Scot he'd make in a tight black t-shirt and a kilt. His arms were well-toned, but she was willing to bet he had some well-defined legs too. None of those were things she should be thinking about, let alone talk about.

James laughed, a big happy sound that warmed her heart. "Would you believe I just happened to leave my kilt at home?"

"And all this time I was just thinking you were wearing jeans to blend in with us Americans." There. That was steering things back on track. Less flirty, more friendly. Good.

She put her sandwich down and looked at him earnestly, suddenly very interested by the idea.

"Have you ever worn a kilt though?"

"Have you got a thing for them?" James's eyes twinkled with interest.

Why did he have to make her heart race when he looked at her that way?

"Avoiding the question?"

He grinned. "I think you do have a thing for them."

"And I think you're avoiding the question."

"Hang on." James pulled his phone out of his pocket and started scrolling. Finally, he handed the phone to her. "I think this'll answer your question."

Paige took the phone and saw a photo of a lovely bride in an elegant white gown standing next to her husband, in a handsome kilt. They were flanked on both sides by their wedding party. The bridesmaids in emerald green dresses and the groomsmen in kilts. One of the groomsmen looked very familiar.

Her imagination had nothing on the intensely hot reality of James in a kilt with a fancy black jacket. Be still her heart!

"Wow!" she said. "You look amazing!"

"Thank you. That's from my cousin Kirsty's wedding a few years back. Did it all over again for Nicola's wedding. So, aye. I do wear a kilt on occasion."

She reluctantly handed the phone back but filed that delicious photo away in her memory.

James made like he was going to put the phone back in his pocket but then exclaimed instead. "Oh. While I've got my phone out, would you mind if I get your number? Would be a lot easier to ask what kind of sandwich you'd like if I could reach you when I'm out."

Smooth. Possibly a little dangerous, but friends needed to have each other's numbers. She had Eric's number, for goodness sake.

Paige pulled her phone out. "Sure. Might as well give me yours too."

They exchanged phones and typed in their info. When they handed them back, James looked at Paige's entry.

"Hmm. There's a 'Paige Librarian' in my contacts. I'm worried she may have given me a fake name and will put my number on her block list."

Paige laughed. "I thought it'd be easier to remember who I am."

"That's no' going to be an issue."

Paige willed herself not to blush, so she took another swig of her drink to try to keep her face cool.

She scrolled through her phone to see how he'd listed his name in her contacts.

James A. MacKinnon.

"You know I have to ask," she said.

"What?" James looked genuinely confused.

"James *A.* MacKinnon? What's the A for?"

He took a bite of sandwich and pointed at his mouth, shaking his head.

Paige playfully pushed his shoulder.

"You're the one who put it in my contacts. You're asking for it!"

He smiled and swallowed his bite.

"Force o' habit. Didn't mean for it to be mysterious. It stands for Alistair."

"I can truthfully say, I've never met anyone with Alistair in their name. How cool!"

"Is it?" James asked.

"I think so. James Alistair MacKinnon. That's an excellent name."

"So what about you, Miss Paige Librarian?"

She laughed. "Calverley is my last name. Paige Marie Calverley."

"That's lovely. Paige Marie." He repeated it slowly as he tapped her real name into his phone. "Does anyone ever call you that?"

"By my name?"

"Paige Marie. Both names."

"No. Can't say that anyone ever has."

"It goes well together. Paige Marie. It rolls off the tongue nicely."

Hearing him say her name over and over was making her spine tingle. It did sound special when he said it like that, with that accent of his.

"I suppose it does," she agreed.

"Paige Marie," he said quietly again before taking another bite of his sandwich.

"James Alistair," she reciprocated, even though he had a point. Paige Marie did roll off the tongue easier than James Alistair, but she liked the way that sounded anyway. It sounded strong. Official.

She loved that they were playing around, having fun getting to know each other in their own silly way.

"So, what are your plans for the day?" Paige asked, pulling a chip out of her bag.

James leaned back and stretched his muscular arms upward and squinted into the bright sunlight.

"No real plans. I'll be needing to drive back to the studio and do some work."

"You can't stay cooped up on a day like this!"

"No?" He cocked his head.

"No. In Michigan, we wait all year for nice weather and then it's here and gone in the blink of an eye. You can't waste a sunny opportunity like this. I know you don't like driving here, but there's a lovely park right across the river from your apartment. There are walking paths and bike paths. Eric has a bike. He hardly ever uses it. I'm sure he'd let you borrow it if you were interested."

That reminded Paige of her text conversation with Kayla that morning, making her laugh.

"In fact, I definitely know Eric would let you borrow it. Kayla told me this morning Eric wondered if you'd go golfing with him sometime."

"I'm no' a great golfer, but that's nice of him to ask. I'd be happy to go with him sometime."

"I'll let him know. Or, better yet, let me do a group text so you'll have each other's numbers and you can plan it out yourselves." She sent a quick text to both of them before she forgot. Paige liked the feeling of James integrating with her best friends so well. Dinner with Kayla and Eric had been comfortable and fun. Now Eric was inviting James to hang out, just the guys. It felt like he belonged here.

She popped the last bite of sandwich in her mouth, balled up the paper in her fist, and shoved it back into the plastic bag. James did the same.

"Thank you, again, for bringing me lunch. That was very sweet of you."

"My pleasure." He grinned and the genuine happiness on his face made her wish she could just ditch work and keep hanging out with him all day, but that was no way to earn a promotion.

Paige glanced at her watch and sighed.

"I should be getting back in."

"Aye, of course. Thanks for spending your break with me." He glanced toward the parking lot, uncertainty coming over his face.

"You can come back in with me and go out the front doors," she said. "Or you can just go around the corner there and you'll be in the parking lot."

"I'll drop by the park and then get to the studio. Better to tear myself away now. I'm sorry."

"No, that makes sense. Enjoy the park for me!"

"I will. Promise."

"Ok. Come here, you." Paige opened her arms for James to fill them with his solid, reassuring presence. If it was possible, his hug was even more comfortable than it had been when she'd dropped him off. They just fit together so nicely, she hated to let him go.

She was the first to pull away, reluctantly. "May the sun inspire you! Go forth and create!" She hoped her silly words masked how badly she wanted to stay with him instead of going back to work.

His gaze didn't waver from her eyes and she actually felt weak in the knees. She thought that was just a literary device, but she definitely felt like she could melt at his feet.

"Want to come by the studio and see what I'm working on? No' right now, obviously. Maybe sometime this week?"

"I would love to see your art! That sounds wonderful. I'm off tomorrow since I'm working today. Is that too soon? I'm also off Thursday this week."

"Tomorrow's no' too soon at all. I'll text you the details later tonight, ok?"

"Sounds great."

She flashed what she hoped was a friendly smile, and turned to go back into the library. Her heart was practically leaping out of her chest in anticipation of spending more time with James, but there were patrons to serve and books to order. Tomorrow couldn't come fast enough.

Ten

PAIGE GOT HOME and collapsed onto her couch. It felt so good to lie down, she didn't know if she'd ever want to get up again. She pulled her phone out of her pocket, not even wanting to sit up enough to grab her TV remote off the end table. She texted Kayla.

Home again. How's it going there?

Kayla

I'm calling you RIGHT NOW!

Paige

Sure enough, the phone rang immediately. Paige answered and put it on speaker so she wouldn't have to bother with holding the phone up to her ear.

"Now we can properly talk about this Scottish hunk of yours!" Kayla practically shouted.

"Uhn," Paige groaned. "It was really busy at work. I'm kind of tired now."

"You cannot bring that delicious man into our house and stay here with him until the morning hours and then refuse to have a proper conversation with me about him."

"We did talk about him this morning. Remember?" Paige asked.

"That was texting. It doesn't count."

Paige rolled onto her back and closed her eyes, draping a hand over her forehead. She certainly didn't mind talking about James, but she could have stood more sleep. Still, she did have news for Kayla. Thinking about it sent a little thrill of energy through her. Maybe she wasn't as sleepy as she thought.

"Well, he did come up to visit me at the library today and he surprised me with lunch."

"I knew it! See? He's the real deal, Paige. We loved him!" Kayla exclaimed.

"Well, I told him at lunch that Eric was asking about golfing together and James said he'd be down for it. So, make sure you tell Eric the bromance is full steam ahead, but James also invited me to come to the studio and see what he's working on tomorrow."

"Listen, Paige. Listen to me right now. Things might be moving fast, but that isn't a bad thing. Plenty of people have whirlwind romances in real life. I say embrace it!"

Paige opened her eyes and sat up.

"Kayla, I love you, but is there a teensy possibility that might be the pregnancy hormones talking here?"

"I'm going to pretend you didn't say that. Instead, I will say, guys like James don't come along every day."

"I know. I know that. But what if he's too good to be true? It's not like we really know much about him. Anyone can make a good impression." She pulled up the memory of that kilt picture. That was a really, really good impression.

"Look, I know you're trying to be reasonable after what you've been through. That's smart and I get it, but I saw with my own eyes that you two light up around each other. I suppose it could just be the blush of new attraction, but it looks like more to me."

Attraction, yes. There was definitely an attraction. Paige could fully get on board with attraction at first sight but it sounded like Kayla wanted it to be love. Paige didn't even know what she wanted. Two months. She only had two months with James anyway. Of course she didn't want to lose her heart and be left with nothing...again. She'd already wasted so much time on the wrong one. Why couldn't there be some sort of lightning crash or blaring trumpets when you met the right one? That would save so many people so much trouble.

"Time will tell." Paige hated herself for even talking about time when there was so little of it.

"Does James strike you as the kind of guy who won't seize an opportunity? Do you think he'd hesitate rather than try for what he wants? He crossed an ocean to follow his dreams, Paige. A whole ocean! He's not going to do what Dylan did."

"Wow—" Paige didn't know what else to say about that. She had enough pressure on herself to figure out what was going on. Kayla may know her better than anyone else, but she didn't need pressure to fall in love from her too. Just because Kayla and Eric were so happy, it didn't mean she could will it to happen in Paige's life. Of course, she wasn't going to say that to Kayla. She knew Kayla wanted her to be happy. How could anyone fault her for that?

"I know. I'm not usually so blunt," Kayla continued, clearly on a roll, "but maybe James was a wake-up call for me too. A glimpse of what you could have. The comparison is startling. Even in the very beginning, you and Dylan weren't ever like you and James were yesterday. I'm not just saying that."

Paige didn't want to compare James to Dylan. She'd known Dylan for years. They had a lot of history. They'd been through good and bad times together, and he'd chosen to let her go. She'd known James for a week. They had a great friendship going on, albeit a flirty one, but that was it for now. There was nothing to compare. As much as she liked him, she needed to keep remembering that.

"James isn't going to be here long. Yes, he's polite, cute, smart, and nice, but temporary, Kayla. He's so very temporary."

Kayla was silent for a few beats before she answered.

"Plans can always change, Paige."

"That's a heck of a decision to make based on eight weeks," Paige said.

"Ugh! Stop being so stubborn! Remember when we were in high school and we used to dream about the future guy who would sweep us off our feet?"

"Of course, but we were kids then," Paige reasoned.

"Well, yes. A lot of it was unrealistic but some of it isn't. It's ok to let yourself be swept along by a good guy. I'll stop now, but I wanted to say it. Someone had to say it to you. You were so happy last night with James. Natural too. You were just yourself and it made me so happy to see. I'm glad you brought him."

Paige remained quiet. When Kayla put it like that, she had to admit it was true. She hadn't felt self-conscious or like she needed to impress James. She felt comfortable and safe with James and her best friends. When was the last time she'd felt that carefree with Dylan? The will he/won't he question had weighed heavily on her for the past couple years. She'd been doing a balancing act of trying to be cool and give Dylan space, while at the same time, expressing her readiness for more. That effort to keep balance had been pulling her apart every day. Now that she was six months away from that, she did feel lighter, more herself, and in touch with what she wanted. She did want James to be around for more than two months, but was that really something she had power over? It was so much to ask.

Suddenly, Paige could feel her lower lip start to quiver and her eyes began to fill.

"I don't know what to do," Paige admitted in a voice that was almost too thin to hear.

"I know," Kayla said, soothing as the mother she was about to become. "It isn't easy. I know you just met him, but the way he treated you. The way he looked at you. It was so genuine. So caring. It reminded me of all the things I love about Eric. And I'm not ashamed to tell you that Eric was the lucky recipient of some hot pregnancy sex after you guys left. It was all so romantic. Made me hot for what I got."

Paige couldn't help but laugh, luckily suppressing the sudden urge to cry.

"Well, good for you guys, but also, don't ever tell me that again."

"Sorry. But if that's what it takes to get you to—"

"Nope. That's not what it takes to get me to do anything other than want to remove that image from my mind."

"You know what I mean."

"I do," Paige agreed. "Seriously. And you're a good friend for having the guts to say it."

"Just think about it."

"I'm definitely thinking."

"Ok, anything else going on today that I need to know about?"

Paige chuckled. "No. It was a busy day, I'm just going to eat something and chill before bed."

"And?"

"And what?"

"Are you going to talk to James?"

"I saw him today. We're going to the studio tomorrow. I'm not going to smother him!"

"Right. Two months though."

"Stop!" Paige said. "You're making me crazy. And I thought you weren't going to talk about this anymore."

"Yes. True. I'm just saying James is great and I hope we all get a chance to see him again. And if he wants to read me a book sometime while I'm doing housework, that would be totally fine."

"His accent is definitely to die for," Paige conceded.

"And those manners! Oh, I just want to call up his mother and tell her she can be so proud of that boy!" Kayla gushed.

Paige remembered the quick peek she'd seen of his mother and wondered what their relationship was like. She wondered again what he'd meant when he'd said things were getting heavy at home. Was it a problem with his mom? Was it something to do with the girl he'd broken up with? There was so much she didn't know about James and his life. As charming and cute as he was, he was definitely a mystery. An attractive mystery that she did want to figure out.

"Hey," Kayla said. "What are you thinking about?"

"You know, I just feel like I'm...I'm…" Paige paused searching for just the right word to describe the turmoil going on inside her. "On the cusp of something."

"You definitely are," Kayla agreed. "And whatever it is, I think it's going to be wonderful."

"Yeah," said Paige. "I think it is too."

Eleven

A WHIRLWIND of thoughts swirled through Paige's mind on her
way to James's studio. Last night's conversation with Kayla was at the
forefront. She may be pregnant and emotional, but what if she was
right? Paige couldn't deny that she was practically shaking with excitement to see James and his artwork. It felt like a very intimate date.
Paige had been a book lover since she was a child. She knew how
vulnerable authors felt putting their words into the world. It must be
similar for visual artists. The best artists, of all types, put their heart
and soul into their work. She respected that it was a big deal for James
to trust her to look inside his soul like this.

She pulled up outside a warehouse-looking building. Not the
murdery abandoned warehouse kind, but clean, well-lit, and industrial.
She spotted James's rental Nissan out front and parked next to it.

Paige grabbed her phone and sent him a quick text to let him know
she'd arrived.

James came out to greet her with one of his signature warm hugs
and showed her into the building.

"I don't know what I was expecting when you said 'studio—'"
Paige gazed all around the building. "But it wasn't this."

The top of the building was lined with windows which let the bright summer sunlight stream through. No trace of fluorescent lighting here. The natural light made the large space feel airy and uplifting.

The perimeter of the space was filled with cubes. Not like the cubicles she had at work, but more like big, square offices. They had no ceilings, so the natural light could fill them too. Some of the cubes were empty, others had artists working away on all sorts of projects. She saw a painter standing at his easel, a potter busy at her wheel, and some spaces were piled with in-progress art and supplies all over. Different sounds emanated from each room. Some had music playing, others had banging, chiseling, or slapping depending on the medium of their artists. The background cacophony of creativity was invigorating. Even though she wasn't an artist, her arms hummed with an energy to be *doing* something in a space like this. The whole place was charged with positive, creative energy. She could see how this would be the perfect environment for an artist.

"It is a great space," James agreed. "We dinnae talk to each other much, but you can feel the creativity of the other artists here. I havenae been in a space like this before either. It's been very freeing for me already."

He led her down to the end of the building. The very last cube on the left was his designated space.

"Here we are," James said, nervously rubbing the back of his neck. "This is what I've been up to so far."

Paige stepped into the room and deeply inhaled the scent of lumber. Her eyes were drawn to the workbench in the center of the room and the wood shavings littering it and the floor. A large chunk of wood stood on the table, but part of it had been carved away to reveal the rough shape of a ship emerging from the larger piece.

Paige walked reverently to the table. The air in the room was still and charged with promise, like in a museum or cathedral.

She leaned down to get eye level with the figure James was exhuming from the log. Even though it was still pretty raw, Paige was amazed by what she saw. While all the rest of the log still resembled a log, this little part had been rough-hewn into the very clear image of a ship. She could see the scoring of the chisel against the wood and the rougher strokes he'd taken to get to this point. If you'd put a chuck of wood and a chisel in front of her, she'd have no idea where to begin. The fact that he'd taken the raw material and already transformed it into the ship she saw before her, blew her mind.

"James," she breathed. "This is incredible."

"Oh, this is early days. Still a long way to go before it looks like anything much."

"But look at this!" Paige gestured at the table. "How do you decide what to cut away and what stays? I can't imagine doing anything like this."

James joined her at the table and pointed at the emerging ship. "It's no' like that for me. When I pick up a piece of wood, I feel the story inside of it. It used to be alive. All living things have a story of some sort. Once I feel that story, it's like the wood guides me to the image inside. I dinnae feel like I'm really the one making the decisions. I just uncover what was there all along."

James's face was so close to hers and his words, combined with the creative atmosphere, made Paige dizzy. All rational thoughts left her mind and she found the full focus of her attention on his lips. They were so close. So enticing. Her eyes began to close.

James's phone buzzed in his pocket, effectively breaking the moment. He groaned and fished it out of his pocket.

"I'm sorry, it's my ma." He shrugged sheepishly.

"No, no. Take it. Should I…" she pointed to the entrance but James shook his head.

"Stay," he said, and answered the call.

"Ye' a'right?" He greeted her warmly. "I'm at the studio with—"

Paige was interested to see how he'd introduce her, but apparently, his mother had cut him off before he got the chance.

"Aye, I'm eating enough." James pointed at the phone and shook his head at Paige.

She stifled a chuckle. It warmed her heart to know that James's mom was the kind of person who wanted to be sure her son was well looked after.

"Ma, I—" He tried again, but it seemed as though his mother wasn't to be deterred from her train of thought. He had said she was stubborn. Apparently, he wasn't exaggerating.

Paige looked around the room to distract herself from feeling like she was eavesdropping. She kicked at a curly pile of shavings on the floor, imagining how James's arms must flex and move to meticulously chip each shaving from the log. It was a nice daydream.

"Aye, I know." James sighed. "There are plenty o' students who can help out temporarily. I talked to David about all this before I left. He has enough help. Dinnae worry."

Paige bristled at James's tone. Just from his side of the conversation, she'd guess that his mother might not be so pleased that he was over here spending time on his art. Not that it was her business, but she felt bad if that was the case. Librarianship was not a career anyone ever entered for the money, and Paige's parents had been nothing but supportive when she'd announced she was going to library school. It was two more years, and thousands more dollars, to earn her Master of Library and Information Science, but they never batted an eye. If it was what she wanted, they'd support it. End of story. She couldn't imagine how she would have felt if they weren't happy with that decision, or if they'd tried to persuade her into something she didn't feel passionately about. She hoped she was misreading the situation, for James's sake.

"Listen, Ma—" He ran a hand over his face. "The exhibit is only six weeks away. If I dinnae have a few good pieces to show, they aren't going to be very happy with me. I appreciate what Uncle Davie's doing, you know that, but can we discuss that when I'm home again, please?"

James was quiet for a little bit before he spoke again, in a lighter tone.

"Aye, the weather is perfect here. Nothing but sunshiny days and warm nights. You could come here and dry out for a bit."

He laughed, and Paige felt that whatever tension the call had started with had dissipated.

"I'm no' alone, Ma. I met a lovely librarian who introduced me to her friends. In fact she's—"

Once again, Paige perked up to see what he'd say about her, but it seemed his mother had cut him off again.

He turned his back and lowered his voice, but in the quiet of the studio, Paige still heard him.

"Ye' ken we're not together anymore, Ma. We're both free to spend our time how we please. That's guid if she wants to go out with Andrew. I've met—"

Apparently, his mom wasn't having any of it.

When James got off the phone, he ran a hand over his face.

"Everything okay?" Paige asked.

"Yeah. Ma was a little concerned since it's the busiest season for my uncle. Sometimes she thinks I should focus less on the art, but it's hard to do that when I'm here specifically for art."

"That's rough, I'm sorry."

"Sounds like Davie hasnae been feeling well these last few days, so they're hurting for my help with the tours." He sighed again, his face clenching with the strain going on inside him. "I can see her point. Davie's got his daughters but the two are married and Fiona is off at university. Kirsty's pregnant with her second child. Nicola moved to Aberdeen with her husband. Davie relies on me. Ma would like me to come home early, but how can I do that? The Arts Council is counting on me. I took a spot that someone else could have had. A twenty-eight year old man should be able to make his own way, at least once."

Twenty-eight? Paige hadn't considered that James was a little younger than her. Lately, she'd preferred not to think of it, but her thirtieth birthday was just around the corner.

"That sounds really tough." She just wanted to hug him until everything was all right, but that wasn't possible. "I can't imagine what it's like to have all that pressure on you from your family to do something you don't want to do anymore, but I can relate to not being where you expected to be at this point. I'm a little older than you. Twenty-nine for another week, and here I am with only a part time job. That's definitely not where I envisioned myself. I thought my life would look a lot more like Kayla's."

"You're doing well for yourself," James countered. "You have your own career. You've got your own place. You're smart and capable. You'll have that promotion in no time and then you'll have everything you want."

"Not everything," Paige said before she could think better of it.

James raised his eyebrows, clearly waiting for an explanation.

If Kayla wanted her to go all in, she might as well put it out there. If James ran now, it would just make it easier for both of them, right?

"Well, as it turns out, I'm one of those stereotypical women who wants to get married and have kids. I thought I'd be on that path right alongside Kayla, but my ex had different ideas. I actually broke up with him six months ago because he asked me to move in with him to 'see if we were compatible for the long haul.' We'd been together nearly six years, so, if he didn't know that already, I didn't think he was ever going to. So, not only do I want the promotion, I want the husband and the pitter patter of little feet. Not very original."

"Why would that be a bad thing?" James asked, genuine concern in his beautiful eyes. "Everyone wants to find love and settle down. I want that too. And, if I can be frank, it sounds like you dodged a bullet with the boyfriend. Any man who would risk letting you go is a daft prick."

Paige's heart warmed. Had James written a manual on what to say to women? He was always getting it right.

"Thanks. Looking back, I think I ignored a lot of red flags because I was too focused on what I wanted. I'm never doing that again."

A hard look passed over James's face for a moment, then faded. They were both quiet for a few moments, privately reflecting on their own demons.

"I think it's very brave that you walked away from something that wasnae working for you. Even if it took a long time."

"Well, I think it's very brave of you to come here for this residency. Especially with everything going on back home."

James looked at Paige and smiled a subdued smile. "I'd intended to let you see me in action, but now, that seems like an egotistical and boring move."

"No, I'd love to see you work. Please do. You won't even know I'm here."

"I doubt that very much, but if you're really interested, I can do a bit of carving."

Paige looked around the room and found a stool off to the side. She pulled it up behind James and sat down. "I'm just a silent observer," she said. "I want to understand how you do this."

James's face relaxed, as if he was pleased with her comment.

"Aye, but do tell me if you get bored and we'll do something else."

Paige nodded, totally sure she'd never tire of watching him do anything.

He turned to a metal cabinet in the back of the space and pulled out a toolbox. He took out a selection of chisels, picks, and mallets, and set them one the table before stepping back to contemplate.

Paige couldn't tear her eyes from James's face as he surveyed the wood. She could see the artistic transformation come over him. The longer he looked at the log, the deeper his eyes focused on it, reading the grain to decipher its secrets. He held out his arms and framed the piece with his hands, moving them this way and that, squinting through reality to reach the creative vision. Then she saw it. A sparkle in his eyes and his posture relaxed. He'd seen it. He was ready to begin.

He stepped to the table and pursed his lips as he contemplated which of his tools would be the right one for the task at hand. He picked a couple up, then set them down, before settling on the combination he needed to begin.

She transferred her gaze to his strong hands as he began to tap the chisel gently into the soft flesh of the log. His movements were careful and precise. She watched the muscles in his arms flex and contract as he worked. Looked like his carving provided all the workout he'd need to keep those arms in top shape.

Paige watched, entranced, as James moved around the piece, finding the right angles to tap out the ship hidden within. It was a form of art, in and of itself, to see him as he worked. Paige had been right. There was raw, vulnerable energy coursing through the room as James tapped into inspiration and went where it led. He'd said he wouldn't forget that she was in the room with him, but she could clearly see that he was in his own world. His eyes only seeing the wood and the vision. The room around them could have been on fire, and he would be too absorbed in his work to notice. He was a being of beauty on a level completely different from sheer attraction. His very soul was exposed before her prying eyes and she couldn't help but feel that her own soul was reaching out to his in answer.

She wasn't aware of how long she watched him work. She was as entranced by him as he was by his vision. The spell was only broken when her stomach growled loudly, startling them both.

James turned to her, eyes large and wild before he blinked and started to shed his artistic cocoon for the reality around him. He set down his tools and ran his hands through his hair.

"Shite, Paige, I did forget you were here. I'm so sorry!"

Paige crossed her arms and kept them low over her traitorous stomach. "I lost track of time myself. It's like you were doing this intimate dance with the wood and the creative flow. I've never seen anything like it. It was captivat—"

Her words cut off when she saw the look on his face. The intensity of his expression drilled deep into her. The fire in his eyes was like a physical touch to her, and her reaction was decidedly more than friendly.

"No one has ever watched me work like this before." He was breathing a little hard. Maybe from the exertion of carving, but the way he looked at her made her think it was something else entirely.

"No one?" Her voice came out in a husky whisper. She took a step toward him.

"No. They've never taken it seriously like you do. It's no' something I've wanted to share with someone until you."

The air in the room changed from the spark of creativity to the increasingly familiar electricity of attraction.

The wildness of creative passion hadn't left his eyes and he took the few strides he needed to close the space between them.

"Paige Marie—" His voice was deeper than normal. "I would love to kiss you in a non-platonic way right now."

She nodded in answer to his gravitational pull, and much to her own surprise, she put her arms around him and pressed her body close.

Tiny wood shavings clung to the hairs on his forearms and the front of his shirt, scratching lightly against the exposed skin of her arms and collarbone. When James's lips met hers, she wasn't aware of any other physical sensation. James held her tight and kissed her with an urgent need she couldn't remember ever feeling with Dylan. Thank God she'd gotten rid of him, if only to have a kiss like this! She closed her eyes and surrendered to the warm, passionate experience of kissing James Alistair MacKinnon. This was undoubtedly what her stomach had grumbled about. It wasn't lack of food. It was the lack of James's lips against hers.

His hand reached up and cupped the side of her face and neck. Tiny curls of wood scratched gently between his fingers and her skin, but it didn't bother her at all.

If she were a character in one of the books she loved to read, she would have skillfully removed his shirt with her hands while they somehow continued to kiss. She'd push him against the worktable, undo his pants, and make the most passionate love of her life right there next to his partially carved ship.

The scene played out vividly in her mind, but in reality, she held on, if only just, to her sensible side. No matter what fantasies her mind cared to indulge, she was still Paige. She wasn't the type for frantic sex in the art studio where anybody could walk by at any time. It was enough of a stretch to be the type who made out with a hot Scottish artist she'd known for two weeks. She half expected alarm bells to go off in her head, warning her that she'd crossed a foolish line and was making a huge mistake. No bells were ringing, but her body was humming.

When they finally pulled away from each other, each was breathless and Paige's legs were wobbly.

"Wow." She tried to steady her breathing and calm her wild heartbeat.

"You're an amazing kisser." James sounded a bit ragged himself.

"You say that like you had nothing to do with it."

James blew out a long, appreciative, breath. He blinked and looked around the room as if surprised to find that he was still standing in his studio space with the world carrying on as if nothing groundbreaking had happened.

"That was definitely not a friendly kiss." Paige tucked her hair behind her ears as her senses started to come back to her.

Worry flashed across James's face. "I'm sorry. I know you just want to be friends. I got caught up with my work and then the way you were looking at me I just—"

Paige shushed him. "That was the best kiss of my life."

"Sooo…you're no' mad at me?"

"I am definitely not mad. In fact, I could definitely use more of that."

As she tentatively leaned in, her stomach took the opportunity to express its displeasure again with a loud growl.

James laughed. "Point taken. Man cannot live on kisses alone, although, with you, I wouldnae mind trying."

Paige smiled and ran her finger over his luscious lips. He gently caught her hand with his and pressed her palm to his lips for a tender kiss.

"Come on. We've got to feed you."

"Way to kill the mood." Paige glared down at her stomach like the traitor it was.

James draped an arm around Paige's shoulders and gave her a squeeze. "I dinnae know about you, but I'll be able to pick up that mood again pretty easily. Meanwhile, let's grab some food. Whatever you want."

Paige leaned her head on James's shoulder, loving the weight of his arm on her and the solidness of his body pressed next to hers. She was treading on dangerous ground. She knew that, but danger had never felt so good.

Twelve

PAIGE COULDN'T STOP SMILING since she'd broken through the friend zone with James. Her mind kept replaying the way they hadn't been able to keep their hands off each other since they'd kissed. They'd picked up a quick lunch to eat in the park and if their hands weren't touching, they were knee to knee, or someone's head was resting on the other's shoulder.

Dylan hadn't been one for PDAs, but it was so natural with James it wasn't even something she thought about. In fact, she didn't understand how she'd been able to keep her hands off him beforehand.

They'd even stopped back at the studio for a mini-woodworking lesson for Paige. She'd laughed as he wrapped his arms around her and put his hands over hers as she learned how to hold the chisel. She'd made a few sad gouges in a spare chunk of wood and he'd been so proud of her that he'd given her a kiss that left her so flustered and breathless that she nearly dropped the chisel onto her toes. That would teach her not to wear sandals in a woodworking studio again. Now her daydreams were so vivid she could almost smell the scent of fresh wood and James's soapy clean scent wherever she went.

Rejuvenated by this newfound connection with James, she felt a self-confidence she didn't realize had been missing. When she got to work and saw Christie was in her office, Paige felt bold rather than nervous. She was ready to make a move.

She knocked on Christie's door and popped her head in.

Christie looked up from her computer. "Hey, Paige. What's up?"

Paige sat down in the chair across from Christie's desk and smiled with confidence. "The book discussion was awesome!"

Christie's interest was significantly piqued at that, so she turned her chair away from her computer to give Paige her absolute full attention.

Paige recounted the lively discussion, the addition of new participants, the success of the dessert idea, and how the group spontaneously asked James to come back and do a Scottish themed discussion. When she was finished, Christie leaned back in her chair looking impressed.

"I knew putting you in charge of the discussion group was a good idea. Nice job, Paige. This is a promising start. We can rebrand the group as Desserts and Discussion, and make sure you submit a reimbursement form for the doughnuts you brought in. It'd be great if you could get local sponsors, but don't sweat it if you can't. There's enough in the program budget to offer monthly desserts."

Things were going well. There wouldn't be a better time to broach the topic.

"While I'm here…" Paige folded her hands in her lap. "I wondered if there's any news about Yolanda's position yet."

Christie's stoic business face was firmly in place.

"John and I are finalizing the job posting. It is going to remain a full time position."

Paige's heart thumped in excitement at that news.

"We'll probably post it next week, collect applicants, and do interviews. I'd love for you to apply. You do excellent work here, as you've just proven again with the discussion."

"Thanks!" Paige tried to keep her mind from going a mile a minute from excitement. It was actually happening. She really had a shot at landing a full time position.

"I'd really love that job. I've been working on more ideas for the book discussions and other new programs too."

"I'm actually about to meet with John right now, but I'd love to hear your other ideas. Knowing you, they're all excellent."

Paige smiled and stood to go. "Great. We'll talk later."

Paige walked back to her cubicle feeling like things were really coming together. Things were going awesome with James and she allowed herself to believe she'd actually end up with the job.

With a spring in her step, she popped into the break room with her phone to see if James was around.

She sent him a quick text.

> **Hey you. I'm still flying high from our time together yesterday. Such a great time!**
>
> Paige

It didn't take long before Paige saw those three little dots signifying that James was typing back.

> **Me too. Let's do it again as soon as possible. What are you up to now?**
>
> James

> **I wish! Actually, I'm at work and I talked to my boss about the promotion.**
>
> Paige

And???

James

She wants me to apply. I think I have a good shot at getting it!

Paige

Of course you do! You're brilliant!

James

Thank you. I sure hope so.

Paige

I can tell her you're the best librarian there is. Would that help?

James

Aww. You're so sweet.

Paige

How long are you working? Should I stop by?

James

I'm in the back for a change. Shouldn't you be making art?

Paige

I have been! Dinner then? My place. I'll cook.

James

How can I say no to that?

Paige

You're not meant to.

James

Then I'll be over when I'm done here. Around 5:30? Ok?

Paige

I'll have it on the table when you walk in. See you then, Paige Marie X

James

Paige put her phone away feeling even more euphoric. James had that effect on her. She could hardly believe how easy it was to be with him. Sure they were just in that happy beginning phase, but they seemed to just click. There was a kindness and attentiveness about him that she wasn't used to. The more she thought about it, the more she wondered why in the world she'd been so focused on marrying Dylan in the first place. They'd gotten along well but it was never like this. This rush of energy she felt with James, it made her feel like a new person. A better version of herself.

Paige grinned. Here she'd been thinking she was sad and washed up, on the cusp of thirty without a full-time job or any prospects of romance and right around the corner she'd run headlong into two unimaginable opportunities. That promotion was so close she could almost taste it. Speaking of tasting, she couldn't wait to see what James would serve for dinner.

Thirteen

PAIGE PULLED up to James's apartment building excited for a homey dinner, just the two of them. She'd stopped off home to freshen up and chosen a tight pair of khaki capri pants and a floaty white blouse with a pink cherry blossom print.

She knocked on his door and he greeted her with a hug and a sweet kiss on the lips before leading her in. She took a moment to appreciate that he was wearing a fitted black t-shirt and cargo shorts.

"Hungry?" James gestured to the little table, where, true to his word, there were two places set with steaming plates of food.

"Smells good in here." Paige inhaled the garlic and tomato tones in the air. "What did you make?"

"I hope you like lasagna."

"You're in luck." Paige rubbed her hands together. "There's very little I don't like to eat. I'm not picky."

"That's my girl." The addition of a possessive gave Paige a thrill. "Come have a seat. I'll just get the drinks."

James poured two glasses of red wine to go along with the meal and they both took a seat at the small table.

"I'm sorry everything's so wee here." James's knees knocked

against Paige's when he sat, driving his point across. "It's no' the best space for entertaining."

"It's cozy." Paige didn't mind her intimate proximity to James at all. "Nothing to worry about."

"Bon appétit!" James raised his glass toward her. She answered by clinking hers with his and taking a sip.

"How did your day go?" James asked, cutting into his lasagna.

Paige thought back to her conversation with Christie before she spoke. "You know how sometimes you just get a good feeling about something?"

"Aye. I do." He looked pointedly at Paige, and she felt herself getting lost in the blue of his eyes.

"Oh!" She snapped herself out of it. She could at least get through the meal before she went all gooey on him. Probably. Well, if she really tried. "I checked out a book about Scotland today. I'm trying to learn more about it so I'll have a better understanding of where you come from."

James smiled broadly. "I feel a bit like an unofficial ambassador. I'm chuffed you're so keen to learn more."

"See? Just like that. 'Chuffed?' I've never heard that before."

James leveled his gaze as if he couldn't quite believe what he was hearing.

"You've no' heard the word chuffed before? How can this be?"

Paige felt a little embarrassed, but only because she felt, as a librarian, she should have a grasp on the English language in all its forms. But she brushed that away, more excited by the chance to learn new things and compare the differences of their heritage.

She shook her head. "I'm afraid not. We definitely don't use that expression here. Sounds like it's a good thing though."

"Aye. It means I'm very pleased."

"Chuffed." Paige tried the word out, liking the way it felt to say it. "So, I could say I'm chuffed that the book discussion went so well?"

"Aye! You've got it."

Paige smiled, pleased that she'd added a new word to her vocabulary.

"It's fascinating! Now that I've met you, I can't believe how little I know about Scotland. It's embarrassing, really."

"No need to be embarrassed. We'll fix that."

Paige bit into her lasagna and enjoyed the cheesy, tomatoey goodness of it.

"Mmm. This is really good."

"I'm glad you like it. I'm no chef, but it's one of the dishes I'm good at."

"Who taught you to cook?" Paige asked, genuinely curious.

"Mostly my ma, but Auntie Cait too. We spent a lot of time with my Auntie Cait and Uncle Davie while I was growing up. They live close and helped my ma out a lot after my dad packed up and left. They're like extra parents to me."

"That's nice that your family's close."

"Aye. Some things are good about it. Some things no' as much."

Finally, they were alone with no time constraints and the subject had come up. Maybe it was her chance to find out what was going on.

"I get the feeling there's something bothering you," she said gently. "If you want to talk about it, I'm here."

"Aye." James lowered the forkful of pasta he was about to eat. "Have you ever felt like you have to be something for someone else that you dinnae want to be?"

One recent example came to mind. She wasn't sure he'd like to hear about that, but in the interest of honesty, she figured she might as well put it out there. At least he'd know they could share important things with each other.

"When I was dating Dylan, I felt like I had to be cool with not moving our relationship forward because Dylan was reluctant. If I tried to have a conversation about it, I felt like a nag. I realize now that I spent a lot of time trying to convince him I was worth sticking around for. I tried to be an extra great version of myself so he wouldn't have reservations anymore. Maybe that's not quite the same…"

He nodded, his face in a grim smile.

"I'm sorry you had to go through that. I dinnae ken what his problem was, but you are worth sticking around for, Paige Marie. I hope you know that."

The words shimmered over her body, making her wonder if he was getting at something by saying that.

"I do now." She had to look away from the intensity in his eyes.

James wasn't done talking though.

"Now that you say it, I think I've been the same way. Trying to subtly get people to realize that I'm no' what they want me to be."

Paige looked up again, now that the heat was off her. "What do they want you to be?"

James blew out a deep breath.

"I'm from a close knit community. Besides my auntie and uncle, there's another family that lived close by that we spent a lot of time with: the MacIntosh family. They have three sons and a daughter. Cora and I are the same age and we grew up together."

"Mmm hmm." Paige tried not to become apprehensive about where the conversation was heading.

"We got on well, and eventually, there was this expectation from our families that we'd be a couple. We were just teenagers, so it was fine at first. But time went by and neither of us found someone else to be with and our families would joke about how we'd get married one day. About a year or so ago, the joking turned more serious. Cora's brothers started asking when I planned to officially become the fourth MacIntosh brother. Her ma would drop hints about good places to host a wedding. My ma made little comments about how I'm far more responsible than my father and that she was sure I'd be settling down soon. She's no' a bad girl. I'm no' here to say anything bad about Cora. I think she was feeling trapped by it all too, but we didnae really talk about it. What do you do when your whole family and all your important people have your life mapped out for you?"

James looked deep into Paige's eyes with a searching look. His expression was so open and vulnerable under the burden of the emotional baggage he was carrying around. Paige wanted to do something to take it all away from him.

"I can't imagine how hard that must be for you, and Cora, to face."

James scoffed and his jaw tightened.

"Aye, it was hard. We did break up but our families havnae completely accepted it's for good. But I've also got the specter of my father hovering over me. He walked out when I was just a babe. I dinnae know him, but he's been the conspicuous absence in my life. His name was like a curse word in my family. 'Dinnae be like Robert.' 'Thank God James didnae inherit Robert's wanderin' ways.' It was like a badge o' honor to be dependable and take care o' everyone else. And I did it. I did it because I didnae want to hurt them again after what my father had done. Davie and Cait took us in, when my ma had nowhere else to turn. They helped raise me so my ma could work and save enough to get us our own wee flat. I could never pay them back for everything they did for me growing up.

"And now Davie's getting serious about me taking on more of his company. I dinnae want to let him down, but I dinnae see it being something I can do my whole life. Everywhere I turn, someone wants a commitment from me that I cannae give.

"And you want to know the best part?" James leaned forward a little in emphasis.

"Hmm," Paige said, not wanting to say anything more for fear that she'd start crying.

"This rogue father of mine is a musician! Robert, the musical artist! And here I am, James the visual artist. He couldnae be tied down to one place with a wife and child, so he kept moving on. They think my coming here for the residency is a slap in the face and they're worried I'm going to turn out like him after all. To be honest, I dinnae know anymore. Maybe I am like him. I like being here. I like waking up and planning my day the way I want. I like spending my days in the studio instead o' the boat. I like being with you. So, now you know. I'm no amazing man, Paige. I'm a wee bit of a lost soul."

James didn't look at her then. His gaze was downcast and his hands rested on either side of his plate.

Paige couldn't abide the distance of the table between them any longer. She walked around it and hugged him, hoping she could make him feel wrapped up in understanding and support.

"That doesn't make you like your father at all," she said.

"The MacKinnons may no' agree with you," he scoffed.

Paige squeezed him tighter.

"No. You're not. It sounds like your father left and never looked back. You care about your family. I'd say your heart is breaking because you're trying so hard not to hurt them. You're an incredibly good son and the most loyal nephew I've ever heard of. You are an amazing man. You really are."

"Maybe so, but running away is a coward's way. I couldnae face them so I left. I'm no' proud of that."

"Sometimes people won't listen to you until you do something drastic. You're following your heart, whether they understand that right now or not. I saw your face when you were carving. You were in another world. You weren't running away then. You were running toward your dreams. Your passion. And you crossed an ocean to do it. That's very brave."

James sighed. "They love me, but they cannae understand why I came here when I could be trying to advance my career alongside Uncle Davie. It's put a strain on things, but they think I'll get it out o' my system and come back ready to toe the line. I'm afraid I'm going to let them all down."

James's broad shoulders slumped down as if he really was carrying the burden of his family's expectations.

"What do you want to do?" Paige stepped back from the hug so she could look at James's face again.

"I know I'm no' going to make a living as an artist. I'm no' daft, but I dinnae want to give boat tours for the rest of my days. I'm no' sure which direction I want to go yet, but I know it has to be something different."

"Well, whatever it is, you're going to find it and you're going to be great at it. I have faith in you."

James's shoulders relaxed and he looked at Paige with a glimmer of hope in his blue eyes.

"I dinnae think I deserve you, Paige Marie."

"Oh, I don't know. I'd like to think we deserve each other."

James reached for her hand and brushed a trail of the lightest kisses across her knuckles.

"Where've you been all my life?" His breath was hot against the skin of her hand.

"Michigan," she answered, echoing his answer from their first meeting.

James squeezed her hand, pushed back from the table and then gently tugged her onto his lap.

"I just dumped my baggage all over you, but I so want to kiss you right now."

She may not have known him for long, but after the conversation they'd just had, Paige couldn't imagine feeling any closer.

She leaned in and pressed her lips to his. She'd thought their kisses in the studio were hot, but there was an entirely new energy now that he'd unburdened himself to her. It wasn't just the electricity of attraction that was jolting throughout her nerve endings, it was a need to be closer. To share everything that was her, with everything that was him.

She wasn't quite sure how it happened, but they fumbled their way from the table and onto the soft expanse of the bed. All the while, his kisses left a deliciously searing path from her lips, along her jaw, and down her neck.

He laid her down with the utmost care and then pulled his shirt over his head. Her eyes were instantly drawn to the tattoo she'd been enchanted by since she'd met him.

James noticed where her gaze had gone and he flexed his bicep to show it off a little more. "You really enjoy that."

"Very much." Paige looked over the intricate knotwork, eyes bright with intensity. "It didn't seem appropriate to roll up your sleeve and run my hand over it the first time we met, but I wanted to."

"Well, it's just us now. Do with me what you'd like."

He lay down beside her, propped on his ink-less arm, leaving his tattoo easily accessible to her.

She rolled onto her side, mirroring his position.

Slowly, she began to run her fingers from his wrist up his forearm, to gently trail a circle inside the crease of his elbow. Then up one of the dark lines of the Celtic knot that spread from above his elbow, over his shoulder, and crept toward his chest.

James kept his eyes fixed on her face, breathing heavily as he enjoyed her discovering him.

"This is true artwork." Her words were neutral but her tone was deep and luscious.

"I'm glad you like it." James kept his eyes on Paige's, watching as she took in the full expanse of black ink on his pale skin. She was utterly entranced.

"Maybe you're thinking of getting one for yourself?" He shivered as her fingers brushed over the sensitive skin at his collarbone.

"Maybe you'd get one here?" He leaned in and kissed her neck right where it joined her shoulder. She tipped her head back in pleasure.

"Maybe," she breathed.

"Or maybe you'd rather get one here." He tugged at the neck of her shirt to expose the top of her shoulder and placed a gentle kiss there.

"Maybe." The word was barely more than an exhale.

"That's my girl."

"Mmm," she murmured. "I love when you call me that."

That was the limit of his restraint.

James's arms smoothly closed around her and pulled her against him. She pressed her hands into his warm skin and melted deep into his kiss. Every kiss with him was delicate and exquisite. Their lips fit together so well, like they were made specifically to kiss each other.

For the first time in a very long time, her mind had no cares in the world. She was focused solely on the sizzling friction of James's skin against hers. His heartbeats. His sighs. The incredible way he made her feel. Like he'd taken her life and turned it up to the full range of color and sensation it could experience.

She wasn't thinking about the future or how long she might have to be with this man. All she knew was that she'd never felt so alive in a moment and she was ready to get lost in it.

Fourteen

PAIGE WOKE up on her thirtieth birthday feeling on top of the world. She and James had fallen into a comfortable routine of seeing each other every day. They'd grab dinner after work, or lunch when she had the evening shift. On her days off, she'd go to the studio and watch him work, or just quietly keep him company and read her new discussion book.

It seemed crazy to think about, but it felt like they'd known each other for years. Things were going so well, apart from that decreasing two month time frame she refused to think about. She got out of bed when the alarm went off, rather than playing tag with the snooze button. Once she switched on her phone, it started pinging like mad. There were birthday texts from her parents, Kayla, and James.

Happy 30th to my beautiful baby girl! Where did the time go?

Mom

Happy birthday, Paige! I'm so proud of you. Hope you have a happy day. Call us when you get a chance.

Dad

Happy birthday, Paige Marie! I hope your day is perfect from the moment you open your eyes until you go to bed tonight. Looking forward to seeing you later. Thinking of you until then. XX

James

Happy 30th! Do you feel old? (Laughing emoji) I've got a rip-roaring good time planned for you tonight. Can't wait for you and James to get here. Love you!

Kayla

She sent thank you texts in reply before setting the phone down and hugging herself tight. As much as she wanted to play hooky and see if she could get James to do the same, the reference desk awaited her, birthday or not.

Paige made it to work and smiled quietly at her desk. The standard issue staff birthday card was propped up on her keyboard so she wouldn't miss it.

The day went on like any other, filled with computer and technology questions. By noon, she'd already helped five people set up their tablets to borrow ebooks, and six people with various computer questions. She'd spent more time standing in the computer area then sitting at her desk. She was counting down the minutes until her lunch break when a delivery man with a huge bouquet of pink roses stood in front of her desk.

"Delivery for a Paige Marie?" He squinted at his delivery schedule.

"Oh my goodness!" Paige exclaimed. "That's me!"

He set the vase on the desk and handed over a clipboard for her to sign.

"This is so beautiful!"

"Hang on," he said. "I've got more in the truck."

Paige's mouth fell wide open in disbelief. The delivery man walked out to get the rest of the order while Paige examined the bouquet. Although the name on the delivery gave it away, Paige found and extracted the little card to see what it would say.

"Beautiful Paige Marie, some flowers to help you celebrate your special day. See you soon, James xx."

It was so sweet, and completely unexpected, she was floored in the best possible way.

When the delivery man came back, he had one large vase in each of his arms.

Paige stared in disbelief.

"Surely, these aren't all for me!" she exclaimed.

"Three bouquets for Paige Marie. That's what's on my list. Either someone really likes you, or someone's really sorry," the delivery man said without humor.

Paige could only gape at the flowers he set on the desk. Each bouquet was different. One of them was a brilliant assortment of orange, yellow, and pink lilies. The other, a dazzling arrangement of blue and purple orchids. There was another card in that one. She pulled it out, certain it would be made out to some other lucky woman.

"Three bouquets to celebrate the three decades of your life. Happy birthday. Love, James."

The delivery man left, leaving Paige flustered, wide-eyed, and staring around the desk looking for a place to put all three of the huge and wonderful arrangements. She didn't miss the wording of that card. He'd used the word. *Love.* Her mind went into overtime. Did he just mean it as a friendly sign off or was he actually saying he loved her? It was too soon to say that, wasn't it? Although, she had to admit, the word filled her with excitement, not misgiving.

"Wow, must be a special day for you today, huh? What's all this?"

Her amazing mood wasn't even shattered when Norm walked up and peered at her around the stalks of flowers.

"It's my birthday." She grabbed a vase and moved it to the shelf behind her rather than up front.

"Is it really? Happy birthday. These must be from your boyfriend. That's a whole garden's worth of flowers."

"I wasn't expecting this."

"Well, when you get these put away, I could use some help on the computer."

"Yeah, I'll be there in a few," Paige said absently, her senses on overload with the fresh, sweet smell of flowers.

Lunch forgotten, Paige was surprised when Christie came up to relieve her.

They shared a moment of shock and delight before Paige gathered her wits and her tote bag and headed back for her break. She left the flowers for Christie to enjoy and walked, in a daze, to the lounge for lunch.

Gossip travels fast in libraries and as Paige opened the fridge to retrieve her lunch, the ladies around the table were already talking.

"Did you see the delivery guy come in with all those flowers?" Jill, one of the circulation women asked.

"No. For staff or a patron?" Ruby, the circulation supervisor asked.

"They were for me," Paige cut in, taking an empty seat at the table.

All the ladies turned to her with bright eyes and surprised "O" mouths.

"*All* of those? There were dozens!" Jill exclaimed.

Paige could feel herself blushing. "There are thirty flowers, for my thirtieth birthday."

"Wow!" everyone murmured and then wished her a happy birthday.

"Are they from your boyfriend?" one of the ladies asked.

Paige wasn't sure how to answer that. Could you call someone your boyfriend if they were set to move across the planet in a few weeks' time? Was there a name for a very brief relationship that wasn't a fling, with a person you felt a deep emotional attachment to?

Depressingly short-term partner? The one who's destined to get away because of the cruel geography of the earth?

"Yeah," Paige said, deciding to just go with the path of least resistance. Her love life with an expiration date wasn't the business of her co-workers.

Interest in her flowers waned as everyone got to the business of eating before their break time ran out.

Paige couldn't stop thinking about it though. No one had done anything like that for her before. One bouquet, sure, but three! It was over the top. It was flashy. It was fun.

After lunch, Paige went to her own desk to work. She considered bringing the flowers back, but there was no way those three huge bouquets would fit on her desk and give her any space to work.

When her shift was over, she had to ask for help to carry the flowers to her car.

"These are so beautiful," Christie said. "I'll have to tell my husband to up his game."

Just as Paige was getting into her car, a silver Nissan pulled in next to her. She glanced over and saw James in the driver's seat waving at her. She got out of her car again as he hurried over to her.

"I just finished up here," she said, but he pulled her into a big, glorious hug, causing her words to melt away. She could smell a hint of cologne. She breathed in deeply. The combination of the musky tones with his warm skin made her squeeze him a little tighter.

"Happy birthday!" he said. "I left the studio a wee bit early to help you carry your flowers to your car, but it looks like I'm too late."

"James, they're amazing! I never expected anything like that. Thank you!"

James smiled, and Paige sensed that he looked rather chuffed.

"You've gone out of your way to be kind to me, I wanted to do something to show you how much I appreciate it."

"I can't drive you to my place." Paige gestured to her car full of flowers. She had the largest bouquet, the orchids, strapped into the passenger seat. The other two were buckled up in the back.

"That's ok. I'll follow you and help you get them into your apart-

ment. I wanted large bouquets but I didnae realize they'd be that big."
James laughed. "Guess you won't be forgetting me any time soon."

Paige shook her head. "No chance of that ever happening."

"Well, birthday girl, shall we head out? Your party will be starting soon."

Kayla loved to have Paige come over straight after work, so that's when she'd scheduled the party to begin. It was just going to be them anyway, so no problem getting the flowers settled at home first.

They got to her building and James hefted two of the big vases into his arms. Paige picked up the last one and hoped she'd be able to unlock the door with it in her arms.

Once they successfully made it into the apartment, Paige looked around trying to see where the best place would be for the flowers. Finding nothing obvious, she gestured toward her dining table. "Let's put them here for now." The modest table was quickly engulfed by the bright colors of James's flowers. A lovely rainbow against the boring white walls of her apartment.

"Maybe I went a little overboard." James laughed, his eyes twinkling.

"Maybe." Paige hugged his arm to her and rested her head on his shoulder. "I like it though."

James shifted so they were facing each other. His eyes turned serious as he basked in their closeness for a moment.

"I like you, Paige Marie," he murmured. "I like you an awful lot."

"I like you too." Paige's pulse quickened in anticipation as she thought about that special little word on the card.

James lowered his face to hers and brushed her lips with his. Every sensation faded away other than his lips on hers. It made her breathless and light, like dancing on clouds.

When they parted, Paige was almost ready to suggest they just stay in and leave Kayla and Eric to their own devices. Almost.

James rested his forehead against Paige's. "You ready to go?"

"Not really."

James smiled and gave her a cute peck on the lips.

"Actually, I wanted to change out of my work clothes first. Put on something a little more festive."

"By all means, Birthday Girl." James made himself at home on Paige's couch and she headed into her room to change. She selected her favorite summer party dress—an ombre maxi dress. The halter top was a gentle peachy hue that turned into a fiery red at the gauzy hem. It made her fair skin, dark hair, and blue eyes pop. More than that, it felt floaty and fun. Just the vibe she wanted to begin a new decade of her life.

She slipped on a pair of strappy gold sandals and grabbed a white bolero sweater, just in case.

Paige stepped out of her room into the hallway. "I just need to brush my hair and I'm good to go."

She ducked across the hall to get her hairbrush and when she came out, James stood in the hall.

"My God, Paige. You're a vision in that dress."

"Thank you. It's my favorite."

"You're absolutely stunning." He leaned in and gave her a hug and dropped a lingering kiss on her cheek.

They parted, slowly, and Paige's heart beat in overtime as they looked at each other, faces mere inches apart.

"Right," James said, coming back to earth first. "I dinnae want to hold you up from your own party."

Paige exhaled slowly, a private smile curling on her face. She wouldn't mind missing her party for him, but she could hold that thought. Somehow, she got the feeling he wouldn't forget it either.

"HAPPY BIRTHDAY!" Kayla and Eric shouted when they greeted Paige and James at the door.

They pulled Paige into a big group hug as she crossed the threshold. She laughed into their embrace, grateful to be spending the evening with such dear friends. James was also greeted with a hug from Kayla.

"James! Great to see you again." Eric clapped him on the back, one step away from a bro hug.

"Thanks for inviting me back," James replied. "I'm glad I get to celebrate Paige's birthday with everyone."

Kayla flashed Paige a meaningful look that said, *you really lucked out finding this one!*

"So…" Eric turned to Paige. "How's thirty feel so far?"

Paige glanced at James. "Well, thanks to this guy right here, it feels downright magical."

"Do tell!" Kayla gestured for everyone to relax in the living room.

After everyone claimed a comfortable seat, Paige explained about the surprise flowers that kept coming.

Kayla was so excited she clasped her hands above her baby bump and squealed in delight.

"That's it!" Kayla exclaimed. "James, the next time you call your mother, do it here. I want to tell her what an amazing son she's raised."

James pushed a hand through his hair, a little unsettled by the praise.

"She's not kidding," Eric said. "She tells my mom things like that all the time."

Kayla rolled her eyes, but then smiled and planted a quick kiss on Eric's cheek.

"Honey, that's called keeping on your mother-in-law's good side."

Everyone laughed.

The doorbell rang, causing Kayla and Eric to exchange exaggerated wide-eyed, open mouthed looks.

"Oh wow!" Kayla said in a fake, stilted voice. "Who in the world could that be?"

"I don't know," Eric answered in the same fake dramatic voice. "I'll just go and see."

Paige put her head in her hands. "Oh no. What have you done?"

Kayla grinned wickedly, clearly pleased with whatever she'd come up with.

"Paige!" Eric called from the door. "It's for you!"

"Am I going to regret this?" Paige slowly got up from the couch, looking to Kayla for a clue.

Kayla shook her head as the giggles started to overtake her.

James stood up and offered Paige his hand.

"Come on," he said. "You never know. It might be another batch of bouquets."

Paige gladly took his hand and walked into the hallway with him. At once, her eyes were drawn to the elaborate Elvis impersonator standing just inside the door. He was decked out in a bedazzled white jumpsuit, complete with sideburns that wouldn't quit, and a wicked cute lip curl.

"Hey, hey," said Elvis. "Very happy birthday to you, Paige. I'm just passing through to sing you a very special birthday song from your friends Kayla and Eric."

Paige covered her mouth with her hands, unsure whether she was going to laugh or scream. What James, and possibly Eric, didn't know was that Paige and Kayla had choreographed a dance number for the high school talent show when they were fifteen. The song they'd chosen was "Blue Suede Shoes." They'd listened to that song so many times, it was seared into her brain forever.

Kayla had reached all the way back to high school nostalgia to book this ridiculous, but fun, singing telegram for Paige. Right there, before her eyes, a pretty good Elvis impersonator launched into "Blue Suede Shoes."

Kayla sidled up to Paige and started dancing, as best she could with her ever-increasing baby belly. They hadn't done the routine in years, but they remembered a surprising amount of it. Their teenage selves had choreographed a lot of jumps, but Kayla just clutched her belly and rose up on her toes for that.

Even Eric and James got in on the action and turned the small foyer into an impromptu dance party with the King. They laughed, bumped into one another, and tried to twirl and dip the ladies.

The King had some mighty authentic dance moves of his own. His pelvis shaking and gyrating might have made her blush had she not already been red-faced from laughing so hard. When he finished, he pressed his palms together and took a deep bow while the friends clapped and cheered like a bunch of rowdy fans.

"Thank you. Thank you very much. Elvis has left the building." He took a bow and made his way out the front door with no further ado. They ran after him and crowded onto the front stoop watching as he got into his vehicle, a sketchy white van with the Elvis impersonator's picture and call to action on the side: "Hire 'the King' for your next event!" He backed out of the driveway, rolled over the curb, and floored it down the road while the party continued to applaud and whistle until he was out of sight.

Paige had tears in her eyes from laughing so hard.

"I can't believe you did that!" she gasped, trying to catch her breath.

Kayla wiped laughter tears away from her own eyes. "I had to. It's now, officially, half our lives ago since we did that Elvis routine. I can't believe it."

"Half our lives ago? Way to make me feel old!"

The ladies hugged each other and dissolved into another fit of laughter, leaving Eric and James to shake their heads.

The party had started with a bang, putting everyone in the mood for silliness and good times. The rest of the evening was much calmer, but just as enjoyable.

Kayla and Eric gave Paige a gift certificate for a girls' night out spa package, so Kayla and Paige could enjoy some pampering together.

"I thought it was just for Paige," Eric said quietly, but the sparkle in his eyes betrayed that he wasn't mad.

"What?" Kayla grinned at Eric. "I'm pregnant. I deserve to be pampered while celebrating my best friend's birthday."

Even James hadn't been finished with his three bouquets. He also gave Paige a beautiful coffee table book of Scotland, a book of Scottish poems, and a silver necklace with a Scottish thistle charm.

James gestured at the necklace box. "May I?"

Paige eagerly handed it over. "Yes, please."

His fingers brushed across the sensitive skin of her neck, ever so lightly, as he delicately lifted her hair and fastened the clasp for her. He also dropped a gentle kiss on her cheek, which caused Kayla to take Eric's arm and nestle into him.

"It's lovely on you." James looked from the charm against Paige's skin to her face. "And the books." He glanced at them. "You said you wanted to know more about Scotland. I thought this might help."

Paige hugged the books to her chest. "Oh thank you! I love them!"

"Wise." Eric nodded appreciatively. "The way to a librarian's heart is through books."

After presents, Kayla sat up and clasped her hands above her bump.

"Ok, I've been patient because it's not my birthday, but I'm sorry you guys. Baby and I need some cake and ice cream right now or we're not going to make it through the night."

"Of course! Bring on the cake." Paige waved her arms in the air as if she could magically conjure the cake that way.

Kayla leaned forward, preparing to heave herself up to her feet but Eric stopped her and jumped up. "I'll get it. Just you relax."

James got up too. "I'll help."

The men disappeared off to the kitchen and Paige nestled up next to Kayla and rested her head on Kayla's shoulder.

"Have I ever told you you're the very best friend in the whole world?"

Kayla rested her cheek atop Paige's head.

"Hmm. You may have mentioned it once or twice over the years. Have I ever told you that you and James are the cutest couple I've ever seen? Seriously. You have landed the catch of the century. You're lucky I'm already married and all tied up carrying Eric's baby."

Paige laughed.

"He is amazing, isn't he? I can't believe he just walked into the library, during my shift."

"Mmm hmm. Like it was meant to be?"

The guys came back with a candle lit birthday cake.

"Oh! That's my cue." Kayla sat up and started singing "Happy Birthday" and the guys joined in.

They got to Paige just in time for the blowing out part.

Paige got it in two breaths. Thirty candles is a lot to blow out at once.

"What did you wish for?" Kayla asked as James set to cutting the cake and Eric ran back to the kitchen for the ice cream.

"Actually…" Paige turned to James. "I wished that someone really meant what they said about taking a little Michigan road trip this summer."

James looked up from the cake he was plating.

"Aye. O' course I did."

Paige couldn't stop the big grin that was spreading across her face.

"I got an email with deals for great last minute Fourth of July trips. I didn't book it though because I wanted to make sure you'd be free. I don't want to ruin your art time."

"From what I've heard, at least two of the other artists are going away for a three day weekend, since the fourth is on a Friday. What do you have in mind?"

Eric rejoined the room and started scooping out ice cream to go with the cake.

"Oh my gosh, you guys!" Paige paused her trip planning when she saw the ice cream flavor. "You got my favorite!"

"Of course we did!" Kayla motioned to Eric to give her a more generous serving. "But we can talk about the ice cream later. I want to hear this amazing road trip coming to life. You two are so cute!"

James handed a plate to the birthday girl and then Eric handed one to his wife. After Paige took a spoonful of the ice cream, she closed her eyes a moment, letting the flavor spread over her tongue. Kayla had remembered to get Superman ice cream. What exactly the flavor was, no one really knew. Paige only knew that it tasted like summer, childhood, and long afternoons spent on various docks, on various vacations, dangling her toes in the water.

"Mmm, this is so good. I haven't had it in forever. Thank you."

"Right, right. You're welcome." Kayla waved her fork trying to speed Paige back to the previous conversation. "But I'm dying to hear about this trip you're taking. I have to live vicariously though you because this big ol' belly is not getting more than twenty miles away from the hospital until this baby's out."

"A trip? Where are you guys going?" Eric settled next to Kayla on the couch with his plate and dug in.

"I dinnae ken." James sat beside Paige, close enough that their thighs were touching. "She got too distracted by the ice cream to tell me." He looked at the rainbow scoop on his plate with interest. "I dinnae think I've ever had this."

"You haven't," Eric assured him. "It's a Midwest thing."

"Enough about the ice cream! I want to hear about the trip!" Kayla's fake outburst got things back on track.

"Three days is enough for a nice little introduction to what we Michiganders like to call 'Up North.' That's all I'm going to say. I want to surprise James, if that's ok with you." She looked at him to make sure he was all right with a mystery road trip.

"If you're the one orchestrating it, I have perfect faith."

Paige was really relishing the idea of playing tour guide, and not just because it meant three glorious days alone with James. She was excited to show off the gems of her state. She knew that movies and TV shows tended to depict the United States as California, New York, and maybe Texas. With fifty states in the mix, that was a pretty poor showing.

"Leave it all to me and I'll see what I can get booked."

"Wait a minute." James held up his hand. "I insist on paying my way."

"That's fine," Paige assured him. "You can pay me back. I just want to get some things booked before they fill up."

"This is so exciting!" Kayla interjected. "I think thirty is definitely your year, Paige."

Looking at the smiling faces surrounding her, Paige had to admit that things felt a lot more positive than she would have expected just a few short weeks ago.

After goodbye hugs were exchanged, and Paige and James made it back to her parking lot, it was almost midnight. Kayla had been a trooper staying up so late, but when it got to the point when she couldn't stop yawning, Paige had known it was time to call it quits. But now, sitting in her car, she didn't feel quite ready to say goodbye for the night.

"I hope you had a good birthday," James said.

"I did." Paige reached across the console and laced her fingers with his. "I got to spend it with some of my most favorite people. I couldn't ask for more."

James put his other hand on his chest and looked at her with an earnest, 'Who? Me?' expression.

"Yes, you," Paige answered his unverbalized question. "You've quickly risen through the ranks to become one of my favorite people."

"I dinnae know how I got so lucky."

"I've been asking myself that same question since you walked into the library."

James turned to Paige, his expression turning serious. "Listen, I want you to know this. I really care for you. We haven't known each other for long, but we just click. I want to spend as much time with you as possible. I dinnae mean this to be a summer thing. It feels like so much more to me. I wanted you to know. So it's all out there."

Paige's heart fluttered like a moth flying to a flame. Only, she was sure this flame would keep her warm, not burn her.

"I feel the same way. There's something about you that's just...whew!"

James flashed a smile. "Aye, I know just what you mean. You're quite 'whew' yourself."

Paige looked James in the eyes and noticed the playful relief in them turn into something else. Something deeper.

"Paige Marie." His voice had turned low and husky.

"Mmm?"

"I have another birthday kiss for you."

"I was hoping you did."

James leaned forward, across the center console of her car. She moved to meet him halfway, closed her eyes, and their lips met. James raised a hand to lightly play with her hair as they kissed. Paige melted into the moment. James's lips moved perfectly in sync with hers. His hand in her hair was gentle and tender.

James pulled away before things progressed past sweet and lovely.

"Can I walk you to the door before I go?"

"Do you have to go?" Paige's eyes were firmly settled on James's beautiful lips. Somewhere in the back of her mind, she knew he needed to be at the studio in the morning. His residency was moving along and he had lots of work to do, but the larger part of her brain could only think how good it would be to end her birthday wrapped in James's strong arms as she fell asleep.

"Are you asking me to stay the night?" The words practically sparked through the charged air in the car.

Paige bit her bottom lip, wishing for more kisses, and nodded.

James ran his finger along the curve of her cheek.

"Whatever you want, birthday girl."

Sixteen

PAIGE CLOSED the trunk of the car. The time had finally come to set off on her road trip with James. She put her hands on her hips and regarded James through her sunglasses.

"I guess that's it. Ready to hit the road?" she asked.

"I was born for this moment. Off we go!"

Paige slid into the driver's seat, ready to let the grand adventure begin. James buckled up in the passenger seat, looking thoroughly hot in his forest green t-shirt and black cargo shorts.

Paige had opted for jean shorts and a white eyelet top. She was going for the delicate summer feminine vibe.

"Here we go!" Paige exclaimed, pulling out of the lot and onto the road.

"Lead on, fearless guide!"

"Well, we aren't on the expressway yet. That's when the magic will really happen."

"I feel pretty magical already." James was staring at Paige, but she kept her eyes on the road. It wouldn't do to get into a wreck right out of the gate because she wanted to gaze at James's handsome face.

"Well, now that you mention it, I do too. I blame you." Paige took one hand off the wheel a moment to poke James playfully in the thigh.

"That's convenient. No' true though. It's your fault." He laced his fingers through hers and pulled her hand to his lips for a kiss. She was excited enough to finally be taking this trip with James, but he already had her body at full attention. It was going to be a long drive, indeed.

She reluctantly took her hand back in the interest of safe driving. James had come so far to be here. Nothing bad was going to happen on her watch.

"This leg of the journey is a pretty quick one. We've got a little over an hour and then we'll be at our lunch destination."

James glanced at his watch.

"I know what you're thinking. Who's going to be ready for lunch in one hour, but there are things to do before lunch. Don't worry. I know what I'm doing."

"I trust you. I'm completely in your hands," James said.

"Ok, you'll have to stop that. No distracted driving."

James grinned. "What?"

"That entire statement is just loaded with meaning."

"Was it? It was a purely innocent statement. Surely, you know I would never tempt you while you're driving." His voice was tinged with laughter.

"We have a long drive ahead. You'll have to behave yourself. Mostly."

"Mostly. Ok. I think I can handle that. I do have a question for you. A completely safe one."

"Fire away," Paige prompted.

"I know you've taken great pleasure in putting together the right stops on this mystery tour. The places are a surprise for me, but can you tell me why you picked the places you did?"

"Hmm," she stalled while she got her thoughts together. She had to be sure she could answer the question without giving away where they were heading.

"I guess you could say it's sort of a trip through some of my fondest memories."

"I like the sound of that," James said.

"For instance, this first stop, I've been going there since I was a little kid. My parents used to take me for a long weekend here and there because it wasn't too far from home, but far enough to feel like we were getting away from it all. It's touristy, for sure. Really, the whole place is kind of manufactured for tourism, but it doesn't feel like a trap, you know? It feels wholesome and happy. Kind of like the way Disney World makes you feel, but on a much smaller scale."

"I think I get what you're saying." James nodded thoughtfully. "Although I've no' been to Disney."

"Oh, Disney is one of my favorite places. It's overpriced. It's hot. But there's pure wonder to it. It's wholly manufactured, but the point of it is to push the envelope to make people forget the real world as soon as they step through the entrance gates. It works too. I like that about it."

"Ok, so our first stop is sort of like that. That sounds good. And your parents took you there often? The mystery place, I mean. No' Disney."

"Yeah. Not really often, but maybe once every two or three years. Enough that it could start to feel familiar, but not so often that it didn't have surprises. If that makes sense."

"It makes perfect sense. And you said we're going for lunch. Is there a special reason it's this place to eat?"

"Yes! The place is well-known for its food. There are some other famous things about the area, but you'll see that for yourself. It's also lucky for us that our proximity makes it a good place for eating. It's definitely a defining moment to experience a meal here. The sort of thing that bonds people. Forever after, someone could say to you, 'Have you ever had the meal at this place,' and you could smile knowingly and say, 'Oh yes. Those little ice creams,' and you'll be in on the secret with them."

"Are there really wee ice creams?"

"Yes, but that's all I'm giving away right now."

"That's enough to keep me going. Wee ice creams. I like the sound of that."

Paige had a vivid picture in her mind of what those simple delights looked like and what it would be like to watch James's face when he saw them for the first time. She could hardly wait.

Seventeen

"WILLKOMMEN TO FRANKENMUTH! Michigan's Little Bavaria!" Paige announced as she took the Frankenmuth exit.

"What was that you said?" James asked.

"Frankenmuth?"

"No. Before that. It started with a 'W.'"

Paige playfully punched James in the shoulder. "Stop it. I don't know the first thing about the German language."

"Evidently," James teased.

"Then welcome to Frankenmuth," Paige amended. "It's our uber tourist tribute to stereotypical German things. Having never been to Germany, I couldn't say how close it comes to the actual country, but it makes us happy and we mean no harm."

"Sounds interesting," James conceded.

"It is. The touristy part isn't very big, really, but it's an extremely popular destination. It boasts the famous Frankenmuth chicken dinners. Not only is there delicious food, but Frankenmuth is home to Bronner's CHRISTmas Wonderland, the largest Christmas store in the world!"

"Come on now. The largest in the whole world? Can that be true?"

Paige shrugged. "Sure it can. Besides, Michigan doesn't get a lot of press in general. Let us have our giant Christmas store."

James smiled. "Whatever you want."

Paige maneuvered her car down the main street and toward the Bavarian Inn. The closer they got, the more the stores lining the street were decorated with alpine facades. It was the best place to leave the car to explore the main drag on foot. She made sure to park in the back so she could give James the somewhat unsettling experience of driving through the old wooden covered bridge. It always made her heart beat a little faster to drive through it, a throwback from her childhood. She couldn't help but imagine the boards falling away under the weight of the car and plunging them into the current of the Cass River below.

"All right," Paige announced after she'd turned off the car. "We're here. How are we feeling? Hungry? Want to explore the Riverwalk first?"

"A walk sounds wonderful. Lead the way."

Paige jumped out of the car and directed James's attention to the modern Riverwalk.

"It wasn't here when I was a kid," she explained. "It's just a glorified shopping area but it has a cute vibe."

As if to punctuate her comment, the deep tones of a horn blared, making them both jump.

"There's a boat?" James asked.

"I almost forgot. That's the Bavarian Belle. It's a riverboat that goes up and down the river for a nice little trip. Only lasts about an hour, if I'm remembering right."

"Is that part of our travel itinerary?"

"Sure. If you want it to be. We'll have to find out when the next tour is heading out."

"A riverboat cruise that I'm not working sounds perfect to me."

Paige smiled and slipped her arm through his, letting her hand run down the inside of his arm until she reached his hand.

He squeezed her hand and they headed off to explore the shops and pick a time for their boat tour.

They had an hour to kill before the next boat went out so they took some time popping in and out of whatever shops took their fancy. They stopped in one of the cafes to grab a couple of drinks and people-watch for a bit.

"You're right," James said. "The actual structure here feels very contrived, but it's a good vibe. Happy and open. I like it."

"Oh good," Paige said. "I hoped you'd agree with me on that."

She pulled James's arm over so she could take a look at his watch. She could have pulled out her phone to check, but it was more fun to touch James instead.

"Ready to head over to the boat launch?"

"Aye, lead the way."

They grabbed their drinks and strolled back to the boat, which had already started boarding. They got settled on the top deck, at the railing facing toward the city. A light breeze blew across the river making for a pleasant boating experience.

"Well, this is quite lovely, isn't it?" James asked, taking in the view over the water.

"It is. Is it anything like being on your uncle's boat?"

"No' the actual boat or the scenery, but see that smiling guide?" James inclined his head toward the uniformed young man who was smiling at passengers as they got settled.

Paige nodded.

"That smile is familiar. Acting like you don't say the same thing all day, every day. That's very much the same."

"So you're the tour guide for your uncle?"

"Sometimes. I do just about everything depending on what needs to be done. I know all of it backwards and forwards by now. Muscle memory. Brain memory."

The boat sounded its loud horn, interrupting Paige's insight into James's working life, and pulled away from the dock. The guide came over the loudspeaker and narrated the history of the town and pointed out interesting business sites and wildlife along the slow trip down the Cass. Paige had heard the spiel and seen the sights before but this time, she tried to imagine James standing with the microphone pointing out landmarks and sharing history. From where she sat, it seemed like a pretty fun job, but she hadn't considered how tedious it must get to see the same sights and be enthusiastic about them all the time. She thought about how soul-sucking it could be to explain the same computer functions to the same patrons over and over. The smile stayed in place but the mind screamed.

"You've been doing it a long time?" Her question popped out when the guide took a breather to just enjoy the scenery, without comment, for a few minutes.

"What now?" James tore his gaze from the treeline to Paige, looking a little confused.

"Working on the boat. Sorry, my mind is a little stuck on imagining what your life is like in Scotland."

"Oh aye." James rubbed the back of his neck as if just talking about it was causing his muscles to stiffen. "It was a bit of a lark when I was a boy but then I started helping out on weekends, or during school holidays, and it just stuck from there. It's the only job I've ever had. Which is part of why I'm tired of it."

"Wow. I hadn't realized it's all you've done. I don't blame you for wanting to move on."

The guide got back on his mic and narrated more of the trip, leaving Paige and James to fall silent and listen politely again.

By the time they made it back to the dock, their stomachs were starting to rumble.

"Are you ready for a famous Frankenmuth chicken dinner?" Paige asked.

"Bring it on!" James patted his taut stomach.

They strolled up to the street and walked along the sidewalk to the Bavarian Inn. The timing was perfect as the larger than life Glockenspiel clock was whirring to action. Paige and James stopped along with the gathered crowd to see the mechanical clock put on its show. The chimes rang out as the figures portrayed the fairytale of the Pied Piper. As a child, Paige had thought the clock was positively magical. As an adult, it was now a reminder of a simpler time in life and how the small pleasures are truly the most important. She slipped her hand in James's as they watched the show. When it was over, she pointed to the lit "immediate seating" sign on the side of the building.

"We won't even have to wait, but we better get a move on. All these clock watchers are probably getting hungry too."

"We cannae have them getting ahead of us. I've come all the way from Scotland to enjoy this meal."

Paige chuckled and led him into the Bavarian Inn and up to the restaurant. The strolling accordion player was making his rounds in full lederhosen. James took in the costumed restaurant staff and looked at Paige with wide eyes.

"You weren't kidding about the little Bavaria thing. This is some serious lederhosen."

"There's no mistaking who works here."

"I dinnae think I could handle a job that required me to wear a getup like that." James gestured to a knobby-kneed waiter bustling by with a large tray of delicious food.

"I hope it inspires good tips. The more awkward you look in your lederhosen, the bigger the tip should be."

"Absolutely no'," James shook his head. "They know what they're getting into when they take the job. I'm no' paying extra for questionable life choices."

Paige laughed. "It's not bad if you're a girl. Their dresses are adorable."

A waitress in a royal blue Dirndl bustled by with a huge tray of food. Paige had always admired these dresses. They pulled in at the waist, flaring out to knee length. Of course, the bodice came up to just under the breasts to accentuate them to full effect, but it wasn't immodest. Everyone had a white, ruffly blouse underneath that kept everything covered. Paige thought it was a lot cuter than the lederhosen the waiters had to wear.

"Definitely more flattering on the ladies. And how are there so many skinny waiters at a restaurant? You dinnae like to see a waiter swimming in baggy lederhosen, now do you?"

Just then, one of the ladies came up and ushered them to a table for two. "Your waiter will be with you shortly." She left them with their menus and hurried off.

"You don't really need the menu." Paige set hers aside. "For the true Frankenmuth experience, you just order the all-you-can eat chicken dinner. If we both get it, it's served family style."

"Sounds like the thing to do. I cannae come here and no' indulge in the true experience."

One of the skinny-legged waiters came up to the table to take their order. James ordered a house ale to go with his meal and Paige ordered water with lemon.

"No iced tea this time?" James asked.

"No. Just water. Saves the most room for food. You'll see."

James raised his eyebrows, wondering just what he was in for. He didn't need to wonder for long. The waiter came back with a tray of breads and jam to start them off.

"This is how they get you!" Paige whispered across the table. "This stuff is so good, but bread is filling. No matter how bad your mouth wants to keep eating it, you gotta limit yourself to one piece. We can take the rest as leftovers. It makes a good snack in the car."

James smiled and shook his head as he reached for a piece of Stollen bread.

"What? You're laughing at me, aren't you?" She helped herself to a piece of bread and slathered it with homemade cranberry relish.

"No' laughing. I'm enjoying your insider information. I can imagine you coming here, year after year. You know the tips and tricks now, and it's simply adorable."

Paige took a bite of her bread. The candied fruits inside were sweet in the fresh white bread, but the crust was her favorite part. Always a deep brown and sprinkled with powdered sugar. Paired with the tangi-ness of the cranberry relish, it was a tantalizing taste sensation, even better than she remembered.

"Mmmm. I want to eat the whole thing. You see? It's a trick."

James bit into his bread and had a similar reaction.

"Aye. This is good. It's only a couple of slices of bread. Surely we can just eat that and move on."

"That's exactly what they want you to think. Just fill up on all that bread and you won't be able to scarf down the chicken, potatoes, salads, vegetables, and noodles." Paige folded her hands in her lap to keep them from reaching into the bread tray for another piece.

James glanced around the large room they were seated in. "I'm guessing by the number of people in this dining room that all those things are just as good as this bread."

"It's fried chicken, but you haven't had fried chicken like this before. I don't know what they do to it, if it's the combination of spices or the way they cook it, but it's just perfect. Juicy, but not greasy. Totally worth foregoing another slice of bread."

"But that bread is practically singing my name right now." James stared at the bread and the little dish of jam.

Paige laughed. She knew exactly what he meant. "It's a siren song. If you listen, it'll destroy you."

"Duly noted." James took his eyes off the bread and looked at Paige's face instead.

"I havenae mentioned it today, but you look beautiful. Road trips suit you."

That was one way to take her mind off bread and jam. She tried, unsuccessfully, to hold in the huge grin the compliment brought on.

"Thank you," she said. "You look gorgeous yourself. Something about that auburn rock star hair of yours complemented by your green shirt." She fanned her face with her hand to drive home her point.

"What? This old thing?" James joked, pulling at the front of his shirt.

"Yeah. That 'old thing.' You know what you're doing." She took a sip of her ice water.

"Says the vision in that lacy white top. You're like a summer dream, floated down on a sunbeam to brighten my life."

Paige set her glass down and just gazed at James.

"Is that a quote from something?" She knew he was well-read. As lovely as the phrase was, she didn't recognize it from anywhere.

"No' that I know of. That's an original James MacKinnon, inspired by the incomparable Paige Marie."

Paige could feel a light blush creeping into her cheeks, but it didn't bother her.

"I didn't know you were a poet too."

"Neither did I. It's all you, my dear. You've got me right here." He placed a hand on his heart.

Before Paige could formulate a verbal response to that, the waiter came back with a large tray of food, all for them.

James gaped at everything set before them: the chicken, a fresh coleslaw, warm buttered noodles, pasta salad, dressing, and mixed peas and carrots.

"Enjoy your meal." The waiter in baggy lederhosen looked expectantly from Paige to James in case they needed anything else, and then left them to it.

"You weren't kidding about holding off on the bread. This is a feast for half a dozen people!"

"It's all so good too. The bread isn't the only thing that begs you to eat it." Paige surveyed the delicious items, deciding what to put on her plate first.

They got to the business of filling their plates and exclaiming over how good everything tasted.

"You were right about this place. Everything is delicious," James said after he'd sampled everything.

The accordion player sauntered into their dining room. Most of the guests quickly averted their eyes, but James and Paige smiled when the minstrel made eye contact. He knew how to read a crowd so he slowly made his way over to their table. The name tag on the strap of his lederhosen read "Wendell."

"Good afternoon," he greeted them, apparently able to hold a conversation and play the instrument at the same time. "Where are you folks joining us from today?" Cognizant that he was speaking to people who were stuffing their faces with delicious food, he casually swept his eyes over their faces and then settled into a vague gaze around the room. Paying attention, but not aggressively so.

"I'm from the Detroit area." Paige held her hand over her mouth as she chewed a bite of juicy chicken.

"That's not too far away." Wendell turned to James, but kept his eyes trained on the background of the room. "Same for you?"

"No. I'm from Glasgow."

Wendell actually looked at James after hearing that answer. "That's quite a trip. First time to Frankenmuth?"

"Aye," James agreed. "My girlfriend here thought I should see it while I'm in Michigan."

My girlfriend! James hadn't referred to her as such before and the words settled over and hugged her like a lovely party dress.

"Ah, well. Thanks for thinking of us." Wendell aimed the comment in Paige's direction. Then, back to James, "How long are you in town for?"

James and Wendell continued on in polite conversation while Paige silently stared at James. Correction, her boyfriend, James. Correction, her unbelievably wonderful boyfriend, James.

Finally, the intensity of her stare penetrated James's attention and he turned back to her. She was looking at him with intense eyes and a quirk of a smile. He smiled back, his eyes sparkling.

Wendell came to the end of his tune and waited for just a beat.

"Thanks for the song, mate," James said. "You're good with that thing."

"Thank you. Enjoy your visit." Wendell wandered off to find another table that would make eye contact.

"What's this sexy look for?" James asked, once Wendell was out of earshot.

"That's just how I look at my boyfriend." Paige emphasized the word, loving how it felt.

Suddenly, James's expression very nearly mirrored hers.

"It just came out of my mouth, but it felt right. You like that, then?"

"I like that very much."

"Excellent," James said. "Then it's good luck we're at the beginning of a three day trip together."

"It's very lucky for both of us."

James grinned at Paige before turning his attention back to his meal. "First up, stuffing ourselves and then spending some time in a food coma. Together, of course."

Those were the magic words. As long as they were together, even a food coma sounded like the perfect way to spend some time.

Of course, once the meal was over and they were both sure they couldn't manage another bite, it was time for the signature finish. The little ice creams Paige had mentioned. She always got the orange and vanilla twist and James followed suit. It was served in an extra small sundae cup with a little plastic character sticking out of the top, a red fräulein for Paige and a dapper blue chap in lederhosen for James.

"Don't worry," Paige said. "It just melts around the other food in your stomach and doesn't take up any more room."

"Here's to the complete Frankenmuth experience!" James raised his glass of ale and toasted Paige's water.

Stomachs stuffed with food, they shuffled back to the car.

"Do you want to walk it off at the Christmas store or do you want to get back to driving?" Paige asked.

James rubbed his stomach absently. "Well, you cannae very well throw around the term 'largest in the world' and then fail to show me. Might seem a bit disingenuous, wouldn't it?"

"Oh, it's the largest. Let's go see for ourselves."

Paige drove the short distance to Bronner's.

"Hmm," James stroked his chin. "It looks big, but I dinnae know if it's really the biggest in the world."

The grounds of the store were a Christmas wonderland even in summer. A giant waving Santa sculpture greeted them. Nativity pieces, enormous candy canes, and scenes from Santa's shop surrounded the store.

"Come on." Paige hopped out of the car. "It's deceiving out here. You'll see once you're inside."

James maintained his skepticism but put his arm around Paige's shoulders and walked into the store with her. They were immediately greeted by floor to ceiling Christmas displays and larger than life outdoor displays of snowmen, Santas, and the Holy Family. Statues, trees, lights, shining tinsel, and Christmas music positively assaulted the senses. There wasn't an area of the store you could look at that didn't contain hundreds of ornaments and sparkly decorations. James blinked in awe of everything he saw.

"I take it all back. This is, undoubtedly, the biggest store in the world."

The greeter offered James a map of the store, and he took it, turning to Paige.

"We need a map? Are we ever going to get out of here again?"

Paige grinned. "If not, we could live quite happily in the Christmas tree forest for a long time."

They strolled through the store looking at absolutely any and every type of Christmas decoration there could possibly be. They took their time in the almost endless maze of ornaments, from delicate and beautiful to gaudy and silly. James picked out a few ornaments that he thought his ma and Aunt Cait would like. There was another he picked up, turning to Paige.

"You must have this one."

Paige reached out and took the delicate glass Scottish flag ornament he held up. Surrounded by the lights and trappings of Christmas, she fell into a daydream of hanging it on her Christmas tree with James standing beside her. Mistletoe kisses. Cocoa with mini marshmallows. Watching the snow fall outside while sitting bundled up together on the couch. Hanging stockings with their names embroidered on them. The images were so vivid in her mind that it nearly took her breath away. The clutch of longing that formed in her stomach was unexpected. How could she want so much after spending so little time with James? If a glass ornament in a Christmas store could make her feel so strongly, how in the world would she feel after he went home to Scotland? The cruel unfairness of it all threatened to make her cry right there in the international ornament aisle.

Instead, she turned away a little so James, hopefully, wouldn't see the tangle of emotion his little gift had caused.

She carefully pressed the ornament to her heart. "It's my new favorite. Thank you."

The nostalgia for an impossible future only grew as they made their way to the Christmas tree forest. There were rows of artificial trees of every shape, size, and color. Some reaching nearly to the ceiling of the store, others just coming to the tops of their knees. A white light show gave the impression of falling snow.

James put his arm around Paige and squeezed her tight to his side.

"Isnae this a lovely slice of Christmas magic?" He kissed the top of her head.

She breathed in the scent of synthetic evergreen and imagined the crisp, clear smell of falling snow. If she closed her eyes, she could imagine that she'd wandered into an enchanted Christmas forest with James, a place where time and distance didn't exist and her holiday fantasies would be reality. Maybe if she wished on one of the twinkling tree toppers, her wish would come true?

Eighteen

THEY'D HAD about a two-hour stretch of driving before Paige pulled off into the city of Grayling. As they'd gotten further from Frankenmuth, the landscape along the expressway changed. Strip malls and urban sprawl began to fade away, replaced by longer stretches between exits and more tree-lined areas showcasing rows of tall white pines, with stunning white bark birch trees reflecting the sun. The trappings of cities and the hustle of life fell away as the more natural miles went on. Even in the car, Paige found herself breathing deeper.

"You feel that?"

"Feel what?" James looked bewildered.

"There's a change in the air around here. Although Yoopers would scoff, the 'Up North' feeling starts here. I can feel it in my bones. It's a slower pace. An unraveling of cares. A greater connection with nature."

"Yoopers? You'll have to enlighten me."

Paige smiled, pleased to be able to share a little bit about her special state. "Yoopers is the nickname for people living in Michigan's upper peninsula. It's because we call the upper peninsula the U.P. Say U.P. enough times fast and that's where Yooper comes from."

"I dinnae think I would have learned that without this trip."

"Then the trip is already a raging success…and here we are at the next stop."

She pulled the car into a gravel parking lot and James stared at the gates and the trench ponds beyond.

"Grayling Fish Hatchery," he read from the sign on the fence.

"Trust me." She turned off the ignition.

"Wholeheartedly."

Paige led him to the little booth where they paid their admission and purchased two baggies of feed that looked like cat food kibbles. They walked out onto the concrete pathway to get to the first pool of fish.

"This place has been a family tradition since I was a kid," Paige explained. "I've been here with my parents so many times. It may seem crazy, but this place is so fun! Just watch."

Paige took a pinch of feed and flung it out over the water. The second it plunked into the water, a frenzy of shining, thrashing fish bodies appeared to snatch it up.

"Whoa!" James exclaimed. "That's intense! Let me try." He dipped into his baggy and pulled out a handful of the fishy smelling pellets. Tossing them into the water, an even larger group of splashing trout writhed over each other to reach the food.

"I feel so powerful!" James exclaimed.

Paige laughed. "That's because we are. We are the food gods of the hatchery. Mwahaha!"

"Oh no!" James laughed. "The power's already gone to your head."

"Don't worry. I'm a benevolent feeder."

"Benevolent with an evil laugh? I'll take your word for it."

They walked up and down the length of each pool, causing an uprising of fish along the way.

Paige was so glad James was enjoying it as much as she was. There was something very satisfying about watching the scales glint in the sun and hearing the frenzied splashing. Even the gentle sound of the food pelting the water. Families with young children, laughing and squealing with delight when they made the fish jump, added to the happy energy of the place.

"I wasn't thinking that you grew up next to a river when I picked this place. Did you have anything like this there?" Paige reached into her bag and tossed out another handful of pellets to the ravenous fish.

"No' quite like this, but I've been to a fishery with my Uncle Davie and the girls. We'd get a boat and fish for our dinner rather than feeding the wee buggers."

"That sounds like fun. I've never actually been fishing. I mean, they have the little fishing pool over there." Paige pointed toward one of the tanks near the entrance of the hatchery. "But that doesn't take any skill. You just get a pole with a piece of bait on it, dip it in the water, and pull up a flopping fish."

James spread his arm out, raining an arc of feed over the water.

"If you ever come to Scotland, I'll take you fishing. It's a nice way to clear the mind, although I probably had more fun messing about with my cousins than reeling in any fish."

Paige felt a twinge in her stomach, not unlike the one she'd felt in Bronner's. She liked the idea of fishing with James in Scotland, but not the reminder that he'd be moving so far away soon. Would she ever be able to go visit him? It sounded like a lovely dream but she knew airfare alone wasn't particularly affordable. She hoped extra hard that the promotion would come through for her. After she figured out where she was going to be living, maybe she could start a Scotland travel fund. Would he still be her boyfriend though, when they were living across an ocean from each other?

James threw a lovely arc of pellets through the air and they plinked into the water making another batch of fish go wild. She could worry about the future later. For now, she had James all to herself and she intended to show him a good time.

It was a bit of a letdown to reach the bottom of the baggy and empty out the last of the food into the water. But there were other experiences to have.

James took a tentative sniff of his hands.

"Och, I smell like a fishmonger."

Paige laughed. "Yeah, that's the drawback of this place, but it's totally worth it, don't you think?"

"To feed those wee greedy beggars? You bet."

They walked over to the outdoor portable sinks. Paige pressed the foot pump to start some water flowing. It was only a trickle, but better than nothing. "The bad news is there isn't a public bathroom here, so this is the best we can do for now. But don't worry. Our next stop is about ten minutes away and has a bathroom so we can really wash the fish smell off."

They got back into the car for the quick trek over to Goodale's Bakery. The unassuming brick exterior gave no indication of the homey little bake shop inside. They clomped up a few wooden steps to get into the shop. To the left were displays of breads, pies, and rolls. There was a glass counter around the back with cupcakes, muffins, pastries, and all sorts of sweet little delights. The sugary and yeasty smells of bread, cake, vanilla, and cinnamon were a treat, especially while they still smelled a little fishy.

On the right was a little dining area with a few small tables and chairs. They took turns in the tiny restroom to wash the fishiness off their hands and then lingered in front of every display browsing the treats.

"This is a quaint little shop, sort of like the one my ma works in."

Paige brightened, liking the new insight into James's life.

"Does she make the same sorts of things as these?" Paige gestured to the shelves of rolls, breads, and pies, and the counter displaying doughnuts and cookies.

"Mostly, aye. But I dinnae see any scones or shortbread here. She makes a lot of those."

"Scones are definitely not common around here." Paige picked up a mixed berry pie. "Kayla had her bridal shower at a tea house and that was the first time I'd ever had a scone."

"Hmm." James examined the shelves to select the treat that called to him. "I would normally pick a scone, but since there are none, I'll take this." He held up a gooey batch of cinnamon rolls.

While they waited in line at the counter to pay, the row of choco-late chip cookies in the case caught her eye.

"You can't have too many cookies," she said to James, then asked the cashier to add a dozen of those for the road. It was a three day trip after all.

Sweets selected and paid for, they loaded them into the car and hit the road again.

Paige navigated back to the expressway. "Just a little over an hour now, and we'll be at our home base for the next two nights."

James looked out the window as they left the little town of Grayling behind. There was even less civilization to see as they flew down the expressway now.

"This is lovely." James gazed out his window, mesmerized by the trees going by.

"See? The 'up north' feeling is getting to you."

"It is a different vibe, isn't it? You can feel yourself loosening up. Like regular life is disappearing."

Right now, at the beginning of the trip, it was easy to pretend it was the beginning of a new life and they would never have to return to the old one.

They drove along listening to the local radio stations and belting out 80s and 90s tunes that they knew as the stations came and went out of range.

Paige was relieved when she finally took the exit that would lead to their hotel. At last, the road veered toward the impressive Lake Huron. Beyond the road, there was nothing but deep, blue water as far as the eye could see. Who needed ocean beaches when freshwater Michigan lakes were so huge and beautiful?

"What a view!" James rolled his window down halfway and let in the fresh lake air. It was all lake to their right and little motels and shops lining the left side of the street. It just looked like a laid back touristy area on the water and Paige couldn't wait to dive into it with James.

Paige inhaled deeply. The breeze blowing in and the scent of the water put her instantly in vacation mode.

"Mackinaw City, here we are!" Paige announced, keeping an eye out for the driveway to her chosen home for the next two nights. Finally, she pulled into the Cabins of Mackinaw.

"Surprise!" she exclaimed. "I booked us a tiny cabin while we're here. I thought that would provide the required character for being 'up north' for your first time."

"That's brilliant!"

Paige got them checked in and they stood in front of their new home for the next few nights. A small orangey wood cabin with a green roof and a little porch provided a fitting welcome to the beauty of Mackinaw. It was one of a line of tiny cabins, but everyone else was either inside their cabin or out exploring the town, so it felt very cozy and private.

The door swung open revealing a clean, rustic retreat. The floor, the walls, and ceiling were hewn from knotty pine. The decor was minimal and sparse, but with a rustic woodsy look. It had two bedrooms, a bathroom, and a tiny living room area with a television, mini-fridge, and couch.

"This is a wee fairytale cabin." James spread his arms looking around the small space before them. "I think it fits two o' me across and maybe three deep."

"It's definitely not fancy." Paige suddenly realized that James might not appreciate quirky charm in his lodgings. "I'm not a Four Seasons kind of girl. Unique charm is more my thing. I hope you don't mind."

"Mind? I love it. I get to be holed up in a private cabin with my girlfriend for two whole nights. It doesn't get any more posh than that."

They set their luggage down and poked their heads into the other rooms of the cabin. They were very tiny. The bedrooms fit a queen bed, which very nearly touched three of the four walls of the room, and a TV on a dresser. That was it.

The bathroom was a modest size but didn't feel cramped. It was more than adequate for getting washed up.

"Which room do you want?" James asked.

"Oh. The two bedroom was all they had left. I didn't mean too…"

"Probably a good thing. I dinnae think both of us can store our clothes in the same dresser or dress in the room at the same time."

Paige looked at the gap between the foot of the bed and the wall. It might be a little cramped for two people to try to reach around each other for the dresser.

She laughed. "It's definitely cozy here."

"Aye. Cozy is just what I like." James leaned in and gave Paige a soft kiss. She wrapped her arms around him and squeezed tight.

"I'm so glad you're here with me. There's so much I want to share with you."

She tried not to let the wet blanket of reality weigh down on her. She had Googled the distance. Ann Arbor to Glasgow was 3,505 miles away. It would be less distance to drive from New York City to Los Angeles, and that was a huge expanse she could hardly picture. James would be even further, separated by an ocean she couldn't drive over whether she was up for the trip or not.

She didn't want to think about any of that. *Stay in the moment. Enjoy right now.*

She gave James another kiss to put herself back in the present. Not a long, lingering kiss. Just enough to ground herself in how wonderful he made her feel. Once she felt herself smiling against his lips, she pulled away and picked up her bag.

"I'm just going to unpack this in here." She nodded at the closest bedroom. "Then we've got a little time to unwind before dinner."

"Right." James followed suit, picking up his bag and heading into the other room.

Paige put her clothing into the dresser, popped her toiletry bag on the sink in the bathroom, and went back into the tiny living room area.

After getting their things squared away, they snuggled up on the couch together, legs stretched out in front of them, to just relax for a while before dinner and Paige's final surprise of the day.

"Why does being in the car make a person so sleepy?" Paige yawned, resting her head on James's shoulder.

"You've been very busy driving. You deserve a wee rest." James reached over and gently smoothed her hair back from her face. "Fair warning, if you fall asleep, I probably will too."

Paige gave a sleepy chuckle and rested her hand on James's chest.

She liked the feel of his heartbeat beneath her palm and his strong shoulder under her cheek.

"I might just close my eyes for a few moments," she said.

"I might as well." James leaned his cheek on the top of her head.

Comfortably wrapped up with each other, it didn't take long for either of them to doze off. An hour had gone by before Paige woke. She'd been using his shoulder as a pillow, but her hand had fallen from his chest to his thigh.

From the rhythm of his breathing she could tell he was still asleep. She gently lifted her head, hoping she wouldn't wake him up. She hadn't counted on her neck muscles being angry with her for leaning against a shoulder instead of using a fluffy pillow.

"Ooh!" She exclaimed, rubbing her neck.

James sucked in a loud breath and his eyes flickered open.

"Sorry. I didn't mean to wake you," Paige apologized.

"Did you get a nice rest?" James's voice was gravely from sleep.

"Yeah." Paige yawned. "Although I think I gave myself a kink in my neck."

"Oh, we can't have that." James sat up and stretched. "Turn around. I can take care of that for you."

Paige looked at him questioningly.

"Turn around," he instructed again.

She swiveled on the couch, putting her back to him. He placed both his hands on her shoulders and began to massage.

She gasped in pleasure at the warm, firm, pressure of his fingers as he found just the right spot to work on. "Oh God. You have magic fingers."

"I do," he agreed. "I know a thing or two about massage. You'll be good as new by dinner."

"Mmm." Paige could only reply with a sound. His hands working her shoulder and neck muscles felt so good she just wanted to dissolve into his touch and never come back.

He kept going, strong enough to be effective but light enough to be comfortable. When he felt that the tension was dissipating beneath his fingers, he left off and placed a gentle kiss at the base of her neck.

"There you go. Feel better?"

Paige didn't think there were meaningful enough words in the language to describe how she felt at that moment. She was sure the spa treatment Kayla had given her for her birthday would have nothing on this.

"Don't ever stop touching me," Paige finally said.

James squeezed her shoulders lightly and pressed another warm kiss on her neck, sending a delightful shiver down her spine. "Is that an invitation?" His lips tickled the delicate skin between her ear and shoulder.

After that massage, there was a number of things she'd like to invite him to do, but she noticed the time on the clock said nearly seven o'clock. They still needed to eat dinner and she wanted to show him a few things before dark.

She turned to him and kissed him lightly on the lips. "Let's grab dinner first. Ok?"

James smoothed down some of Paige's hair that had gone astray while they napped.

"Aye. Let's go."

They got back into the car and drove the mile or so to the first cluster of shops and restaurants they found, after the long stretch of lodging and coastline. Once they managed to find a parking spot, they strolled down the sidewalk, hand in hand, peering in souvenir shop windows, past a little ice cream parlor, and a fudge shop with the sweetest smells wafting out from it.

"That smells like a dream." James inhaled deeply of the candy-scented air.

"Mackinac is known for its fudge and salt water taffy. We'll see lots of sweet shops while we're here."

"I'll gain half a stone while I'm here, won't I?" James rubbed his stomach.

Paige wasn't exactly sure what the equivalent of a stone was, but she did recognize it as a unit of weight from some of the British television shows she watched with Kayla on girls' nights in.

"No one would notice if you did." Paige took a glance at his fit body.

They found an Italian place that tempted them with its savory aroma of garlic.

After the meal, James sat back and patted his stomach. "Well, this has certainly been a day of rich eating."

"A delicious day for sure," Paige agreed. "How would you like to walk it off with me?"

"Roll me out of this restaurant and I'll catch up with you."

Paige stood and reached out her hand for James. "It's only a short walk. You can recover once we get there."

As sundown was nearing and it was the Fourth of July, foot traffic had picked up considerably. It was busier than she would have liked, but not even that could diminish the impact of the place.

As they walked past more kitschy tourist shops, ice cream parlors, and fudge shops, the breeze picked up off the water, sweeping into town. They turned a corner and then they could see it. The massive towers of the Mackinac Bridge swelled into the sky ahead of them.

"Wow!" James exclaimed once he saw where they were headed. "That's impressive."

The Mackinac Bridge towered high before them and stretched away, farther than the eye could see, over the Straights of Mackinac, with Lake Huron to their right and Lake Michigan to their left. The sky above was a lighter shade of blue than the deep, ocean hue of the lake.

"Isn't it something? I've only crossed it once in my life, and it was terrifying. It connects the lower and upper peninsulas of Michigan. So, the other side of the bridge is where the actual U.P. and the real 'up north' are. This bridge is the fifth largest suspension bridge in the world…I looked that up before we came. It's nearly five miles long but it feels like it'll never end when you're going over it."

"Are we going to cross it?" James's eyes lit up like an eager boy.

"Oh God. I don't know if I could actually drive it. I was a kid when my dad drove our van over it so we could visit the Soo Locks in Sault Ste. Marie. I pretty much kept my eyes closed and prayed the whole way over it."

James gazed at the towers of the bridge and the road between them, supported by thick beams that plunged into the dark, stormy blue of the Straights of Mackinac. "What's so scary about it?"

"Well, the only thing I could think about was the car that had gone over the edge and plunged into the water, killing the driver, in the 1980s."

James's eyes widened in horror.

"Are you sure that isnae just an urban legend?"

"No. It's real. Can you imagine?" Paige shivered. "Ugh, I couldn't stop imagining it when we drove over it. They have to close the bridge when it's too windy because it would be too hazardous to drive over."

"Amazing." James gaped at the wonder of construction before their eyes, as they reached the rocky beach. "So, we're going to walk across it then?"

"No way! Although, they do shut it down for people to do that over Labor Day weekend. I don't think I could handle that either. I mean, if I'm worried about a car flying off the edge, just imagine a teeny little person." Paige shuddered just thinking about it.

"So, a walk on the beach enjoying the view of the bridge?"

"Yes!" Paige exclaimed. "That sounds far safer."

The beach was crowded with people enjoying the sunshine and scenery, but Paige and James made it to the water's edge. They wove a lazy path between children squealing as they waded in the cold water. The waves landed roughly on the beach, crashing impressively. Everything about the place screamed size and power. The pair stared out over the water, at the monstrous bridge, at the dark choppy waves, and remained in awe of it all.

They meandered along the bustling shoreline picking up interesting rocks and shells. The water in this area wasn't known for being warm. Even though it was July, the water felt refrigerated as it washed over their bare toes, causing Paige to grit her teeth and call, "Woo, that's invigorating!"

As dusk began to fall, crowds thickened, and they went back to the car to retrieve a quilt and a fleece blanket to stake out a spot on the beach to watch the fireworks display over Mackinac Island. Paige figured the breeze would get chilly off the water once the sun went down, and she wasn't wrong. She was glad she'd also brought a hoodie and a pair of sweatpants to pull on over her shorts. She might not be winning any cute points, but at least she wouldn't be too freezing to enjoy the display.

They huddled together under the fleece and watched the sky grow darker and the stars get brighter. There was far less light pollution than at home so there was a dazzling spread of stars in the sky.

Finally, the first pop and explosion of dazzling color filled the night sky and everyone turned their attention to the fireworks. Paige sat between James's legs, her back to his chest, head resting against his shoulder. He wrapped his arms around her, to share body heat as much as to enjoy being so close to her.

The colors streaked and sizzled across the sky, reflecting in the water as well, giving the illusion they were completely surrounded by a blaze of rainbow colors amidst the blackness of night.

James leaned his head over Paige's shoulder. "The fireworks are like Hogmanay back home, only this is a lot warmer."

"Hogmanay? I've never heard of that."

"It's how we ring in the new year. Ma and I go to a big family party at Uncle Davie and Auntie Cait's and then we go to the fireworks."

Paige thought back to the photo she'd seen on James's table and tried to picture a loud, boisterous party with James and his family.

The roaring of the waves was powerful competition for the blasting of the fireworks, and Paige nestled into James's arms and felt immersed in the wonder of the moment. The only things she was aware of were the dots of light, the rhythmic noise of the waves, and the warmth of James's body wrapped around hers. She was surrounded by all she wanted and she luxuriated in the satisfaction of loving exactly what she had.

The fireworks lasted about forty-five minutes, but it felt long enough to fundamentally shift reality. The crowd on the shore erupted in cheers and applause after the thunderous grand finale.

"That was an impressive display," James whispered in Paige's ear as the people around them began to pack up, but James and Paige remained rapt where they sat.

She squeezed his arms.

"How was that for your first Fourth of July celebration?"

"I dinnae think anything could top it."

Reluctantly, they started to pack up their blankets and head back to the car. It was too chilly to remain with the stragglers on the beach. Paige was looking forward to snuggling into their cozy little cabin for the night. It had been a long day, but she wasn't the least bit tired. Something about the lake air and her proximity to James had invigorated her like nothing else could.

The drive, although short in distance, was long on time with all the crowds dispersing at the same time. As they sat in the slow moving traffic backup, the beach mood remained intact.

"Is the Fourth of July always like this?" James asked.

"I have to admit, this is the most magical Fourth I've ever had."

"Seriously?"

"One hundred percent."

"How so?"

The air in the car was charged with electricity. Paige hoped that James had asked the question for her to clarify that they were feeling the same thing. It wasn't like her to be bold in relationships, but bathed in the glow of brake lights, she didn't feel her normal reserved caution.

"Well, I've probably spent more Fourths at family barbecues. There are usually backyard potlucks. Lots of pasta and potato salads. Hot dogs. Hamburgers. Chips. Watermelon. All that good stuff. The kids run around with sparklers to keep them occupied before the local firework show starts. But today felt a lot different than those celebrations."

"Yeah," James encouraged quietly.

Paige took a deep breath and went ahead and said it.

"Being wrapped up on the beach, with you, watching the show, I felt like we were the only two people in the universe. So that's why this one is special. It's all about being with you. I'm really falling for you, James."

Her heart pounded in her chest. It was risky to say that, no matter how she was reading the situation. However, if she'd learned one thing from her time with Dylan, it was that saying what she felt was more important than staying quiet out of fear. She might as well put it out there, no matter what might come of it. She gripped the wheel and stared ahead of her, waiting for his response.

James took a moment to distill his feelings into verbal form before putting her out of her nervous misery.

"I wondered if it was ridiculous how strongly I feel for you after just these few weeks, but I promise you Paige, I feel the same. From the moment I saw you sitting at that library desk, I felt drawn to you. It was like you understood me before we even spoke. It sounds crazy, I know…" James struggled to find more words that would accurately convey what he was trying to say.

Paige didn't need to hear any more. She understood him perfectly. She leaned over and used her kiss to say all the things they were both trying to express. She didn't pull away until the car behind her honked.

She jumped and moved the car up the couple of car lengths that had opened while she and James were kissing.

Paige laughed quietly. "I guess we'll have to save that until we get back to the cabin."

"Safety first," James said. "But I'd much rather be kissing you than sitting in traffic. To be clear."

"Same."

James ran his hands through his hair. Paige tapped her fingers on the steering wheel. It was the best option she had to dispel the mounting energy in her body. They were only half a mile from their cabin. If they got out and walked, they'd probably make it faster than waiting for the cars to clear out.

"Well," Paige started in an attempt to continue the drive with a less enticing line of conversation. "What do you think of Michigan after today?"

"I love it, o' course!" James said. "It was wonderful to see some o' the places that shaped you. I got a feel for what your childhood was like and a glimpse o' your happy memories. Now I have memories o' your special places too. That's amazing to me."

So much for steering to more neutral conversation. Paige couldn't tell if she'd rather keep listening to James say such wonderful things or keep his mouth occupied with kisses.

"You know, one could say you almost seem too good to be true," Paige remarked.

"I hope no'," James said. "I have plenty of flaws. I dinnae mean to sound like a hero in a movie. I genuinely care for you, Paige. No matter what, I want you to know that. You're much more than a pretty girl I met on my summer in Michigan. You're the kind of girl who makes me want to make plans."

"Plans?" Paige asked, a lump forming in her throat as her head began to buzz with excitement.

"I dinnae want to scare you."

Paige finally got to pull into the driveway for their cabin.

"I like plans." The calm certainty in her voice was in direct opposition to the wild rush of feelings inside. She turned off the car, but neither made a move to get out.

James picked at the vent on the dash in front of him. "Maybe it's just because there's a deadline looming on how long I'm supposed to be here, but I dinnae want this summer to be it for us. I really like who you are, Paige Marie. I want more of that in my life. More of you."

"I feel exactly the same way about you," Paige said in a voice trembling with emotion. "I didn't know things could be this easy, you know? Like you said, it's like we just clicked together from the beginning. It was never like we hadn't known each other. You sort of feel like a welcome home."

"Aye! That's what it is. I dinnae have to hide anything with you. Dinnae have to pretend. I'm just me and you seem to like that."

"I love that." She pulled the keys out of the ignition and nodded toward the cabin. "Want to head in?"

"I cannae believe I get to share a cabin with you." James smiled. "I'm a very lucky man."

They got out and Paige made quick work of getting the door unlocked. A dim light emanated from the bathroom. Apparently, it had one of those glowing light switches. It was all the light there was in the cabin and Paige didn't mind keeping it that way. As soon as the door closed behind them and James locked it, they found their way to each other and their kisses said what words could not.

She tugged him into the closest bedroom and they collapsed on the bed, not even bothering to close the door.

Nineteen

PAIGE WOKE up in the morning with images of James and the nighttime beach in her mind. It took her a few minutes to figure out if it had all been a dream. Once she remembered the events of the previous day, she couldn't keep the smile from her face. When was the last time she'd woken up so happy? She couldn't remember, but she didn't care. She was happy now and that's what mattered.

She stretched out like a starfish in her bed before she realized James was no longer next to her. Finally, her brain kicked in enough that she noticed the muffled sound of water splashing in the shower.

She had moved to the couch in the mini-living room when he emerged from the bathroom with nothing but a short towel wrapped around his waist.

"Morning, beautiful," he said, making her spine tingle all over. "I hope I didnae wake you."

"Morning, handsome," she answered. "No, I didn't even hear you get up."

"Good. I want to see what you have planned for us today." He took the few steps over to the couch and leaned in for a good morning kiss.

"I do have a fun day planned. How about we get ready to head out, grab some breakfast, and then we'll make our way to the next stop."

They did exactly that and, soon enough, found themselves in line to catch their ferry to Mackinac Island. The water looked calmer than it had the evening before, but not exactly smooth. Paige hadn't been to the island since she was a child and didn't really remember what the ferry trip had been like. She hoped the choppy waves wouldn't make her seasick. That would put a damper on her plans.

She needn't have worried. Although a few points in the trip made her stomach drop, it was no match for her elation over sitting next to James, holding his hand. The boat docked and they got off on the island. Paige didn't have clear memories of the place in her mind, only images from the family photo album. Once they made it away from the dock to the main street, Paige felt that they'd stepped back in time.

The shop-lined streets had lovely old-timey storefronts that radiated mid-1800s charm. The tourists looked like futuristic time travelers, walking along car-less streets snapping selfies with their smartphones.

"There are no cars on the island," Paige explained as they folded their way into the crowds strolling down the main street. A clip-clop sound came up from behind them and they turned to see the source. "But there are carriages. Do you want to take a carriage ride with me to Arch Rock?"

"Of course!"

Paige figured he'd say that.

They hurried to a ticket station and booked a carriage ride. They browsed the shops while they waited for their appointed time.

"We're going to want some fudge and salt water taffy while we're here, but we'll wait until we're heading back. Less to carry."

James inhaled deeply. "Interesting combination. Smells of horse and warm sugar."

Paige laughed. "And the fresh lake air too. Is it crazy that I think it smells wonderful?"

To her, all of it combined to create the luxurious holiday smell. Nothing smelled like regular life. The simple act of breathing helped to remind the brain that it could relax and enjoy these vacation vibes. Paige couldn't ignore the call of the island.

They made an action-packed day of it. They hopped off their carriage ride to see a rifle and cannon demonstration at historic Fort Mackinac. James laughed at how cute Paige was when she jumped and covered her ears when the cannon blast boomed, rattling their teeth. They listened to the presenter, wearing his reenactment uniform as he explained how the fort had been captured by the British in the War of 1812.

Paige wandered through the buildings with James beside her. "It's hard to take in the history of it. I mean, this building has been here since the 1700s. Now we're in the 2000s. It's mind-boggling."

James gazed at Paige, gentle amusement twinkling in his eyes. "Then you really willnae believe that the oldest building in Glasgow was built in the 1100s."

She nudged him playfully with her shoulder. "I know, I know. I live in a baby country. I can't imagine how it would feel to stand in a building built in the 1100s. Does it feel like you're standing in the same place that nearly a thousand years' worth of people have stood in?"

James considered her question.

"You dinnae think about it every day, but I suppose you get used to history being all around. It becomes part of your story."

"Well, it's not like that here." Paige turned back to look at the display with a grainy old photograph of a regiment stationed at Fort Mackinac long ago. "Here, a neighborhood is considered 'old' if the houses were built in the 1950s. Definitely historic if it's from the 1920s or earlier. This fort is pretty much ancient history to us."

"Aye. Well, it is, in the scope of your country's history. It's no' better or worse for being younger."

Once they'd had their fill of Fort Mackinac, they finished the carriage tour, complete with an obligatory selfie with Arch Rock, then rented bicycles and peddled around the island, enjoying the breeze in their hair and a return to simpler times. They capped their day on the island wandering through the butterfly house and then ate ice cream while sitting on the green and gazing at the magnificent blue of Lake Huron.

"It's nice to be here with you," James mused. "The breeze off the water reminds me a wee bit of home. It makes me want to show you around Scotland."

The words struck Paige squarely in the soft, vulnerable part of her heart. Her heart ached to see where James was from. To touch, smell, taste, and hear the place he'd grown up. Their conversation at the fort stayed in her mind. She wanted to know firsthand what it felt like to stand in a building erected in the 1100s. She wanted to see it all so badly, and yet, the reality was it was so expensive and so far away. Even if she did manage to afford it one day, what would it be like to see it with a guy she used to be with? Would they still have feelings for each other by then? Would they be with other people? She didn't want to imagine that.

Paige snapped herself out of her bittersweet reverie to answer. "I'd love to see it. I've been working my way through the books you gave me. There are quite a few places I have to see for myself."

"I'm pleased you're enjoying it. It's mostly Scottish countryside in that book. I'd have to show you my city too. There's a lot to keep you occupied there."

She thought back to the pictures he'd shared with her on his phone. Not only would she like to see the wild vistas and impossibly ancient castles, but she would love to see the places of James's everyday life. It made her appreciate how James might be feeling about this trip. They weren't in her regular stomping grounds, but revisiting special touchpoints from her past. It was a nice way to connect with the parts of each other they could never see firsthand.

By the time they'd boarded the final ferry heading back to Mackinaw City, they could scarcely keep their eyes open. Paige yawned and leaned her head on James's shoulder. James kissed the top of her head and took the bag of taffy from her hand.

"I'll wake you when we get back to the dock."

"Mmm," Paige murmured, already half asleep from a long day of activity on the island.

When they got to the dock, James gently helped her get to her feet. She leaned heavily against him.

"I can drive," James offered. "It's only just down the road a bit."

Paige readily surrendered her keys and climbed into the passenger seat. James had no difficulty maneuvering the car the short distance to their destination and helping Paige inside.

"I'm sorry," she yawned. "I'm not used to being so active and out in the sun. I'm exhausted."

"You're fine, Darlin'," James assured her. "I'm knackered. Let's call it a night. Thanks for another amazing day."

Twenty

SUNLIGHT PEEKED in between the slats of the blinds, heralding a new day to spend with James. After blinking her eyes into focus, she turned away from the window to see that James was already awake and gazing at her with an adorable little smile on his face.

"How's my girl this mornin'?"

Paige could get used to waking up and having her heart immediately melted by James.

"I'm amazing. How's my boyfriend? Sleep well?" She liked how it felt to call James her boyfriend. It was exciting, but natural too.

"Aye. Exploring the island tired me right out. And today, I get to spend another day with the most beautiful woman in the world. What's your plan?"

"I thought we'd enjoy a day at the beach before we head home."

"Sounds perfect." James leaned in and gave Paige a lovely kiss before sliding out of bed to get ready.

Paige got first dibs on a shower and James walked to the hotel office to pick up some juice and bagels for a light breakfast. When he got back, he showered while Paige ate her bagel. Sufficiently clean and fed, she pulled out the floaty peach, turquoise, and yellow sundress she'd packed specifically for this day. A carefree day at the beach was exactly what they needed before starting the drive home.

Both were in high spirits when they left the cabin. When she'd booked the trip, Paige had figured they'd decide together which beach to spend the day. After their conversation by the bridge, she realized there was one place she really had to take him.

They got into the car and Paige took a deep breath. She could do this. She had to do this.

She pulled out onto the street and headed north. Heart pounding in her chest, her palms and underarms prickled with sweat.

"Let's listen to some music." Paige connected to the Bluetooth system in her car and put on her most soothing playlist from her phone. The familiar notes of a calming Coldplay song came on and she tried to focus on the beat of the music rather than the beat of her heart.

James was taking in the scenery from his window until he realized what was happening.

"Paige! You're heading toward the bridge."

"Yep." She nodded, staring straight ahead. Trying to imagine that the lovely rectangular towers of the Mighty Mac weren't getting closer and closer because she, herself, was driving straight for them.

"You said you were terrified to drive it!" James leaned forward in his seat, alternating between staring at Paige and turning back to the rapidly approaching bridge.

"I am."

"Paige, you dinnae have to do this for me." He put his hand on her thigh, to be reassuring, to ground her, or to stop her. She wasn't sure which.

"I know. I think I need to do it for myself. If you can fly over an ocean to a place you've never been to try new things, then I can drive over a bridge."

"Are you sure? It's no' too late. You can pull over and I can drive."

Paige shook her head. Her adrenaline had kicked in now. She was doing this. She may not be able to control the price of her rent. She may not be able to ensure that she'd get the promotion. She couldn't even guarantee that she and James would be in the same country ever again, but this was something she could do. True, she did want to do it for James. If he had come all this way to stand before the Mackinac Bridge, it would be pretty pathetic to not even cross it, but more than that, she wanted to prove to herself that she could. She would drive the terrifying five miles over that bridge and live to tell the tale! She hoped.

As the road began to slant up from the ground, Paige gripped the wheel tight.

James looked at the view, but also at Paige.

"Can you tell me what it was like in that city you visited on the other side o' the bridge? I forget the name you said."

Paige kept her eyes straight ahead on the lane she was driving in. She'd chosen the inner lane, as there were two lanes in each direction. The outer lane was way too close to the edge and she really couldn't handle that. The railing didn't seem high enough or strong enough to do much good from the towering heights above the water. And water was all there was to see. It felt like driving over an ocean.

"Sault Ste. Marie. It's known for its locks system. My parents took me to see them in action. I remember the rushing sound of the water as it filled the lock so the boat could safely make it to the other side. I also remember thinking it was crazy that the spelling of the city and pronunciation are completely off. It's pronounced Soo Saint Marie." Then she spelled out the name of the city to illustrate how an outsider would never get it right. "Same with Mackinac. You may have noticed on the road signs that it's spelled with a 'c' at the end, but it's pronounced Mackinaw. The city we're staying in spells it with the 'w' at the end. But the island and the bridge have the 'c.' It's all very confusing. You have to be a Michigander to know the difference. Even then, probably most of us are pretty confused too."

She did feel better when she was back in tour guide mode, but just as Paige was getting more comfortable, the pavement in her lane changed to an open grating. If she looked at it closely, she'd be able to see the water below them. She didn't care to think about the lack of pavement between her wheels and a two hundred foot drop into freezing cold water.

"That's a little terrifying don't you think?" Paige didn't want to panic, but she could feel herself starting to freak out. She laughed nervously but she wasn't fooling either of them. Bridges like this were scary. It was just the truth of the matter.

"You're doing very well. We'll be there soon. And I'd have no idea that's how you spell Sault Ste. Marie. If I read it, I wouldnae know it was the same place. Feeling ok?"

All she knew was that she couldn't wait to be on the other side of this ridiculously long bridge.

"I'm ok. Are you enjoying the view?"

James turned his attention to the view from his window.

"Aye, it's beautiful. Such a nice clear day. Perfect beach weather. Can you tell me anything about the beach we're going to?"

"I can't, actually. I just Googled it on my phone this morning once I decided we had to go over the bridge."

Thankfully, the grate in her lane turned back into pavement and she could feel herself relax a little. Maybe the worst was over.

"Do you know you're lovely when you're conquering your fears?"

"What?" Paige hadn't expected that question but it did bring a small smile to her face.

"You are. You look determined and capable. Like a woman about to get a promotion and take on the world."

She did like the sound of that.

"One terrifying bridge at a time, I guess."

"Aye. That's the spirit."

Paige eased up her grip on the steering wheel just a bit. You'd never catch her saying how much she enjoyed driving over bridges but, apparently, she was capable of doing it anyway.

"Have you ever driven over a bridge like this?" The end was in sight and they hadn't blown off to their death. She was feeling confident enough to ask the questions now.

"No' as long as this, but I have driven over the Queensferry Crossing. It goes between Edinburgh and Fife."

Paige had no idea where Edinburgh and Fife were in relation to

Glasgow, or anywhere else in Scotland to be honest. She was pleased, at least, that she'd heard of both places before.

"It didn't make you nervous at all?"

James leaned back in his seat a little and looked out at the view again. It was a fantastic sunny morning and the deep blue water sparkled in the light, a nice contrast to the lighter, brighter blue of the summer sky.

"No' nervous. I'm used to being on the water. Driving over seems more stable than floating on top of it. I'm comfortable either way." He turned back to Paige. "Have I mentioned you're doing great?"

Paige chuckled. "Yes, I believe you have. I appreciate it though. And look! We're coming up to the toll station. You're about to go to the Upper Peninsula of Michigan for the first time."

"Because you were brave enough to drive me. Thank you, Paige Marie. I mean that."

Slowing down for the toll lines, Paige's heartbeat returned to normal and she felt a sense of exhilaration. She'd actually driven over the Mighty Mac. She never would have done it if it wasn't for James, and he'd been a very calm and supportive companion on the journey. She'd have to tell her parents about this. They'd hardly believe it, but they'd be so proud.

Paige paid the toll with a beaming smile on her face and then continued the short drive to Straits State Park, where they could enjoy a nice stretch of time sitting on the beach of Lake Huron.

"It's lovely here," James said as they lounged on the sand, the breeze ruffling his hair. "So different from Ann Arbor. Like another world, really."

Paige pulled in a deep breath of the fresh lake air and exhaled slowly. "Yeah, it just slows you down. You can't help but let go of everything here. It's good to recharge."

"Aye, it is." James leaned back on his elbows, but kept his eyes on the vibrant blue lake water and the boats that drifted by.

"Does this give you any ideas for your art?" Paige watched the path of a sailboat as it followed along the coastline.

"It does. The breeze, the clean lake air. It reminds me of the spirit of the water and the rich history of the people who've made it their lives. It's good to tap into that. It keeps the connection to the larger story intact."

Paige enjoyed the warmth of the sun on her skin, the breeze in her hair, and the breath of the waves. It slowed her heart rate and calmed her into believing that everything was just as it should be. Sitting on that blanket, with her toes curled into the cool sand, she could easily trust that the job promotion was in her reach and that things would work out between her and James.

"What are you thinking about?" James asked, taking in the Mona Lisa smile on Paige's face.

She closed her eyes and tilted her face to the sun.

"I was just thinking about how everything feels right when you're on the beach. It's just peaceful, like the whole world's in balance."

"Aye," James agreed. "It feels even more right when you're sharing a blanket on the beach with your dream girl." He traced a finger down from her shoulder to her wrist and Paige opened her eyes to survey his face.

"I mean it," James said, when he saw her expression. "I never want this to end. No' just this." He nodded to indicate the idyllic beach scene around them. "But this." He gestured back and forth between the two of them. "You have such a beautiful heart, Paige. I saw it the minute you decided to share your library card with me."

"Oh that." Paige looked away to the water, remembering that first meeting that felt both years ago and just yesterday.

"Aye, that," James insisted. "It may sound foolish, but it was like you were willing to stake your reputation for me. You didnae know if I'd come in again, but you did it to help me. That's beautiful, Paige, and most people wouldnae have done it."

"I'm not that wonderful." Paige sat up and crossed her legs. "I wouldn't have done it for just anyone. If lecherous Norm had the same problem you did, no way would I check out books for him. It greatly helped your cause that you're so charming, not to mention good looking."

James smiled, but shook his head. "There's more to it than that. It reveals your kind heart, even if you wouldnae have done it for someone who makes you uncomfortable. You took a risk with me to be nice. And—" he continued emphatically before she could object, "You invited me to Kayla and Eric's for dinner to be nice. You cannae deny that."

"Again," Paige chuckled, "you're so good looking and you seemed really nice too. I didn't want you to go have dinner alone when I could bring you along with me."

"Aha! See? You didnae want me to be alone. That's a caring heart, Paige."

"But I wanted to spend time with you because I was attracted to you. That's actually self-serving."

"No, this is self-serving." James leaned over and dropped a gentle kiss on Paige's lips.

"Mmm," Paige mused after they pulled away. "I don't know. Depends on whose perspective you're looking at. To me, that was an act of kindness."

James smiled and gazed out over the water. They fell silent and just listened to the crashing of the waves, in and out, on the shore.

Eventually, James broke the silence with a question.

"How did you decide you wanted to be a librarian?"

Paige kept her eyes on the waves as she answered.

"I've always been a reader. I was one of those kids who always had a book in hand, but I didn't realize I could make a career from that. In high school I did a lot of babysitting and got a part-time job in a pet store."

"A pet store!" James exclaimed. "That sounds like good fun."

"A lot of it was, except for cleaning out cages and tanks. By the time senior year rolled around, we had a career day at school. One of our guest speakers was a librarian and she was so cool! She wasn't your stereotypical librarian. Her hair was short and dyed Cookie Monster blue. She had a nose ring and a rose tattoo on her arm. She talked about all the fun programs she ran at her library and I thought I wanted to do what she did. In college, I got a job at the university library as a checkout clerk."

"And that solidified it, did it?"

"Well, little known fact, librarians have to get a master's degree in library science. So after undergrad, I got a full time job as a social media manager for a local realtor and took night classes to get my library degree. Little did I know the social media experience would help me in libraries, too."

"Sounds like a dream to me. The chance to try out different things and hone a skill set along the way. All I know is boats. No' much of a transferable skill."

Paige squeezed James's hand. Her heart broke for him. She tried to imagine how she'd feel if she'd only ever worked at her first job, or transitioned from babysitter to a family daycare center. A lifetime did seem like too long to have the same job. She didn't even know if she'd want to be a librarian until the day she retired.

"Don't be so hard on yourself. You do know more than boats. I've seen you in the studio, remember? You know a heck of a lot about woodworking. And you're amazing at it too."

James smiled, if a little weakly. "I wouldnae say that."

"Well, I'm saying it for you. You know public speaking and customer service, too. Those are certainly desirable skills that transfer to a wide variety of jobs."

James tilted his head as he soaked in her words.

"I hadnae thought of it that way."

"Have you been thinking about what you'd like to do? After you're done with the tour boat?"

James breathed a heavy sigh. "*If* I'm done with the tour boat. I dinnae really know what else to do."

Paige looked James in the eye.

"Listen to me, James. I know that change is scary, but it's possible. No matter how tough it seems, it's possible and you'll get through it. I one hundred percent believe in you."

James swallowed hard and pulled Paige close for a hug.

"You make me so happy. What are we going to do?"

Paige wasn't really sure how to answer the question. He'd have to go back to his complicated life of expectation in Scotland. She lived here. Was there really any way to reconcile that into a scenario that kept them together, while living on opposite sides of an ocean? It didn't seem likely. But the breeze danced across her skin, seeming to carry doubt away with it. Against the odds, their paths had crossed. Feeling the rhythm of the earth all around her, Paige couldn't deny there were more possibilities and connections in this world than could be seen. Maybe there was a natural solution to all of it, if they just trusted and followed the flow.

"Right now," she said quietly, "It feels like anything's possible, doesn't it?"

"It does," James agreed.

"Maybe we just go with that."

"Maybe we do," James echoed.

Twenty-One

AFTER THE LONG DRIVE, Paige and James were relieved to be back, but also sad to leave behind the easy flow of sunny vacation days.

"Wow," James said when they pulled into his driveway. "Paige, I hardly know what to say. That was an amazing trip."

"I loved it too," she said. "I'm so happy I got to be the one to show you some of what Michigan really has to offer."

"Do you have time to come in?" James asked.

They both had to work in the morning, but she wasn't particularly looking forward to the solitude of her apartment.

She pulled the keys from the ignition. "Sounds perfect."

They got into James's place and collapsed on the bed together. The post-drive weariness was upon them again, but not so much that Paige didn't have any energy left.

She rolled over and pulled James tight for a welcome home kiss.

He leaned in and kissed her back, but before things could get any steamier, Paige felt James's pocket vibrating.

"Ugh. Let's get rid o' that." James pulled out his phone to toss it on the nightstand until he caught sight of the name. He frowned as he looked at the screen and sat up.

"I should take this. It's gone midnight there."

"Of course." Paige slid a little further from James to try and give him some privacy.

"Hey, is everything ok?" James answered.

Even though she wasn't trying to eavesdrop, Paige was close enough to hear the fairly loud and distinctly distraught answer from the other end of the line.

"They've just taken David to the A & E."

James sat up at the edge of the bed, his face going white.

"What happened?"

"He was complaining o' chest pains and then fainted. Cait called 999 and they've just left with him now."

James sprang to his feet and started pacing the room as Paige remained on the bed feeling helpless.

"Is Cait gone with him? What can I do?"

"You can come home, Jamie. We need you!"

"Right. I'll be on the next flight."

Paige didn't register anything else after that. Her brain snagged on 'the next flight.' Although she'd just overheard that his uncle was being rushed to the hospital, she couldn't believe this is how their night was going to end…maybe how everything between them was going to end. She wasn't ready for this. She needed more time with him, if only a little.

James held the phone to his ear, even though Paige was sure his mother had hung up. One look at his face reminded her that this was no time to worry about the future of their relationship. She needed to help him, however she could.

"Are you ok?" Paige stood up and put a gentle hand on James's arm.

James looked at Paige, his face bereft of the warmth and kindness she was used to seeing there.

"They've taken David to the A & E. Sounds like it could be a heart attack. I think I've got to go back."

The words pierced Paige in the heart with all the delicacy of a rusty bread knife. So many questions swam through her murky thoughts. Was it really possible his uncle would die, now that James had finally gotten a summer away to explore his art? What was the right thing for Paige to do? And heaviest of all, if he did leave, would he ever come back?

The new memories Paige had made with James assembled like a collage in her mind, and then shattered like broken glass. There didn't seem to be enough air in the room anymore. How could everything have changed with one frantic phone call at the end of a beautiful day?

She couldn't give voice to any of her questions. None of that would help James, and the lost look on his face clearly indicated that he needed her help.

"Ok…" Paige started cautiously. "What do you need to do? Is there someone I can contact at the residency for you tomorrow? We should look up flights and I can drive you to the airport."

James shook his head and blinked, as if reality was just coming back to him.

"Right, yeah. Uh, Beverly Streeter is the head of the Arts Council. I've got her number. If you could ring her in the morning, that would be a big help. Just tell her…" His face crumpled as he tried to think of what to say.

"I'll just tell her there's been an emergency at home and you had to go back. For a few days?"

James ran his hands through his hair and exhaled. "Maybe? I have to be here for the exhibit."

Paige couldn't deny the little glimmer of hope she felt that James was thinking he'd be back for his exhibit. Of course, that was all dependent on what happened with his uncle. She would have to tell her mother and her prayer group to focus on Uncle David.

"Well, don't worry about that. One step at a time." She squeezed his shoulder and offered a little half smile as gentle encouragement. He returned the expression and rested his hand on hers.

"I guess I should check for flights." The last thing Paige wanted to be doing was helping him search for a last minute flight to whisk him to the other side of the world, but she knew it was the right thing to do. She understood that James's uncle was like a father to him. What would she do if she were in Scotland and her dad was struck with a potentially fatal illness? She'd want to go home right away too.

He started searching on his phone for flights and she sat beside him, feeling numb.

"There's a flight tonight at 10:17." He pointed at the screen as if the flight would disappear before his eyes. Do you think I can make that?"

Paige looked at the clock on the wall. It was nearing 7:30. The airport was about forty-five minutes away. He wouldn't get there with the recommended amount of time for an international flight, but he should definitely be able to make it.

"Yes. We'll make it there. Don't worry about that."

"Right." James looked around the room like he was running a quick mental check of what he really needed to have. "I'll just bring my bag from our trip. Dinnae need anything else. I have plenty o' clothes at home. Should we go?"

He left her Beverly's contact information so she could take care of that for him. He also left her the keys to his apartment, in case she needed anything or if Beverly would want them back while he was gone. Finally, they set up a free messaging app on Paige's phone so they'd be able to stay in touch easily while he was gone.

Before she knew it, she was pulling up to the international departures terminal of Detroit Metro Airport with her heart hammering in her chest, not because she was scared to drive this time, but because she couldn't shake the feeling that she was losing something irreplaceable.

Normally, cars were only supposed to drop off and leave immediately, but at that hour of the evening, it wasn't very busy. Paige put the car in park and hopped out. She couldn't let James go without a proper hug and kiss.

She came around to his door and he got out slowly, patting his pockets. "I've got my passport, right?"

He pulled it out, answering his own question before putting it right back again.

He slung his carryon bag over his shoulder and looked sadly at Paige. They gazed into each other's eyes without saying anything for a moment. Stress and regret were etched all over James's face.

"Paige, I'm so sorry…"

"I know." The moment crashed down on Paige all of a sudden. She was saying goodbye to James. She'd known she would have to eventually, but there was still a silly part of her that had held out hope this would never really happen. Now, everything James had been trying to escape was back stronger than ever. How could she ever expect to compete with a sick uncle? What if the worst happened to David? Wouldn't James step up to fill the position his uncle had left in the business? She'd only known him a short time, but she already knew how important family was to him. Even if he did make it back for the exhibit, he would have to leave again. Permanently.

She crushed James into a hug, fighting hard not to cry. His uncle was in trouble. She couldn't make this about her.

"Have a good flight," she murmured into his neck.

She pulled away, but James didn't let her go. Face to face, he kissed her, slow and sad. Their lips still fit together perfectly, but it wasn't a magical kiss to realign the heavens. It felt final.

"I hate to go like this." His voice was low and heavy.

"It's ok." She said the words, but they felt like a lie to her. "I hope your uncle is all right."

The mention of his uncle seemed to ignite him with a sense of purpose. He kissed her forehead and squeezed her shoulders before pulling away.

"I'll send you a message as soon as I land. I'll be back, Paige Marie. I promise you."

She nodded and turned back to her car as he headed into the terminal.

As she pulled away, it felt like she'd forgotten her heart there on the curb. She didn't have to be strong for James anymore, and she cracked. Tears poured down her face as she maneuvered her way into traffic.

I'll be back, Paige Marie. I promise you. The words echoed around her mind and as much as she wanted to believe them, she just didn't know if she could.

PAIGE HARDLY SLEPT ALL NIGHT. She tossed and turned, her mind going over everything again and again. When she got up for the day, she couldn't eat more than half a slice of toast and a couple sips of orange juice. As she sat at her table, picking at breakfast, her gaze lit on a letter that had been slid beneath her front door.

She got up to retrieve it, vaguely hoping that somehow it was from James.

It was not.

In fact, it was from the apartment complex. It was a reminder that they wanted her to state her intentions by Friday, whether she was going to stay on with the increased rent or if she would not be renewing her lease.

How had she managed to ignore that part of the original letter?

For lack of anything more uplifting to do, she put on a decent outfit and walked over to the leasing office to see if she could straighten things out.

The woman in the leasing office smiled when Paige opened the door.

"Good morning!" She sounded genuinely happy. At least someone was. "What can I do for you?"

Paige pulled out her letter. "Well, I wanted to talk about this. The thing is, I'm not going to know by Friday if I can renew my lease or not. I'm hoping to get a promotion at work. If I get it, I'll be able to afford the rent increase, but if I don't, I won't be able to stay here. But I'm not going to know by this Friday."

All this time the receptionist had been nodding sympathetically, but now she frowned. "Oh, I'm so sorry. We really need to get a commitment as soon as possible."

"But I've been a tenant here for years. Surely I could get a couple more weeks."

"I get it, I really do. But it sounds like if it's going to be that close to call, you might be more comfortable somewhere in your price range, right?"

"This is in my price range!" Paige could feel her color rising. "It has been for the past few years, but now you're raising the rent, by a lot I might add, and I recently broke up with my almost fiancé, and I need that promotion. I'm probably going to get it, but I don't know for sure. I've never even been late with my rent. Can't you work with me a little bit here?" She probably shouldn't have included that much detail, but Paige was feeling fragile and the tears were threatening to flow any second. Coming off as emotionally unstable probably wasn't the best way to negotiate with the leasing office, but she couldn't help herself. Everything was coming down around her.

The lady made an over the top sad face, big pouty lips, round pathetic eyes. "I absolutely understand. Sounds like you're going through a rough time, but I'm afraid we need to know your intentions so we can fill the space as quickly as possible if you don't stay. Maybe we can allow for an extra week, but that's about all."

Paige sighed, exasperated. An extra week didn't help anything. It wasn't like she could march into Christie's office and demand to be promoted by the end of the week.

"An extra week. Thanks so much." Paige's voice cracked so she turned and walked out of the office hoping to retain some amount of dignity.

She pinched the bridge of her nose as she walked across the asphalt parking lot. *Don't cry. Don't cry. Don't cry.*

When she got back to her apartment, she tossed the notice on her table and picked up her phone.

There was a message from James from around 7am, when she was showering.

**Made it safely. Exhausted.
Heading to see David.**

James

She wanted to call him immediately, but he was probably with David that very moment. She didn't want to bother him. She just sent a quick text so he'd know she was thinking of him.

That reminded her, she needed to call the residency lady. No one answered, so Paige left a message. Telling Beverly that James was gone twisted the knife in her heart a little deeper. How could he be so far away when she'd just kissed him hours earlier? Why had she been so stupid? This was exactly why she'd said they were better off as friends. Better to have loved and lost…what a crock of shit! It was definitely better to not know what you were missing.

By the time Paige walked into work, she felt like a zombie, only mechanically going through the actions of her life.

"Hey Paige," Christie called when Paige set her things at her desk.

"Hmm?" Paige answered, in a lackluster haze of sadness and sleep deprivation.

"When you get your stuff put away, could you come see me for a minute?"

"Sure." Paige tried to leave her personal problems behind. This could be an important conversation. Hopefully good news. She could really use a shot of good news.

Paige walked into Christie's office.

"Go ahead and close the door," Christie said.

Paige felt like her heart was beginning to beat again, if just a little.

She took a seat and tried to stay calm.

Christie smiled in an official manner.

"Paige, I just wanted to let you know we're ready to interview for Yolanda's position. Let's get something set up."

"How many are you doing?" Paige asked.

"Just one besides you, and it's an out-of-towner. We didn't get any other in-house applicants."

Paige nodded to herself, barely processing the information. She was in the top two. She should have been ecstatic, but that wasn't an emotion she could access at the moment.

Christie got John on the phone and they decided to do Paige's interview that afternoon. It was a little unconventional, but Paige assured them she didn't need to prep anything. It was her job. She knew everything she needed to know about it.

She walked back to her desk for the couple minutes she had left before going out to reference. Her phone vibrated in her pocket and she pulled it out to see a message from James.

Can I call now?

James

Paige's spirits rose for just a moment before she realized she wouldn't have time to talk to him.

So sorry. I'm about to go on desk.

Paige

Right. Sorry. Forgot about the
time difference.

James

How's David?

Paige

She bit her lip as she sent the message. She had to ask, but she was afraid of the answer.

He's weak, but stable. It was a
heart attack.

James

I'm so sorry. How are you
holding up?

Paige

Paige could see that James started and stopped typing a few times before he finally answered.

Gotta go. Sorry. Talk soon. xx

James

Ok. Talk soon.
xo

Paige

Paige headed up to reference cursing the unfairness of time zones and countries across oceans. Maybe the interview would perk her up, but it was difficult to see how when her heart was currently walking around Glasgow without her.

Twenty-Three

WEDNESDAY MORNING, Paige found herself at Kayla and Eric's for brunch. Kayla was sprawled out on the couch looking large and miserable.

"This kid is killing me," Kayla moaned. "I'm awake half the night, exhausted, but can't get any sleep. I think they're lying vertically, head in my bladder and feet in my chest. I never knew antacids would be more of a treat than chocolate, but here we are."

"You're almost there." Paige tried to be soothing. She was sympathetic, even though she didn't have any firsthand experience with the hardships of pregnancy. She thought Kayla looked adorable. Her skin had been glowing since she first got pregnant. Now, she had a big belly full of baby and a pronounced waddle in her walk, but her hair looked amazing. Kayla didn't see it herself, of course. Although, Paige had to admit if you were at the point where a bottle of antacids seemed like a treat, it'd be hard to feel your best.

"Seven more days, max," Kayla said. "If little one doesn't come out on their own by then, it's induction time."

"Seven days! That's so exciting!"

"Yeah, it'll be nice to be the only person in my body, but, you know what? I will kind of miss having them here." She stretched her hands over her bulging belly. "It's like a fun secret just Baby and I can share. I know when they're being active and when they're sleeping. If I choose to share, other people can know, but it's nice not to tell sometimes."

Paige was struck with misty eyes. The intimacy Kayla was already sharing with her unborn baby was like a kick in the uterus. While she was nothing but happy for her friend, it was also a reminder of how far she was from her own dreams of getting married and starting a family.

"Ha!" Kayla continued. "That little stinker. I'll tell you. They're trying to wiggle around in what space they've got left. Want to feel?"

"Of course!" Paige sprang up and knelt next to her friend.

"Right here," Kayla said, taking Paige's hand and pressing it into the side of her stomach. Paige's hand was filled with a mass that was slowly pushing against her. She could see the bulge shifting across Kayla's abdomen. It was a little like watching a scene from a sci-fi movie except she knew a beautiful little version of Kayla and Eric was inside, not a hideous alien monster.

Paige kept her hand on the baby bulge until it got comfy again, or gave up, and sort of sunk back into Kayla's stomach area.

"Wow," Paige breathed. "I know you're uncomfortable, but that is really amazing."

"It is. I know that during the day. Not so easy to keep sight of at 1:00am. And then 2:30. And then 3:00."

Paige moved back to her own seat.

"Anyway," Kayla said. "Entertain me. I want the latest on your exciting love life."

Paige had known she'd have to tell her friend what had happened with James, but she just hadn't wanted to relive it.

"Oh no!" Kayla sat up so she could look at Paige properly. "Why do you look like that? I thought the trip was amazing."

"It was," Paige agreed. "But then something else happened."

She told Kayla everything. From the pressure James felt to take over his uncle's business to dropping him off at the airport, and she managed it without crying. Barely.

Kayla put her hands over her mouth, absolutely shocked by the whole thing.

"So he's not here anymore? You drove him to the airport and you didn't call me immediately? Paige! You know I'm here for you!"

"I know, but you've got the baby coming. You can't sleep as it is, I don't want to dump my drama on you."

"That's what best friends are for. Oh honey, come give me a hug. You need it!"

Paige moved into Kayla's open arms and blinked back a couple stray tears that threatened to turn into more.

"Has he called yet?"

Paige shook her head against Kayla's shoulder. "We've texted a little, but with the time difference, my work schedule, and him dealing with his uncle, we just can't connect for a call."

Kayla clasped Paige a little tighter.

"That sounds absolutely awful, but there's got to be a time that'll overlap for you sooner or later."

Paige sniffled, feeling wracked with hopelessness. "It was always going to happen like this anyway. He was bound to go back home and I'd just be left again. I knew a long distance relationship like this wouldn't be able to work. I should never have let him kiss me."

Paige couldn't hold back any longer and she succumbed to the tears that threatened to drown her. Kayla stroked her hair soothingly, until Paige realized Kayla had gone totally rigid.

Instantly, her tears dried up and she pulled away to look at her friend.

Kayla's jaw was clenched and her eyes were closed.

"Kayla, are you ok?"

Kayla exhaled slowly and blinked a few times. "Whew! That was something." She rubbed her belly.

"Was that a contraction?" Paige asked.

"Nah. Stuff like this has been happening on and off. At this point, there are all sorts of twinges and uncomfortable sensations. Hard to know what might be something and what's just another passing thing."

"Are you sure? That looked sort of intense."

Kayla waved it off.

"You know what would make us both feel better?"

Paige looked at Kayla, still concerned about what had just happened.

"Ice cream," Kayla continued without hesitation. She started the process of heaving herself up off the couch.

"Hey." Paige put her hand out. "You stay here. I can get ice cream if that's what you want."

"Of course." Kayla nodded. "You're feeling bad, I'm wildly uncomfortable. Ice cream helps."

Paige was wary, but trusted that Kayla knew what she was doing. Paige left Kayla on the couch and went to get them both a bowl of ice cream. When she came back, Kayla's eyes were closed and her hands were spread over her belly.

"Are you ok?"

Kayla's eyes popped open and she reached for her bowl. "I'm fine. Just tired. I didn't sleep much last night."

Paige eased down next to Kayla and handed over a bowl.

"Sorry about that," Kayla said taking a spoonful of ice cream. "We're supposed to be talking about you, not getting involved in baby drama."

Paige sighed. "I don't know that there's anything more to say. His family needs him. He's a good man, he's going to help them. That's why he's so wonderful."

"Surely other couples have found a way to make it work." Kayla thoughtfully licked her spoon.

"And other couples have called it quits for less."

"You don't have to be so defeatist—ooh!" Kayla dropped her bowl on the couch next to her and clutched her stomach.

"Another one?" Paige wished Eric was there. He'd faithfully attended the birthing classes with Kayla. He knew what to do more than Paige did.

"Kayla, this has to be contractions. Are there breathing exercises you're supposed to be doing? Should I be rubbing your shoulders or something? What can I do?"

Kayla didn't answer. Her face contorted as she rode the throes of the contraction.

Feeling utterly useless, Paige moved Kayla's bowl off the couch and texted Eric.

Paige

Paige stared at her phone, anxiously awaiting those three little dots. They didn't come.

When the contraction passed, Kayla leaned heavily back on the couch looking totally wiped out.

"These things are no joke. Maybe I won't have to wait seven days after all."

"I texted Eric but he didn't respond."

"He's got a presentation today. That's probably why he isn't answering. It's ok though. This can last a long time. We might as well get comfy and watch Netflix or something."

Paige grabbed the remote off the coffee table and handed it to Kayla. "Whatever you want."

Kayla started flipping through reality shows and romcoms, making sarcastic quips about any of the previews she stopped to watch.

"I don't know how you're so calm right now." Paige stared at her friend, totally in awe.

Kayla turned to look at Paige. "Can I tell you a secret?"

"Of course!"

"I'm kind of freaking out."

Paige took Kayla's hand and squeezed. "Listen to me. Whether this is a false alarm or the beginning of the real deal, you're going to do great. You're going to meet this awesome little person soon. Maybe today, maybe not for another week, but whenever it is, you'll do what you need to do."

Kayla blinked away a couple tears. "I think this is it. I didn't sleep well last night because I didn't feel very good. Now this."

"Maybe you should call your doctor? She'll know what to do."

"Good idea. Could you grab my phone? It's next to my bed."

Paige did as she was asked, eager to do anything that would help her friend.

Kayla took the phone. "I better call Eric too, just so he knows what's going on."

She heard Kayla leave a voicemail for Eric and then call her OB/GYN. While she was talking to her, she got hit with another contraction. Paige wished she could do something for Kayla to help her through but she couldn't think of anything.

When the contraction subsided, Kayla finished her conversation and hung up the phone. She leaned back on the couch and blew out a long breath.

"What did she say?" Paige asked.

"There's a small pink duffel bag on the floor of my closet. It's all packed and ready to go. Would you mind taking me to the hospital? She thinks Baby's on the way."

PAIGE HAD NEVER BEEN MORE scared in her life. After sitting through quite a few contractions with Kayla, the nurse looked at the readout on the belt monitor she'd put on Kayla and frowned.

"I'll get the doctor," she'd said ominously and hurried from the room.

Paige held Kayla's hand and smoothed the damp hair back from her face. "You're doing really well. You got this, Mama."

The doctor came in quickly and looked over the readout and checked Kayla.

"Well," the doctor said. "I don't like that. The baby is showing signs of distress. We have an open OR. I'd like to get you prepped for a c-section and get this baby delivered as soon as possible."

Kayla looked at the doctor with wild eyes. "Is the baby ok? My husband's not here yet."

"I don't want to risk it." The doctor looked at Paige. "The nurse will get you a gown for the OR."

Now it was Paige's turn to have wild eyes. "The OR? I don't know how to—" But the doctor was already on her way out the door.

Kayla was lost to another contraction and Paige held her hand and tried to talk her through it with encouraging words. She'd never seen

Kayla turned so intensely inward in her life, but she tried her best to make sure Kayla knew she was with her every step of the way.

A team of medical staff burst into the room to prep Kayla for surgery. A nurse took Paige aside and handed her a cap, gown, and booties.

"You're going to be accompanying her in the OR? You'll have to put your hair up under the cap and wear these to preserve the sterile environment of the room."

"Her husband is on the way. Shouldn't he be the one to go with her? I have no idea what to do."

The nurse smiled wryly. "No one ever knows what to do. She's going back now, so it looks like you're it. Stay behind the curtain with her. You'll be fine."

Paige gaped at her, but started to get her gown on anyway. It looked like things were about to get real.

Once they'd arrived at the hospital, Eric had called Kayla back. He'd given a presentation in Detroit and, of course, there'd been a huge accident on the expressway and traffic was absolutely crawling. It was a forty-five minute drive in good conditions. He would be there as soon as he could.

Paige wanted to call Eric to see if he was anywhere close yet. She wanted to call her mom to get some advice about helping someone through childbirth, but there wasn't time for either. After she got everything put on, the nurse whisked her off to the OR and sent her in.

The room looked like a scene out of a sci-fi movie. Paige had never had an operation so she'd never been in an operating room before. It all looked bright and metallic and smelled like chemicals and sterility. Kayla's arms, chest, and head were the only things visible. She was laying on the table, with her arms out to the sides. A curtain rose from just below her chest to block the view. There was a little stool up by Kayla's head, which the nurse gestured for Paige to take.

Extremely careful not to look beyond the curtain, Paige sat down.

Kayla's eyes were closed. Paige wasn't sure if she was awake or not. Her voice was thin when she asked, "How are you doing?"

Kayla's eyes snapped open.

"Thank God, you're here. I'm so scared."

Paige moved the stool around a little so it would be easier for her and Kayla to look at each other. Paige could hear monitors beeping, the surgeon talking to her assistants, and the hum of the high powered lights in the room. She hoped Kayla wasn't listening to what the doctor was saying. She couldn't imagine lying awake hearing a doctor talk about cutting her open.

"It's ok." Paige tried to be convincing. "You're doing great and Eric's on the way. You're about to meet your baby. The moment's finally here!"

Kayla smiled faintly. "Yeah. The baby's coming. I didn't think it would be like this."

Paige squeezed Kayla's shoulder. "You're doing really great, Kayla. I'm so proud of you."

Kayla couldn't help the tears that fell across her temple and trailed right into her ear.

"Thank you so much for coming here with me." Kayla sniffled. "I couldn't do this alone."

Paige dabbed at the tear trail with the sleeve of her gown.

"Of course. I'd never leave you alone." She was getting teary too. The emotion of the moment, paired with seeing her best friend so helpless and afraid on the operating table, threatened to overwhelm her.

"Kayla? How are you doing?" The voice of the doctor came from over the curtain.

"I'm ok."

"That's good. You're about to feel some pressure while we get the baby out."

Kayla's mouth made the movements for "Ok," but no sound really came out.

The doctor muttered some things in an authoritative tone and the next thing they knew, the room was pierced with the loud crying of a newborn.

"Kayla, that's your baby crying!" Paige and Kayla looked at each other and their expressions said everything words could not.

There was a flurry of activity on the other side of the curtain.

Someone called out, "Seven pounds, fourteen ounces!"

Other numbers and stats were shared and then, all at once, a nurse was thrusting a tiny, wrapped bundle into Paige's arms. "Congratulations. It's a girl."

The instant Paige laid eyes on the scrunched, red face with a damp shock of dark hair, she knew what love at first sight really meant. This tiny creature had just come from her best friend's body minutes ago and was the most beautiful thing Paige had ever seen.

She turned to Kayla and pressed the baby's tiny head up close to Kayla's cheek.

"Kayla." Tears shone in Paige's eyes. "This is your daughter."

"My daughter." Kayla said the words in wonder. She kissed the baby for the first time and Paige's heart burst with joy.

"Hi baby." Tears were streaming down Kayla's face now. "I'm your mommy. This is your aunt Paige. Your daddy will be here soon and we all love you very much."

Paige dropped her purse and keys on the table and collapsed onto the couch in her own apartment. It had been a very long day. Although Paige had been transfixed by the beautiful baby, she'd quietly excused herself shortly after Eric arrived. She knew it was a special time for Eric and Kayla to admire their daughter and learn how to be a family of three.

She'd been feeling low when she'd gone to visit Kayla, and the birth of the baby was an incredible high, but as she looked around her lonely apartment, she felt worse than ever. Kayla and Eric's home was about to be filled with the joy and activity of a brand new human life. Her apartment was filled with books. Much as she loved them, a book would never welcome her home with a hug and kiss, or talk her through driving across the Mackinac Bridge.

She picked up her phone to look for messages she may have missed while she was at the hospital with Kayla.

She decided to send James a message about what had just happened.

She waited a few minutes to see if he was around to chat.

Nothing.

Then she thought to check the time. That explained it. She'd spent all day with Kayla from brunch to baby and it was after 10pm in Scotland. If he'd also been at the hospital all day, he was probably exhausted and might already be asleep.

Still, she wanted to talk to somebody.

She dialed her parents' number knowing they'd be so excited to hear about Kayla's baby. But it just went to voicemail. Even they were probably out with their friends while their daughter sat home, completely alone.

Hadn't she known this would happen? She knew she shouldn't have fallen for James. This was squarely her fault. She'd gone ahead and gotten herself attached to another unavailable man. Not unavailable because he couldn't commit, but because he didn't live in the same country. This is the only way the situation could have played out —Paige alone in her apartment feeling like her heart had been ripped out of her chest and thrown away. The remaining hole gaped and pulsed, aching to be put back together.

All she wanted to do was curl up on the couch with James and explain everything she'd just been through with Kayla. To feel his arm around her and his fingers in her hair.

She was dying to hear his voice. To know how he was doing. Was his uncle ok?

Out of all the people in the greater metropolitan Detroit area, why was a visiting Scotsman the one who tugged at her heart like this?

She looked around her apartment, which she very likely wouldn't be staying in for much longer, and it was all too much. She curled up on the seat cushions and gave in to the wracking wave of sobs that overtook her.

Twenty-Five

THE DAY WENT by in a blur. Patrons came and went. Questions were asked and answered, but Paige just kept watching the minutes pass on the clock and wondering when she could get back to her apartment for a sad date with her pajamas and a pint of ice cream.

She mindlessly went through the steps to help a lady upload her resume to a job site. The woman was extremely appreciative. She grabbed Paige's wrist and squeezed. "Thank you so much! You don't know how much I need this job."

It always made Paige feel good when someone truly appreciated her help, but it didn't provide much of a lift this time. She kept thinking she saw James out of the corner of her eye, but when she looked, it was a young father bringing his son for story time, or a man carrying a stack of books for his wife. She knew he couldn't possibly be there, but she still felt disappointed all over again when she saw it wasn't him.

She strolled back to her desk feeling like an enormous failure. Even if she did get the promotion, what did that solve? She'd get to stay in her apartment and continue to be alone. That wasn't what she wanted. She wanted to visit James at the studio and watch him breathe life into chunks of wood. She wanted to take more trips together and eat sweet bakery treats. She definitely wanted to kiss him again. Many times. As much as he would let her.

Her melancholy pity party was interrupted by the voice of the circulation supervisor behind her.

"There's cake in the lounge for Yolanda's retirement. Come on."

Ah. The retirement party. Paige had definitely not been thinking about that, even though she'd signed the card that had made the rounds amongst the staff.

"Thanks for reminding me. I wouldn't want to miss that." Paige got up and walked to the lounge. Everyone was gathered around, including Christie and Yolanda, who were standing at the head of the table in front of the cake.

"I'm not going to get too mushy," Christie started, causing a murmur of chuckles in the room. "But it's been an absolute delight working with you, Yolanda. You're so attentive, and kind, and you know absolutely everything there is to know about genealogy. We may find someone to fill your job title but we'll never find someone to take your place."

Everyone clapped and Yolanda got misty eyed. "Oh, you guys are like family to me. I'm going to miss seeing your faces every day but I'm excited to move on to my next role as full-time grandma!"

That elicited a lot of cheers. Paige smiled. She was happy for Yolanda. It sounded so nice to be able to spend time with family, and especially a new baby. She still hoped she'd be able to move into Yolanda's position, but it felt a million miles away from her grasp.

"Now let's dig into this cake!" Yolanda picked up the cake cutter with a big smile.

Paige waited in the line to get her piece of cake and vaguely listened to the ladies chatting with Yolanda.

"How's your daughter-in-law feeling?" LeeAnn asked. "Other than exhausted."

Yolanda chuckled. "They're really looking forward to me coming to stay with them. In the meantime, I told them it's perfectly fine to subsist on ice cream. The calcium is great for mama."

The ladies who'd already had children of their own laughed, but suddenly Paige was struck with an idea.

She got her piece of cake and hurried over to Christie.

"I'd like to print out some flyers for the book discussion and drop them off at a few places in the city. I'm not on desk this afternoon. Would that be alright with you?"

"Sure. Sounds like a good idea to me."

Paige finished her cake, gave Yolanda a big hug and wished her well, and went back to her desk to make up some flyers. Maybe driving around town with discussion promos would keep her busy enough to stop brooding about James. Probably not, but at least it would keep her out of the building where they met.

After spending her afternoon dropping off flyers, she came home to her empty apartment for a lonely dinner. Short lived as it had been, James had really become a part of her daily routine. They'd had so many meals together, it felt extra sad to be back to Lean Cuisine for one. She couldn't even pop by Kayla's house because she was still at the hospital.

Paige was clearing away the trash from her pathetic dinner when her phone pinged with a new message. She wiped her fingers and pulled the phone out as fast as she could.

A chubby cheeked baby in a white, pink, and blue cap filled her screen.

Hi Auntie Paige. I have a name now! Amanda Paige DuPont. Me and mommy are doing great. Come up and see me as soon as you can.

Eric

Paige covered her mouth and tears pricked at her eyes. Amanda Paige! She had no idea they would include her name and she couldn't stop staring at that angelic little face.

One tear got big enough to roll down Paige's cheek. She grabbed a napkin and dabbed it away.

> **I just finished dinner. Is it ok if I come up now?**
>
> Paige

> **Absolutely.**
>
> Eric

> **I'm on my way.**
>
> Paige

Paige gathered her purse and hurried out the door. As she reached her car, she realized she couldn't just show up empty handed. From the moment she'd found out Kayla was pregnant, she'd imagined showing up in the maternity ward to meet the baby with balloons and gifts. Since she'd met the baby a lot sooner than she ever expected, she'd missed out on greeting her for the first time with gifts, but she could remedy that.

She made a quick Target run on the way and picked out a card, a cute pink sleeper, a handful of board books, a box of chocolates for

Kayla, and a selection of coffee for Eric. She figured he'd need to be caffeine powered for the foreseeable future.

She walked into the hospital and stopped at the reception desk to get a visitor badge.

New grandparents were walking in with giant pink or blue balloons, bouquets, and big smiles. She could identify the new fathers coming down the hall because their eyes looked exhausted, surprised, and terrified.

She got to the door of Kayla's room and peeked in.

"Knock knock!" Paige said.

"Come in!" Eric greeted her, standing up to relieve her of the gifts.

Kayla was lying in her hospital bed. Her face was pale, there were shadows under her eyes, and her hair looked like it was clinging to her head for dear life, but Paige thought she'd never looked more beautiful. Kayla held Amanda in her arms, just gazing at the little bundle.

It was a little weird to see her best friend as a mother. Visions of shenanigans in high school, college parties, road trips, and late nights laughing together popped into her mind. None of them matched up with the reality of the tired, but proud, woman cradling her newborn. It was new territory for all of them.

"I gotta see her sweet little face!" Paige's spirits improved vastly with a newborn in the room.

Eric set down the gifts and came to join Paige at Kayla's bedside.

"Hey there, Amanda," Kayla said in a soft voice. "Auntie Paige is here to see you."

Paige gazed down at the little baby and her heart swelled. Babies truly were a miracle and Paige's heart melted instantly as she beheld Amanda's perfect, sleeping face.

Paige slipped her arm around Kayla's shoulders and gave her a kiss on the cheek.

"She's so beautiful, Mama. How are you feeling?"

"Exhausted. Sore. But I can't stop looking at her. She's the prettiest thing I've ever seen."

Kayla leaned her head toward Paige's shoulder, but didn't take her eyes off the baby.

"She is," Paige agreed. "She absolutely is. Takes after her mommy."

Kayla smiled. "Do you want to hold her?"

"Of course! Are you willing to give her up for a bit?"

"Only for you." Kayla carefully transferred the precious bundle from her arms to Paige's. She breathed in the one-of-a-kind newborn scent. So milky sweet and distinctive.

"Hello, Amanda Paige," Paige cooed, marveling at the tiny button of a nose, little pink bow mouth, and impossibly small eyelashes and eyebrows. "Your parents gave you my name so we'll always have that in common."

"Of course." Kayla carefully readjusted herself on the bed. "You really stepped up when I needed you. If you hadn't been at the house, who knows how things would have happened."

"Besides—" Eric stepped over and put his arm around Paige's shoulders. "Amanda Paige sounds really good together."

Amanda slept on, completely calm and sweet in Paige's arms. It was hard to say if she looked much like one or the other of her parents, but it didn't matter. It would be amazing to watch her grow and change and turn into her own little person.

Kayla smiled, although her eyes were droopy with exhaustion.

"Any idea when you get to go home?" Paige asked.

"Tomorrow," Kayla said. "I don't mind having one more night of round the clock help."

Paige felt Amanda twitch in her sleep and looked down to see Amanda's tiny lips making a suckling motion.

"Aww!" Paige beamed at the baby, totally enraptured by her tiny, honorary, niece. "She's sucking in her sleep! That is so adorable."

"Don't wake up hungry yet," Kayla said. "Mommy wants a rest first."

Paige sensed that the visit should be wrapping up to let Kayla recover. She hadn't planned to stay long anyway.

"I'll let you guys rest. Let me know if you need anything. Day or night, seriously."

"We will. Thank you." Eric stood up and wrapped Paige in a hug before taking Amanda from her.

"Congratulations," Paige said again, giving Kayla a hug too. "I'm so happy for you guys."

When Paige got back to her apartment, she changed into her pajamas and got to that ice cream she'd been thinking about earlier. She imagined Kayla and Eric bent over their newborn, secure in their new family unit. Paige couldn't admit it to anyone, but holding that beautiful baby had really made her ache for a family of her own. She felt physically empty. She wasn't filled with hope. She didn't have the possibility of a future like Kayla's. Now, all she had was the certainty that men like James existed, but she couldn't hold on to him either.

An image of James popped into her mind, cradling a baby in his strong arms. She bet he would make a wonderful father one day.

Then another image came to her. The photo of James's mother and uncle in Glasgow. They were so candid in that photo, but what were they like now? What if David was fighting for his life? Worse, what if he'd already lost the fight?

She grabbed her phone and looked for messages. She had missed one from James. It had come when she was preoccupied visiting the baby.

Do you have time to talk?

James

It was about an hour old but maybe there was still hope.

Just home for the night now. I'm free.

Paige

This time, the response was almost immediate.

I'm calling.

James

Twenty-Six

THE PHONE barely got through its first ring before she answered.

She heard some shuffling around before she finally heard James's voice. "Paige?" He sounded so weary she feared what he might say.

"Hi." She said the word gently. "I've been thinking of you and your uncle. Didn't want to bother you though. I know you must have so much going on."

"I'm so sorry I havnae been able to call. It's been absolute chaos since the plane touched down."

"Don't worry about that. I knew you'd be busy." She steeled herself for the question she dreaded to ask. "How's your uncle doing?"

James let out a long breath before he answered. "He feels like he's been hit by a lorrie, but he's stable. It was a heart attack and he's had surgery. Likely a few days more for him to stay before he's released home."

"So he's going to be ok?"

James was silent for a moment and Paige's heart dropped as she anticipated what he'd say next.

"He's expected to recover, aye, but he's been advised to take it easy. Ma and Cait take that to mean immediate retirement."

"Mmm." Paige didn't need him to say more than that. She knew what was coming.

"That makes sense." She tried to stay strong and diplomatic. It's not like she expected him to come back after this anyway. He was only confirming what she'd already known.

"Nothing's set in stone, but there's a lot o' work to handle right now. Fiona is helping me settle what to do with the business for now and the others are attending to David."

"Yeah, of course. That's good you have Fiona's help."

"Paige, I'm so sorry, but I'm no' going to make the next book discussion."

Paige nearly laughed, she was so surprised he'd even mentioned such a thing.

"Don't even worry about that a little bit. It's my job. I can handle it."

"I feel terrible though. You were counting on me to be there and I hate to be letting you down."

Her arms ached to hold him in that moment. All the pressure of his family was crashing down on him and he felt bad about her book discussion.

"It's going to be fine. You need to focus on your family. I totally understand and so will our regulars. You know they'll be wishing the best for you all."

"Aye. They're good people." James sighed and she heard a scratch against the phone like he was running a hand over his face. "I miss you so much, Paige Marie."

His words caught her off guard. To protect herself, she'd let herself think he was so busy worrying about his uncle that he didn't have any energy left to think of her. His voice was so genuine and unguarded, she knew he meant it completely. They were both suffering without the other, but what could be done?

"I miss you too. Every minute."

James cleared his throat. Paige held her breath to keep herself from crying.

"Och, this is too gloomy. It's wonderful to speak with you. Tell me about the baby. That's braw news."

It was a good diversion. Paige finally got to tell him the story of Amanda's birth and James was duly impressed.

"Sounds intense, but I'm no' surprised you were a great help," James exclaimed, sounding a little more like his old self.

"I did the best I could. Anyway, Eric was there waiting once the baby was born. They named her Amanda Paige. She's the most beautiful thing I've ever seen."

"Tell them congratulations for me. Hopefully, I'll be able to meet her soon."

"Really?" The word jumped out of Paige's mouth before she could think to conceal her enthusiasm.

"Aye. I've been talking with Fiona. As I say, nothing's set, but she's at least willing to step in on the boat so I can make the exhibit. I dinnae ken exactly when I'll get back, but I'll no' miss the exhibit."

Even though she knew it was just a temporary fix, the thought of seeing James again made her heart soar.

"That's wonderful! Way to go, Fiona!"

James laughed. "Shall I tell her you said that?"

"Why not? Who wouldn't want a random librarian in a foreign country cheering them on?"

"You're no' random. She knows all about you."

"She does?" Damn that growing glimmer of impossible hope taking root in Paige's heart.

"O' course. She's very impressed you drove over the bridge. She doesn't care for them either."

"Oh." Paige didn't know what else to say. Not only was he still thinking about her book discussion, he was telling his family about her. It warmed her up inside.

Paige heard a voice in the background calling for James.

"Just a minute. I'm on the phone," he called back before coming back to Paige. "I'm sorry. I have to go. Ma just got back from Cait's. It's been so good to hear your voice again. I'll be back as soon as I can. I'll be in touch."

"Great talking with you too. I'm glad David's going to be ok."

"Bye my dear."

"Bye."

Paige stared at the phone in her hand unsure how to feel. There was no denying it was so good to talk to James again, but he was at a crossroads. His uncle's business was being put into his hands whether he liked it or not. But what did it mean that he was talking to Fiona about her? What exactly had he said? It was like they were pretending they could still have a future, yet their lives were diverging more and more.

She crossed her hands over her heart as if she could hold him there, make him a part of her forever. He hadn't been in her life for long but he'd already become a permanent part of her. Like Kayla had observed, she did feel lit up around him. Like herself, but better.

While her brain was short-circuiting from trying to analyze the reality of her relationship with James, her eyes lit on the Scotland book he'd given her for her birthday. She fingered the thistle necklace around her neck. She scrolled through her photo roll, pausing at every picture she had of James. His smile was infectious even in digital form.

He had a knack for inspiring impulsive ideas in her. Even though he wasn't there, Paige found herself developing another outrageous idea. But as the idea took shape, she found that she didn't want to talk herself out of it. It hit her with as much force as when she'd first offered to share her library card, and again when she invited him to Kayla and Eric's. Those things had turned out well. Might as well shoot for three out of three uncharacteristic ideas. Besides, she'd have tomorrow for regrets. Today, she just wanted to do something to prove that they'd been together once and that he'd meant so much to her.

She spent a little time researching on the internet before she grabbed her purse and ran out the door. It might have come to her quickly, but she was sure.

Twenty-Seven

A FEW DAYS LATER, Paige wished it would rain. Full sun, singing birds, and the din of traffic didn't provide the appropriate backdrop for wallowing. She was on her way back to the leasing office, with her decision in hand. Time was running out for her everywhere she turned, so she figured it was best to at least take matters into her own hands where she could.

The same woman was sitting at the desk when she walked in. The woman looked up and smiled, although Paige could swear it was a little more of a smirk this time.

"Oh hello," said the woman. "How can I help you?"

Paige handed over the envelope. "I decided not to renew my lease."

The woman took the envelope and set it on the desk in front of her. "Oh, I'm sorry to hear, but thanks for letting us know. We can offer a one month extension on your lease if you need—"

"No. I'm good. I'll be out by the last day of my current lease. You don't have to worry about that."

"Ok then. Is there anything else I can do for you today?"

"Nope. That covers it."

Paige walked out of the leasing office with less fear than she'd expected. She had a few weeks to figure out what to do before her lease was up. It would be fine. She was fine. Fine. Fine. Fine.

She absently touched the delicate skin of her collarbone and smiled to herself. Maybe she was going through a rough patch, but she was doing things for herself for a change. That part, at least, felt good.

It was a good way to start the big book discussion day. Now there was no pressure. She could completely bomb the program, which seemed likely since James wasn't going to be there. But hey, that was fine too! She was going to find a new place she could afford anyway. A sad little place that would suit her sad little life. She just hoped it would be close to Kayla and Eric so she could still easily stop by to help with Amanda, since that was likely the only baby she'd have in her life. But that was fine. She probably didn't want to be a mom anyway. It was just societal pressure from an overbearing culture, propagated by people like Norm yammering at her all the time. What was fun about heart burn, contractions, or a c-section? She was really dodging a bullet by staying single. She'd had a farewell to coupledom with James. What a lovely send-off it had been. Now she could comfortably settle into spinsterhood with an apartment full of books and an honorary niece to dote on.

She fastened her birthday necklace from James around her neck and admired it in the mirror before she left. Her patrons had wanted a Scottish themed book discussion and now they were down one Scotsman. That was ok. She'd have to be a secondhand Scot for them. She didn't have the delightful accent, but she'd learned a few things from James. It would have to suffice.

She just needed to stop by the local bakery and pick up the desserts she'd ordered. It was funny that she'd been so excited he was coming back for another discussion but he'd actually ended up in Scotland again. Ha, ha! That was a good one, universe. It really seemed like everything might somehow work out but then the rug got yanked out from under her. Classic.

Paige popped into the bakery and got her shortbread order. She'd ordered enough for thirty-five people. She'd felt optimistic at the time but now she wasn't so sure. Was that underestimating? Was that way too much? Oh well. She'd find out. If it ended up being too much, she'd just put her stretchiest pants on when she got home and have shortbread for dinner. It would be F. I. N. E.

As she got closer to the library, her brain started to settle into work mode. She had done a good push around town, dropping off flyers at a number of businesses she thought would attract the kind of people who'd enjoy the event. She'd been sure to incorporate a big picture of the dessert in addition to the book cover. If bribing people with dessert was what it took to get them in the door, so be it. She'd done everything she could to entice people to the program, and it was up to them now.

Paige walked into the library, doing her best to pretend there wasn't anything riding on this program. She did not want to scream. Absolutely not. Her confidence wavered between knowing it would be a success to certainty no one would come. She knew Kayla and Eric wouldn't show up this time. There was just too much on their plate. If it was just the six regulars she would burst into tears. No, that wasn't right. She would laugh. Yes. She would laugh because it would be so cliché if she lost her apartment, her boyfriend, and her chance at the promotion. It'd be like one of the silliest romcoms she'd ever read. It seemed comfortably unbelievable when she read about it in books, but this was actually happening! Maybe if she didn't get the promotion she should just quit her job and write her life story as a romcom. Of course, all good romcoms have a happy ending, so there would have to be a hero to end up with. Maybe for a twist she'd have it be someone like Norm. Complete with the short shorts. That would be unexpected. Possibly award-winning. The thought nearly made her gag.

Christie was standing at the staff photocopier when Paige walked by. Christie smiled brightly. "Mmm. That smells good. All set?"

Seeing Christie made Paige feel less like an imposter in her own life and more like she had to pull herself together and do the best job she could. Enough with the snark and the self-pity.

"Let's do this," Paige said.

Christie grabbed her copies. "I'll join you in a minute to help set up the room."

Paige dropped her stuff off at her desk and carried the shortbread cookies into the program room.

Christie came in shortly afterward to help her push the tables into the preferred configuration. They took down thirty chairs and placed them around the tables. Paige hoped she wasn't being overly optimistic with the number. There had only been ten, counting her, last time. An extra twenty people was quite a jump, but she needed it. Frankly, she felt she deserved it, but that wouldn't make anything happen.

With the chairs set up, Paige got water heating for tea and Christie set out the shortbread on a nice platter. Just in case anybody didn't like tea, she also set out pitchers of ice water and lemonade.

To go with the Scottish theme, Paige had printed out some photos to spruce up the room. She paused as she tacked up the picture of Glasgow Cathedral. According to her research, it was built in 1197. She thought back to the day at Fort Mackinac when she and James had talked about the age of their countries. This had to be the building James had told her about. How she wished she could see it with her own eyes, hand in hand with James.

She suppressed the melancholy spreading through her as she thought of their trip. It felt like it had happened months ago. Instead, she scrolled through her phone and the Scottish playlist she'd put together for background music. She put out her portable speaker and started it up. Everything looked cozy and enticing. Paige could only hope she'd get a good crowd to come and enjoy it.

Christie took a picture of the room, including a close up of the shortbread. "I'll put this on our social media pages in case we can get any last minute stragglers looking for something to do today."

"Thanks," Paige called after Christie's retreating figure. It was just her and an empty room. She hoped against all odds it wouldn't stay that way for long.

Before she could forget, she ran in the back and grabbed a package of name tags, a handful of markers and pens, and a stack of program evaluation forms. She hoped for a lot of new faces. Name tags might make it feel friendlier. And if her promotion was riding on the success of the program, some positive evaluations would quantify her cause.

When she got back to the room, she was delighted to see a confused looking pregnant woman milling around the door.

"Hello, are you here for the book discussion?" Paige asked.

"Yes, I guess I'm a little early."

"No, you're right on time. Here, fill out a name tag and help yourself to the refreshments."

Shortly afterwards, two more new faces showed up, a pregnant woman and her friend.

"Is this the dessert discussion?" one of them asked.

"It is!" Paige said. "Come in and make yourselves comfortable."

"Cool," the lady said. "I saw the flyer in my OB/GYN office and thought it sounded like a great idea. I liked that the book was short stories. I don't get a lot of time to read, but I figured I could try this."

"Plus, free dessert," her friend chimed in.

"Yes! That's the idea. Help yourselves," Paige welcomed them, gesturing to the refreshment table. Inside, she was cheering and jumping up and down. Her gamble had paid off! Between Kayla and her ice cream and what Yolanda had said about her daughter-in-law, they'd sparked the idea for Paige...pregnant women and desserts! She had hit the local OB/GYN offices, prenatal fitness, and birthing classes. If even a handful of women were anything like Kayla, they might have some sleepless nights and a craving for sweets. Why not fill those nights with a good book and then get rewarded with free dessert for their troubles?

Three new faces. This was promising. She hoped it would keep up, at least a bit more. If all the regulars showed up again, at least she'd replaced Kayla, Eric, and James. Holding steady at nine plus herself was better than going back down. She didn't know if that would be enough to wow John, but at least she could say she'd tried her best.

The regulars came in and smiled at the new faces. Sandy and Carol even went over to introduce themselves.

More and more people came into the room, many of them pregnant women. Some had brought friends and family along with them, others tentatively walked into the room alone.

She could hardly believe it had worked! Even without James, she'd managed to pull in a bunch of new attendees just by thinking outside of the box. She replaced the pity she'd been feeling with pride. She may be alone and in need of a new apartment, but at least she was good at her job.

Newcomers kept wandering in for a good five minutes after the program was supposed to start. She even had to get down some additional chairs.

Finally, she called everyone to attention and got things underway.

"I do have to apologize. We were supposed to have a very special guest at today's discussion. James was visiting from Scotland but had to go home suddenly to attend to a family emergency."

"Oh, that's a shame," Phil interjected. "I hope everything turns out all right. He was such a nice young man. I was looking forward to his take on the book."

The other regulars nodded in agreement, while all the new members just looked politely blank.

"Me too," Paige admitted. "But we have a full house today so I think we'll still have a lovely discussion. This is the first time we've done a short story collection but I enjoyed it because it was easy to pick up throughout the day whenever I had time. Did anyone—"

Just as Paige was about to pose her first question to the group, she noticed her phone vibrating in her pocket.

She ignored it and carried on.

"Did anyone get a chance to read all of the stories or just a few?"

Some of the newcomers mumbled answers about one or two. It didn't matter. She was just happy they were there.

"Does anyone want to start off telling us which story you liked best?"

Carol was quick to jump on that question as Paige felt her phone buzzing again. That was odd. Two calls back to back immediately made her think of her parents. Or Kayla. What if something was wrong?

While everyone was focused on Carol, she surreptitiously pulled her phone out to peek at who was calling. When she saw James's name on the screen she was confused and worried. He'd mentioned the discussion himself when they'd talked. Surely he knew she was running it at the moment. But maybe something awful had happened to David? She didn't want to ignore him.

She quietly excused herself to the person sitting nearest to her and popped out of the room.

"Hey," she answered in the hallway. "Is everything ok?"

"Aye. Sorry, I didnae think of it earlier. Are you in the discussion? You can put me on speaker. It's no' as good as being there, but I can still participate."

With all he had going on, he was still thinking of her and her program. If he'd been standing there she would have grabbed him tight and refused to ever let go.

"James! You don't have to do that. You have so much going on—"

"Please," he interrupted. "I want to. Honestly, I could use the break too."

Paige smiled quietly. She understood.

When she came back into the room, everyone turned to look at her expectantly. She held up her phone.

"Guess what everyone, change of plans. James may not be able to be here personally, but he's just called in from Glasgow to join us!"

The regulars gave a little cheer and shouted their greetings to James. Paige switched her phone to speaker and turned the volume as high as it would go.

"Hello, everyone," he said. "Sorry to be late, but I just had the idea to call in."

"Ok, let's try this again," Paige said. "I'm pleased to say we're celebrating a Scottish theme today because we *do* have the pleasure of having a real Scotsman in our midst."

"Thanks for asking me, Miss Paige. It's always an honor to spread the love o' my great country. I think the book you've chosen is a fine medley of two very important subjects, Scottish authors and the power of stories."

Paige couldn't have asked for a better segue to get back to talking about the book.

"As a librarian," she started, "the subject of this book is near and dear to my heart. I thought it would be a good read, not only because it's written by an award-winning Scottish author, but because everyone interested in a book discussion program is a book lover. We don't need to be scholarly book critics to have an opinion on the way books and stories make us feel, so even if you haven't been able to read any of the book today, I hope you'll still feel free to share your feelings about books. Would anyone else like to dive in with a favorite story from the book?"

"I'd like to read a bit from my favorite story, if you dinnae mind," James piped up.

"You can read us the whole book! Your accent is just beautiful!" one of the women called out, causing the room to erupt in laughter and murmurs of agreement.

Paige grinned. She knew what he was doing. He knew this program was important to her and he was going to ham it up as much as possible. Give the people what they wanted and they'd repay Paige with glowing program evaluations.

At one point, Paige noticed Christie walk by outside the room and peer in the door. She caught a glimpse of the lively crowd and gave Paige an enthusiastic thumbs up before wandering back to her office.

James even offered to jump on a video call to show everyone what it was like where he was. He'd kept everyone rapt with his stories while Paige had hooked up the equipment so his video would show on the big projector rather than her tiny phone.

The program normally ran for a little under an hour. With a full house and James's irrepressible charm, it went for nearly two. They had an insightful discussion on the stories and the role of books in their lives, but the last hour morphed into a question and answer period with James. The questions ranged from all sorts of topics, from whether or not James owned and wore a kilt, to what his thoughts were on Scotland ever gaining independence. Phil even asked about his artwork and whether his exhibit would be open to the public.

"If anyone's interested, you're all more than welcome to come to the exhibit next week. See Miss Paige for the details, I'll be sending them along to her in a moment. Also, I think we should all thank her for the enjoyable discussion today. She's been working very hard to make this program a success and I think she's definitely done that today."

Everyone gave Paige an enthusiastic round of applause. She led them to do the same for James before letting him go, with the quiet promise of being in touch after work.

"Thank you all for coming," Paige said. "Please fill out a quick evaluation before you leave. I hope you liked the short story theme because our next book is a collection of short stories about vacation mishaps. See you next time."

The group murmured in assent and started to clear out. Most of them did fill out an evaluation and a cursory glance at the ratings showed that the program had dazzled them.

By the time the last patron left Paige could hardly believe it had been such a raging success.

"Is it finally over?" Christie asked as Paige put up the last chair. "Looked like everyone was having a great time."

"That was probably the best program I've ever done."

"That's great." Christie smiled at Paige, looking genuinely happy. "Well, why don't you stop by my office for a few minutes."

Paige fanned through the evaluations in her hand. "I got a good twenty of these back and it looks like all of them are positive. Just a quick glance here, this one says the only thing that could have made it better was more dessert. Next time, I'll be better prepared."

"Twenty evaluations! That's amazing. How many people ended up coming?"

"Thirty-seven. And that's not counting me this time."

"Thirty-seven!" Christie exclaimed. "I knew there were a lot but I couldn't count them all from the door. That's an impressive jump in attendance. What did you do?"

Paige described her epiphany about pregnant women and dessert and her targeted stops around town.

"It looks like you just tapped into an underserved market. Was the group full of pregnant women?"

"There were a lot of pregnant women, but not everyone. Maybe sixty/forty."

"Good for you, Paige. These are the kinds of strong numbers John wants to present to the board."

"Do you think it'll get me the job?"

"I can't say anything for sure without talking to John first, but I can say I'm very proud of you. You really showed initiative and drive. A numbers leap like this solely based on implementing your ideas is a very strong case for you. I'm sure we'll be making our final decision early next week."

"Okay." Paige left the evaluations with Christie and went back to her desk. She'd done the very best she could. All she could do now was wait.

Twenty-Eight

WITHOUT JAMES around and Kayla and Eric settling into family life, Paige found herself solely responsible for how she spent her time. She'd always had someone else to think of, whether it was Dylan or Kayla, but since deciding to find a new place and her little spontaneous act of rebellion that she still hadn't mentioned to anyone, she was feeling a lot more comfortable on her own.

She could tell things were getting a little smoother for James too. He was able to text with her during the day more often and they'd even found time for a phone call since the discussion. The exhibit was looming, but Paige wasn't worrying about that either. She knew he'd be there and that she'd be able to see him and kiss him again soon.

She filled her down time browsing apartment rental websites and heading out for viewings. At her current income, the prospects were pretty dismal. Not to mention that the best choices in her price range were outside of town. It was looking like she'd have to move a good half hour away to get something decent that she could afford.

She hadn't told anybody yet that she would be moving. She didn't want to worry her parents, and Kayla and Eric had to take care of a lot more pressing things. Until she had something workable squared away, she preferred to keep it her secret.

The next time she walked into the library, she felt a renewed jolt of success from her discussion. She still hoped she'd get the promotion, but either way, she knew she'd knocked that program out of the park.

The desk phone beeped with the ring of an internal call. Glancing at the caller ID, she saw it was John. Her heart rate picked up immediately. This was it. She was finally going to find out one way or the other.

"This is Paige."

"Hi Paige, could you pop by my office in a minute? I'm going to have someone come out and cover the desk for you."

"Yep. Be right there."

One of the children's librarians came out and Paige set off to seal her fate.

John and Christie were chatting in lowered voices when Paige walked in.

"Why don't you grab the door and have a seat." John smiled and gestured to the remaining empty chair.

She did as instructed and folded her hands in her lap to keep from fidgeting.

"Let's get right to it, shall we? We've been impressed with your work ever since you started here, but you really went above and beyond with revitalizing the book discussion program." He shuffled through her latest program evaluation forms and read a few out. "'I've never been to a book discussion before, but this wasn't what I expected. It was friendly, informative, and fun. Will come again.'

"'Very well organized. The questions were smart and encouraged great discussion.'

"'I loved having a Scottish dessert to go along with reading a Scottish author. I had a lot of fun.'

"And the list of praise goes on. You have a consistent track record of reliability and exemplary customer service. We'd like to offer you the full time position."

Paige was screaming with joy on the inside, but she distilled her excitement to an enthusiastic smile.

"That's great! I accept."

There was a little paperwork to fill out, and then Christie and John both shook her hand and congratulated her on a job well done.

Just as Paige was about to head out, Christie stopped her. "As a bonus for today, you don't have to do the rest of your desk shift. Get cracking on that next book discussion of yours."

"Thank you. I will!"

Paige hurried to her desk and pulled out her phone.

Paige

It didn't take long for James to reply.

James

Paige

James

Had Paige read that right?

> **Wait, what?**
>
> Paige

> **I was going to surprise you. Too excited. I'll be back tomorrow.**
>
> James

Paige thought the promotion was great news but it had nothing on the way James's news sent her through the stratosphere.

> **YOU ARE?!?!**
>
> Paige

> **Aye. Things are sorted here for now.**
>
> James

Paige was so excited she wanted to scream, but somehow she managed to keep it in. She wasn't thinking that there was still an expiration date on their time together. Her mind was filled with kisses and wood shavings and his beautiful blue eyes.

What time are you getting in? Do you need me to pick you up?

Paige

Beverly is going to get me. We have some things to talk about. As soon as I touch down, you'll be the first to know. I was thinking we could meet at my place?

James

I'll be there. I'm already ready.

Paige

Me too, my dear. I've missed you so much.

James

You have no idea how much I've missed you.

Paige

How she was going to focus for the rest of her shift was a mystery to Paige. Book discussions and collection development were the farthest things from her mind.

She texted Kayla and her parents with the news too.

Probably the only thing that would help her stand the hours until she could see James again was baby snuggles.

Wellll, if you're offering...

Kayla

Of course I'm offering. What do you need?

Paige

Kayla sent over a small list of essentials they were running out of in their post-baby haze. Paige was more than happy to help them out.

She may not have sorted out the bigger issues in her life, such as her future with James and where she was going to live, but she felt like the tide was turning anyway. Job security was hers and there was a sweet little baby waiting to see her anytime. It felt like anything was possible.

Twenty-Nine

SLEEP HAD BEEN A NEARLY impossible state. Her brain was too wired thinking that she'd actually gotten the promotion, marveling at how precious Amanda was, and that James would be back in mere hours. Who could sleep with a heady cocktail of joys like that?

It was a day off so she didn't have work to pass the time. A visiting nurse was supposed to stop by Kayla and Eric's to check on Kayla's healing and remove her stitches. The idea made Paige squirmy, so she was more than happy to stay away during that.

She needed to get out of her apartment or she'd spiral down the rabbit hole of checking the time every thirty seconds.

Grabbing her laptop, she did a search for apartments in the location she wanted within her new budget and set off for a day of apartment searching. It did a good job of keeping her mind occupied, especially when she managed to find something she could absolutely imagine herself living in. It was a wonderful upgrade from where she was. It had a balcony overlooking a manmade pond and a little green space, complete with a dog run for residents. She'd also have an in-room washer and dryer rather than having to cart her laundry to the basement to use the coin operated unit. She'd been so resistant to moving from her little place and here she'd found something even nicer that she was excited to claim for herself.

She stopped into the leasing office and filled out her application, with deposit, so it wouldn't slip through her fingers. The only hitch was that it wouldn't be available until three weeks after her current lease was up. It wasn't an outrageous amount of time. She knew Kayla and Eric would let her crash with them. Given the state of them when she'd visited, it looked like they'd truly appreciate some live-in help while they found their footing with a newborn. If they'd accept it, she'd pay them rent. If they didn't, she'd keep the house filled with groceries on her own dime.

It was dinnertime when she finally headed back to her place. Just as she was contemplating what to eat, her phone pinged. She couldn't get the phone out of her pocket fast enough.

I'm back. Are you free?

James

Paige had never typed so fast in her life.

Yes! Do you need dinner?

Paige

Bev stopped at a drive-through on the way back. I got something for you if you haven't eaten. I'm eager to see you.

James

Me too. I'm leaving now.

Paige

She had exaggerated a bit. Ever since her secret outing, she'd been planning exactly what she'd wear when she saw James again. She hurried to her closet and pulled out the dress she'd been saving. The seafoam green sundress had spaghetti straps and a ruched bust that framed her upper chest like a canvas, which was exactly what she was going for.

She quickly applied some coral lip gloss and touched up her hair. There wasn't time for a standard date night makeover. It was more important to be with James than to transform her look too much.

One final glance in the mirror and she dashed off so she wouldn't miss another minute with James.

She knocked on James's door, her heart hammering at her chest. The door opened quickly, as if he'd been standing right there waiting for her. As soon as she saw his face again it was like her entire being rushed forward to erase all space between them. Still, they hovered for a moment, just taking in the sight of each other.

At last, James's gaze lit on her collarbone and his eyes widened.

He pointed and stared at Paige incredulously. "Is this real?"

Paige nodded. "One hundred percent real."

A huge smile transformed James's face to pure joy and he pulled her into a tight embrace.

She snuggled her face into his neck and breathed deep of his soapy fresh scent. He must have just showered before she got there.

After they'd held each other for a bit, James stepped away to examine what Paige had done.

"You got a tattoo without me?"

Paige laughed. "Well, you weren't here and I was missing you badly. I looked at the book you'd given me and felt the necklace around my neck and I suddenly realized what I would want to have on my body permanently."

James's eyes shone with the depth of his emotion. He moved his face closer to her chest to examine the artist's handiwork. Paige had selected just a small image, a stylized Scottish thistle with Celtic knotwork as the stem and leaves. She'd had the knotwork done in black, just as James's was, and the head of the thistle was a lavender purple, like the real thing. To her, it was absolutely beautiful and the perfect reminder that James had been part of her life.

"I dinnae know what to say." James brushed his fingers lightly over the tattoo, sending a jolt of electricity throughout Paige's nerve endings. "Have I really inspired your first tattoo?"

Paige took James's hands in hers, understanding how lucky she was to have him in front of her, to be able to touch him again.

"It's felt like pure magic being with you this summer. We may live on opposite sides of an ocean, but this was something I could do to keep a piece of you with me always. Once I got the idea, I just knew I had to do it." She looked down, his intense gaze making her feel shy.

"That's amazing, Paige, but no' just because you got your first tattoo."

He stepped back a moment and pulled off his t-shirt. At first, Paige was confused, but he quickly turned around and patted his shoulder blade. There, beside the knots of his Celtic sleeve, was a new design.

Paige gasped and put her hands over her mouth.

There, in bold black ink was a perfect little representation of the Mackinac Bridge. It had been stylized to fit in next to his knotwork and it left Paige speechless.

"I guess we both had the same idea." James looked over his shoulder to see Paige's reaction.

She couldn't stop staring at the bridge, now a part of his skin forever.

James slowly turned back around and took Paige's hands from her mouth and kissed them.

"Come." He gently pulled her toward the couch. "There's something I need to tell you."

The tone of his voice was low and serious and it immediately made Paige's heart thump. She agreed that they needed to talk but she was a little afraid of what might need to be said. She tried to steel herself for whatever the conversation might be.

They sat on the edge of the couch turned inward toward each other. Knee to knee, James ran his hands through his gorgeous hair and blew out a breath. Paige quietly rested her hands in her lap, palms up, wondering what this conversation would mean for them.

"Is your uncle okay?" she asked before things could get any further along.

"Aye. He's well. I had a long talk with him before I left. And my ma too."

The words sent a shiver up Paige's spine. That definitely sounded like a very serious talk.

"Is that good?"

"Well, it definitely needed to happen. My uncle's heart attack put things in perspective for all of us. I hadnae seen my ma cry in a very long time but this did a number on her. David's her big brother and he's been her rock since my father left. It was scary for all of us."

Paige nodded silently. That all made sense.

"I didnae want to upset my uncle in his condition, but he broached the subject himself. He sent everyone else out o' the room and said, 'Jamie, how are you getting on in America?' So I told him everything. I explained how the art makes me feel alive, but more than that, how you make me feel alive. That I've never met a girl so charming, kind, and supportive and how all I want is to spend my time with you. I even told him how you helped Kayla have her baby. You dinnae shy away when people need help. When I was done talking, David looked me in the eye and said, 'Sounds like you love her.'"

James took Paige's hands in his and clutched them to his chest. She stared at him with trembling lips, not daring to speak yet.

"When he said it, I thought o' when you told me I was allowed to have my own dreams. You didnae mean I could have my own dreams as long as they fit in with everyone else's. You didnae mean I had to please everyone else. You meant I could follow my own path. And when that path led me back home, you took me to the airport without a second thought because you knew it was important for me to help my family. You make me feel like I'm capable, and good enough, and I just want to make you as happy as you make me."

He paused and looked deep into Paige's eyes. "He's right Paige Marie, I do love you."

She couldn't help it now. His earnest declaration, his strong hands in hers, the intensity in his blue eyes, it was too much to contain.

"I love you too, James." The words burst out without a hint of hesitation. "You've already made me a stronger person than I ever was before. I never could have driven the bridge without you by my side and I certainly wouldn't have gone to get this tattoo, but I'm so glad I did. You've expanded my world and the idea of what I can do. I'm totally in love with *you*…the wonderful person you are." She paused as reality crept in again. "But how is this ever going to work? I live here and you'll be working at your uncle's company there."

Tears spilled out as she succumbed to the highs and lows of emotion she was riding in quick succession.

James squeezed her hands.

"Dinnae cry, my love. That isnae all my uncle said. I said he was right; I do love you. That made him smile big. The first smile I'd seen from him in the hospital. 'Get your ma,' he said. So I did and he said to her, 'Lorna, I dinnae want your boy to take over my business.'"

Paige inhaled sharply, surprised and disbelieving at what she was hearing.

"What are you saying?"

"I'm saying David has given his blessing for me to let go o' the boat business. I had a lot o' long talks with Fiona too. I think she first planted the idea in David's mind that the business might no' be for me long-term. Fiona's braw. You'd get on with her."

Paige laughed incredulously, trying to keep up with what she was hearing. "I'd love to meet her one day."

"Aye. She'd like that. She's already a big fan o' yours. Anyway, I dinnae know what I'm going to do now, but my uncle finally understands that there are other options for the business."

"That's amazing, James!" Paige couldn't find the words for what she was feeling.

"Aye. David said the health scare made him realize he'd been putting off things that he intends to do as soon as he's feeling fit again. He figured my residency is like me doing things before it's too late and if I dinnae feel the business is for me, I shouldnae feel pressured to do it."

"And your mom didn't mind?"

James cocked his head.

"Well, I wouldnae say she was overjoyed, but she said if David and I were happy with the arrangement, then she was too."

"So who's going to take over the business?"

"It's no' clear yet although I did talk to the crew and sort some things before I came back here. There's a lot still to determine but I feel like a weight's been lifted off my chest."

Paige's mind was whirring with this new information. If James loved her, and didn't have to worry about the business anymore, what did that mean for them? Could it mean what she hoped it did?

Paige wrapped James in a giant hug. "I'm so happy you had a good talk with your family and you don't have to worry about that anymore."

James squeezed her tight and kissed the side of her face.

"Aye. Something very good has come out of a scary time."

After a good cuddle, Paige finally dared to ask the question that was really on her mind.

"But where does that leave us?"

"I've still got things to take care of, but I mean to stay. If you'd like me to, o' course."

Her heart lifted on tremulous wings.

"Are you kidding me?" Paige threw her arms around James again. "I could hardly stand having you gone. I never want to do that again."

James chuckled into her hair. "I hoped you'd feel that way. You've absolutely changed my life."

"And you've changed mine. I'm so happy, I could drive over an enormous bridge right this minute and not even be nervous!"

"Should we go find one?"

Paige shook her head and pulled out of the hug to look James in his sparkling eyes.

"No. I'd rather kiss you until morning."

"Me too."

Finally, they melted into a kiss that promised all the hope of a new future together.

Thirty

THE BIG NIGHT HAD ARRIVED. Paige slipped into a little black dress that showed off her new tattoo and strappy red sandals for the reception before James's exhibit. She stood in front of the bathroom mirror, applying her makeup. It was finally his moment and she was so excited to see him shine.

Her phone pinged with a new text. Satisfied that she'd done the best she could with her makeup, she grabbed her phone.

What are you wearing tonight?

Kayla

My black cocktail dress. Why?

Paige

I don't fit into mine anymore. Probably should have figured this out a few days ago.

Kayla

I'm just dressing for the reception. You don't have to go that fancy for the public exhibit.

Paige

That's good. I have a maternity skirt that still fits. It'll have to do.

Kayla

James is going to be so happy you're there.

Paige

We won't stay long. Hoping Amanda sleeps through it, but we have to support James.

Kayla

Paige loved that James fit in so well to their little group.
She glanced at the time and took one more look at her reflection.
"Showtime."

Since James had last minute things to take care of at the gallery, they'd arranged for her to meet him at the reception. She grabbed her little black sequined wristlet, a black shrug, and headed out for the night.

The gallery was in a different location than the studio so she wasn't expecting the smart, modern building she pulled up to. She walked around back, as James had instructed. The reception was being held in a beautiful outdoor patio area covered with a flowery pergola. The pergola was gorgeously draped with morning glory vines. A jazz trio was set up in one corner to provide classy ambient music.

She quickly spotted James, the center of a small group of men and women who were patting him on the back, undoubtedly congratulating him for a job well done. He wore black dress pants with a charcoal gray button down shirt with a black tie. He looked handsome and confident.

This is his world, she thought, looking at his glowing face. Seeing him so happy and the object of everyone's affection filled her with pride and admiration. Against all odds, he'd made it to this night. It was his time to shine and Paige felt like the luckiest woman alive to share it with him.

He looked up, saw her watching him, and excused himself from the group to greet her with a hug and a light kiss on the cheek.

"You look incredible."

"Thank you." She linked her arm through his. "I saw you holding court over there. They were hanging on your every word."

"It's the accent," he joked. "They cannae understand me unless they pay close attention."

James could see the protest in her eyes, so he moved his arm around her waist and led her over to the group.

"I'd like to introduce you to my girlfriend, Paige. She's a librarian at the local library here. She's so good, she just got a promotion."

The group looked at her with feigned interest and a smattering of "Congratulations" and "Good for you."

"Paige, these are the folks I had to impress to get here. You've already met Beverly Streeter, and here's Ben Erston, Russ Greenwald, and Keya Bhattacharji."

Paige shook hands around the group, feeling a little out of her depth. They certainly nailed the eccentric artist stereotype. Beverly had her hair free this evening, the wavy gray strands stopped nearly at her elbows. She had an ankle length navy blue dress with a light knit wrap in rainbow colors. Ben had black plastic glasses that matched his black hair and goatee. He wore khaki pants, black suspenders, and a light blue oxford shirt with a bright orange bow tie. Russ had his brown hair pulled into a neat ponytail. His glasses were wire framed and reminded her of something Ben Franklin would have worn. His shirt was a purple, green, and white paisley pattern with forest green pants. Keya's outfit was the most breathtaking to Paige's eye. She wore a short sleeved shell blouse in a deep ruby color. Her skirt matched perfectly, red with gold brocade. Her left arm was practically a sleeve of delicate gold bangles.

She felt like she and James were appropriately dressed compared to the others, but she wished she'd thought to put a little more artistic flair into her own ensemble. Oh well. Live and learn.

Conversation went back to art techniques and artists Paige had never heard of. If they'd been talking about books, she would have had plenty of names to drop and opinions to give, but she mostly nodded and smiled. She was pleasantly surprised to see a new side to James as he held his own in the conversation. He mentioned artists he'd seen back home that the others hadn't heard of and they seemed genuinely interested in his thoughts and opinions on their work.

Paige excused herself to get a drink and some hors d'oeuvres. There was another little group congregating around the food table. When Paige walked up to get her food, a woman in a wide-legged, white jumpsuit with a halter top and a tight geometric bob did a double take of her.

"Oh my gosh!" The woman exclaimed. "That's amazing."

Paige would have assumed that the woman was talking to or about someone else, except that she couldn't stop staring at her.

"Excuse me?" Paige asked.

"I'm Miki." The woman walked over and shook Paige's hand. "I'm one of the other residents alongside James this summer. He does incredible work. You must be pretty close."

"I'm his girlfriend." Paige wondered what in the world Miki was alluding to. She might have thought jealousy, but the woman's eyes were wide with curiosity, not narrowed to size her up.

"Ah, that explains it." Miki nodded appreciatively.

"I'm sorry, I have no idea what you're talking about."

Miki laughed. "I guess that is pretty cryptic. Sorry, but you'll see soon enough."

"Okay." Paige took her plate of refreshments and made her way back to James, thinking about how eccentric creatives could be. She didn't mind though. She'd had far stranger conversations with patrons at the library.

"Sorry, I should have gotten that for you," James whispered in her ear when she came back.

"This is your night. Don't you worry about a thing."

"No excuse no' to take care of my girl, but you're wonderful. You know that?" He gave her another kiss on the cheek and turned back to the conversation.

"Well, James—" Beverly looked at her watch. "I think your public is ready to see what you've done for them. Shall we?"

James clasped his hands in front of him and looked toward the studio doors.

"This is it!"

Paige detected a nervous edge to his voice and she slipped her hand into his and squeezed. He turned to look at her and she gave him a reassuring smile.

"I can't wait to see how everything turned out. Relax. This is going to be great."

"We'll see." He walked into the studio, holding Paige's hand for support.

Once they got inside, Paige felt like they were walking the red carpet before the Oscars. There were photographers from the local college newspapers and the Ann Arbor News. There were pedestals around the room with art on them, but Paige didn't want to look at them yet. She wanted to wait until James got a moment to show her around a little himself.

Beverly, who was definitely in charge of the whole thing, went to talk to the photographers and reporters quickly before guiding James up to the front door of the building. There was a nice crowd of people gathered outside and James tensed next to Paige when he caught sight of them.

"Relax." She squeezed his hand again. "They're going to love you."

"We're about to find out."

"Let me just steal him for a moment." Beverly cut in and led James to the left side of the gallery, into a small gathering area.

"Go ahead and open the doors," Beverly instructed and Russ did the honors.

He and the other two people who had been in James's group shepherded the crowd into the gathering area, "For artist remarks."

She hadn't known James was going to speak. In fact, she didn't really know what was going to happen, other than seeing his pieces. She'd been to art museums, of course, but never an exhibition like this before. It was an all-new experience.

After everyone gathered into the room and became reasonably quiet, Beverly switched on a portable microphone and got things underway.

"Thank you everyone, for coming tonight. I'm Beverly Streeter, head of the residency selection committee this year. It always makes my heart happy to see such a good crowd out to appreciate the various perspectives that art gives us. It is my great pleasure to introduce you to tonight's artists. First, we have James MacKinnon. When the panel and I received his application, we instantly knew we had the opportunity to accept someone truly unique for this year's artist residency. The artwork had high technical quality, of course, but the great emotion of the pieces was evident, even from the photographs. Art is a subjective experience, but all four of us could admit we'd been touched when we saw this application and we wanted to see what else this fine artist could do right here in Ann Arbor, Michigan. Of course, the competition was fierce, but we kept coming back to his work. It just resonated with us and I'm very pleased to introduce you to the man who touched us all with his artistic vision, Mr. James MacKinnon."

The room erupted into applause, Paige clapping the most enthusiastically of them all.

James reluctantly made his way to the front and took the microphone from Beverly, who was positively beaming at him.

He looked out over the small group gathered before him and ran a hand through his hair.

"I dinnae know what to say. When I applied for this, I was hoping for a chance to see a wee bit o' the world and do my art. Now, seeing you all here, I'm very grateful. It's been a lot o' hard work this summer and I hope you'll enjoy it. And while I'm up here, I'd like to thank Beverly, Ben, Russ, and Keya for the opportunity to be here. This trip has honestly changed my life. I'll never forget it and I'll always be grateful. And also, I must thank my beautiful girlfriend, Paige, for showing me the meaning of kindness and grace. The art tonight wouldnae be what it is without you. Thank you."

A few heads turned to find Paige in the crowd, but she kept her eyes glued to James. She never expected that she'd merit a mention in his work for the exhibit and she was touched by it. Since she couldn't be by his side that moment, she blew him a kiss. He smiled at her and handed the microphone back to Beverly.

Beverly introduced the other three artists, including Miki, who had greeted her so strangely before. They gave their talks but Paige couldn't take her eyes off of James.

"All right everyone." Beverly gestured to the side of the room. "As you can see, the entrance to the gallery is on your right. The Ninth Annual Ann Arbor Arts Council Residency Program exhibit is officially open. Please take your time and enjoy all the pieces. Our artists will be circulating and mingling, so be sure to let them know if you have any questions, and lastly, everyone have a great evening."

There was a smattering of light applause and the murmuring that all groups of people seem to be shrouded in. Most of the group moved into the gallery space, but a few people were already congregating around James and the other artists. Paige moved off to the side with the intention of waiting for James, but Miki appeared in front of her.

"That was so sweet. There's nothing more heartwarming than a guy who's totally into his woman and isn't afraid to say it."

"Yeah." Paige nodded. "I had no idea he was going to say anything about me. It was a nice surprise."

"Hey, since James is occupied, do you want to look around at the art with me?"

Paige glanced over at James again, the group around him only getting bigger.

"Don't you want to talk to the others?" Paige noticed a group that had their eye on Miki.

Miki shook her head. "Not yet. I'd rather see your face when you notice."

Again, this woman was a little odd, but not unpleasant, so Paige just decided to go with it.

They headed into the gallery together and Paige tried to make small talk.

"What kind of art do you do?"

"Pottery. I went to a lot of museums as a child and I was always drawn to the ancient pottery exhibits. By the time I got to middle school, I decided to try making it myself."

"That's cool. I think I've seen your space. I walked past a spot with a pottery wheel on the way to James's."

"Yeah, that's mine. Close to the front door."

"I never saw you in there. I would have remembered that cool haircut."

Miki's face lit up in a genuine smile as she reached up to touch her hair.

"Thank you. I like to make a statement."

They approached the first pedestal in James's collection with a small wooden ship on it. Paige recognized it as the piece James had been working on that first time she visited the studio. It could easily fit in the palm of her hand, but James had also carved a large base of waves around it. The boat itself was very detailed, but the waves were a level of intricacy that blew her away. She could see movement in the rippling cut of the wood. It called to mind the crashing of waves and the sensation of being tossed around by the might of the sea. How he'd achieved it was a mystery to her. It was no wonder he'd landed the residency with work like that.

"Are you an artist too?" Miki asked as they made their way over to the next pedestal.

"Oh no. I'm a librarian."

As if on cue, a small group walked over to Paige to say hi. They were from her last book discussion program, including regulars Phil and Judy.

"Hey you guys! That's so sweet of you to come. Did you get to talk to James yet? He'll be so happy you came out for this."

Judy was all wide-eyes and smiles. "We wanted to see what he was all about. And wow, that one of you is amazing, isn't it?"

"What?" A shock spread up Paige's spine.

Miki smiled knowingly next to her. "That's what I was talking about earlier. You gotta see it."

"You haven't seen it yet?" If Judy had been wearing pearls, she would have clutched them in surprise. "Oh, I haven't spoiled the surprise, have I?"

"You're the potter." Phil pointed at Miki. "Do you sell any of your work? That green vase you made would look just lovely in our living room."

"Meet me over there. I have to show Paige what we're all talking about first."

Miki led Paige past the pedestal they were approaching and around to the other side of the room. There, Paige found herself eye to eye with a wooden bust that was undeniably her. He'd managed to match the curve of her eyes and lips. She was astounded by the level of detail he'd brought out of the wood. The two Paiges stared at each other in wordless silence.

"See what I mean?" Miki stood back and folded her arms as she admired the piece. "He captured your likeness perfectly. He's very talented."

Paige was struck speechless by the piece. He was supposed to be paying tribute to his heritage with his artwork, and here, he'd taken the time to immortalize her. She was still staring at it when she felt a tap on her shoulder.

"Sorry, we're a little late. What a great turnout. James must be so proud."

Kayla stood before her with Amanda in an olive green baby wrap, which was color coordinated with Kayla's white blouse and olive green skirt. Eric was close behind her looking around at the crowd and the artwork.

Paige gave Kayla and the baby a careful hug.

"I'm so glad you guys are here. Look at this!" She turned and pointed to her wooden likeness. "I had no idea he made this."

"That's incredible!" Kayla exclaimed. "It looks exactly like you!"

"Wow!" Eric leaned in to get a better look. "Look at the detail. I don't even know how you'd do this with wood."

"But it's me!" Paige held her arms out to the bust like she was going to lay her hands on either side of it. "I can't believe he made me as part of his exhibit."

Kayla smiled and put a hand on Paige's arm. "Of course he did. He really loves you."

"Aye, I do." James put his hands on Paige's shoulders and squeezed. "What do you think? It's nowhere near as beautiful as the original."

Paige whirled around.

"I don't know what to say! I never dreamed you'd carve me. It's amazing!"

James smiled. "What can I say? You inspire me. I cannae get you out o' my mind so I decided I might as well go with it. It did turn out rather well, I think."

"Understatement of the year!" Paige said.

Kayla laughed. "We just got here, but I'm going to go out on a limb and say this is my favorite piece in the whole exhibit."

"I didnae know you were planning to come. You've got your hands full with the wee one here."

"We wouldn't miss it." Eric clapped James on the back. "Besides, gave us a nice excuse to get out of the house for something other than a quick grocery run or a pediatrician appointment."

"Anyway, congratulations." Kayla surveyed the room. "Look at the crowd here! Do you feel famous?"

James looked down, like a bashful boy.

"No. I'm surprised all these people came out. It's a bit of a shock."

A pedestal with a carved seagull holding a loop of rope was drawing Eric's attention. "You've got talent, man," Eric said. "It's no wonder they brought you here to do this."

"Thanks." James colored slightly from all the praise. "I'm glad you're enjoying it."

The group from the library swept in to catch James's attention, so Paige and her friends stepped aside to let James mingle with his new fans.

Miki had moved to the outskirts of the group to let them talk, but she was still close by. Paige made a quick round of introductions between them.

"I love your vibe." Kayla took in Miki's whole ensemble with an impressed smile. "Are you an artist too or just an art lover?"

Miki filled Kayla in on her work. While they chatted, Eric quietly led the group over to the seagull statue that had caught his eye.

On closer inspection, the seagull was carved but the rope in its beak was real. There was also a base of rocks around the gull's feet. Just looking at it made Paige feel like she was at the beach. She could practically smell the breeze coming off the water, feel the wet sand between her toes, and hear seagulls screeching. For a deceptively simple piece, it really resonated.

James's final piece took up nearly the length of a wall. Free standing arms were carved to assemble an interlocking wooden boat frame. It was like watching workers' arms, frozen in time, on a project that would never be finished. The arms were strong but scarred. Working man's hands that James had somehow managed to carve out of chunks of wood. Paige marveled at the workmanship and the emotion that the piece conveyed. Looking at it made her feel like the workmen weren't valued as people, only as muscles and labor. Like this, they could never work hard enough or fast enough to get the job done. She wasn't sure if that was James's intent in making the piece, but at least it made her feel something. All of his pieces had elicited an emotional response from her. She didn't feel that way strolling through an art museum. Only some of the pieces broke through their medium to touch her heart and mind, but James had done it with all of his. Even if he hadn't been her boyfriend, his exhibit would have impressed her.

"I'm going to go find that guy who wants to buy my vase. It was nice meeting you guys." Miki bowed out of the group and headed over to her green vase where Phil was still admiring every angle of it.

Kayla glanced down at the baby sleeping on her chest. Eric draped his arm around her shoulders and squeezed her close.

"You about ready to go?"

"Yeah. Sorry, Paige. I still get sore if I walk around too much. I think we need to head back to our cave."

"That's okay. Thanks so much for coming out. I know that's a big thing with a newborn." Paige leaned in for a group hug with all three of the DuPont family. "I'll be over to visit again soon, if you're up for it."

"Anytime. Really. You've known me long enough. You're allowed to see the horror of new baby house."

"It wasn't that bad."

"Things change hourly." Kayla gave her a 'you don't wanna know' look.

Pleasant goodbyes were exchanged all around and Paige wandered off to find James again.

He was in the process of being interviewed in front of the piece with the arms.

Beverly noticed Paige standing off to the side and came over to talk to her.

"You must be so proud of him." Beverly smiled.

"I am. He's really done an outstanding job on all of these pieces. I can't believe he did all this in less than eight weeks."

"He certainly flourished at this residency. I suspect he's been very inspired." She cast a knowing glance at Paige.

Paige couldn't help but blush under the insinuation. She couldn't deny she'd had at least some influence on his work. Her wooden double was all the proof necessary.

"No need to be shy." Beverly patted Paige's arm. "Every artist needs their muse."

"Oh, I'm no muse," Paige said. "He's been making art long before he met me."

"Don't underestimate the importance of being in the right place at the right time."

"Any chance you could keep him on for another year or so?" Paige asked.

Beverly smiled knowingly but didn't say anything.

The interviewers were wrapping up with James and he gestured for Paige to come join him.

Paige stepped away from Beverly. "Excuse me. The artist is beckoning."

"By all means."

James wrapped Paige in a hug when she made it back to him.

"Tonight's been too busy. I haven't been able to see enough of my girl."

Paige hugged James tight.

"Everyone wants to bask in your glory. You really did an amazing job on all these pieces."

"You really like them?" James asked.

"Of course I do! There's so much emotion in all of them. Each one makes me feel something. They tell a story. I don't know if I'm getting the exact story you intended, but I'm definitely getting something."

"Honestly? I cannae think of higher praise than that."

"I'm glad everyone got to see how talented you are. And now you're going to be in the papers. Even more people will hear about you. You'll take Michigan and then the world by storm!"

"I dinnae know about that, but I'm happy for tonight. I'm glad you're here with me."

They looked around the room. The crowds were thinning but there were still a few clumps of people admiring the pieces on display.

"Hey, are you ready to take off?" James murmured in her ear.

"Now? There are still people here."

James shrugged. "There's only one person I want to be with now."

Paige couldn't argue with that.

Thirty-One

PAIGE SAT at the reference desk, trying not to resent that she had to be at work instead of being with James.

"Hey, what happened to that sunny smile of yours?"

Paige looked up from the computer to see Norm standing in front of her, as he'd done so many times before. This time, thank goodness, he was wearing a reasonable outfit of knee length jean shorts and an appropriately fitting t-shirt.

She gritted her teeth into the approximation of a smile. "I'm just sitting here working. Not much to smile about."

"You know," Norm continued, "I haven't seen that foreign guy of yours around here lately. He was a little pushy."

"Is there something I can help you with?" Paige asked. Her days of humoring Norm were long gone and she was absolutely not going to talk to him about James.

"Did you ever watch that show I told you you'd like?"

Paige sighed. For a minute, she thought she'd be held captive by Norm for the next twenty minutes. Then she thought about what she'd accomplished. She didn't have to sit here and take whatever Norm wanted to dish out. She was the type of woman who drove over five mile long suspension bridges. She went out and got a tattoo all by herself because she felt like it. She could set boundaries too and today was the day to do it.

"Listen, Norm, I don't like true crime and I'm not interested in that show. I also have a lot of work to do when I'm here because this is my job. If you don't have a library related question I can help you with, I really need to get back to my work."

She looked Norm square in the eye to show she was serious and not messing around with him anymore. He stared back, incredulous.

"You were a whole lot friendlier before." Norm humphed and turned to take his place in the computer area.

Inside, Paige was celebrating. Why had it taken her so long to stand up for herself? She may still have some training ahead of her since she'd let Norm walk over her for too long, but this felt like the start of a brand new, empowered, Paige.

She was still congratulating herself for her small victory and didn't even look up when her peripheral vision caught the movement of a patron approaching the desk.

"Excuse me, Miss, is this where I get a library caird?"

Startled, Paige looked up into James's grinning face.

"I thought you were busy cleaning up at the studio. What are you doing here?"

"Well, I'm hoping to get a library caird."

Paige looked at his poker face, utterly confused. "What are you doing?"

"Can you tell me what I'd need to get a caird here?"

Paige stared at James, completely unsure what was going on, but her years of library service kicked in anyway. "Um, yes. A photo ID and some sort of proof of address."

"Hmm. So this wouldnae be good enough then?" James pulled something out of his pocket with a flourish and handed it to Paige.

"What's this?" she asked, looking from the folded paper in her hand to James's face.

"I think if you open it up, it'll all become clearer."

Paige slowly unfolded the paper with sweaty palms. Whatever James was doing, she wasn't quite following.

In her hands, she held a copy of a work visa application, dated a week prior. She also held an employment contract for the community college.

Her mouth dropped open, as her mind and heart warred with each other to reconcile what she was seeing.

"Will that do?" James asked.

"How? When?" Paige couldn't get out a complete thought as her mind reeled trying to comprehend what she was seeing.

James smiled broadly. "When Beverly picked me up from the airport, we talked about why I'd left and what I'd discussed with David. She said she might be able to get me a part-time lecturer job at the community college if I'd like. I dinnae have any teaching experience but she said she'd help me. Turns out she was an art teacher before she retired and became president o' the Arts Council. She knows a lot of people and she did it. I'll be teaching my first woodworking course in the fall semester. I'll still need to get a place, but I can worry about that later."

"A place to stay?" The idea was coming to Paige in a rush and flying out of her mouth before she could think about it.

"I didn't tell you I didn't renew the lease on my apartment. I'm getting a new place myself at the end of August. Maybe we could…"

Now it was James's turn to stare at Paige incredulously.

"Are you asking if I'd stay with you?"

Paige bit her lip, worried that maybe she'd gone too far too fast. What was it about James that just made her blurt out rash decisions?

"I just thought since we're both in need of a place—"

"And we'll be spending most of our time together anyway. It makes sense." An adorable smile spread over James's face. "I would love to live with you, if that's really what you want."

"We can talk about it more, but I'm definitely up for it." Paige couldn't believe this was happening. She'd have to hug Beverly the next time she saw her, which she hoped would be soon.

"Excuse me." Sylvia peered around James's shoulder. "Could you help me on the computer?"

Paige shook her head. "I'll be back in a minute." She got up, came around the desk and grabbed James's hand. She pulled him right out the front door of the library.

"Are you ok—" James tried to ask, but she was all too happy to stop that in its tracks with a passionate kiss. James threaded his fingers into her hair and kissed her back deeply. Paige released all of her pent up anxiety about how things would end up between her and James. Pregnant Kayla had been right all along. Her perfect man had been just around the corner and she never would have found him if things hadn't turned out as they had with Dylan. To think, she'd thought her prospects were ending, but the best was yet to come.

When they pulled away, Paige looked into James's eyes with a big smile on her face.

"This is the best summer of my life."

James cupped Paige's face in his hands.

"It's only the beginning, my love."

She couldn't wait to write the rest of the story. Together.

Acknowledgments

Quite a few years ago, Karen and I were circulation clerks at a public library. A very handsome man, with a gorgeous New Zealand accent, walked in and asked her about getting a library card. My dear readers, I've seen many reviewers who enjoy trashing the "instalove" trope. I assure you, on the day Rhys set eyes on Karen, everyone could see that love at first sight is real. It wasn't even directed at us, but we could all hear the symphony playing and see the sun shining when those two were together. Not only did Rhys get his library card, but he truly found the love of his life.

It was an honor for me to see their real-life romance unfold. I was an aspiring writer then, and the two of them always told me I should write their love story someday. Now, Paige and James are not meant to actually portray Karen and Rhys, but I hope I managed to capture that same beauty of discovering your soulmate in an unexpected place. Even in a different country!

I'll never forget that incredible time. You two will always hold a special place in my heart.

I also owe a big thank you to Derek R. King and Kiley Dunbar for being my Scotland consultants. I was very concerned with James being an authentic character and not an Americanized stereotype. The input from Derek and Kiley was priceless to me. Thank you so much for answering my questions and suggesting dialogue tweaks. I hope I'll make it over to Scotland one of these days and I can thank you in person.

Chloe Massarello and Heather Hollister cleaned up the embarrassing mistakes authors never want readers to know we make. I am so grateful for your help. I can't thank you enough.

Gigantic thanks go to my husband, Jeff. Thank you for supporting this crazy dream of mine, even when it's frustrating.

About the Author

Alana Oxford is a Michigan author of romcoms, sweet romance, and humorous women's fiction. She wants her stories to bring sunshine and smiles to her readers. She enjoys improv comedy, moody music, everything book related, and has an ongoing love affair with the United Kingdom.

Connect with me:
https://www.sjlomas.com/alana-oxford

Subscribe to my newsletter:
http://eepurl.com/hv4fRb

Thank you for reading this book. If you have a moment, please leave a review on your favorite review website to let other readers know what you think. Thank you so much!

 twitter.com/AlanaOxford

 instagram.com/AlanaOxford

tiktok.com/@alanaoxford

Blue Skies: A Sweet Romcom Novella

"I loved this sweet romance! The chemistry between Seth and Patrice was palpable, and I was rooting for them from the beginning."

LACIE WALDON AUTHOR OF *FROM THE JUMP.*

"I couldn't put it down! It was just what I needed, to get lost in a story with characters I couldn't get enough of, taking me on a journey of wild fun and romance."

ALLYSON MARTINEK, MORNING HOST 100.3 WNIC AND AUTHOR OF *LIVING ON AIR.*

Life isn't always a walk in the park, but when Patrice takes her Pomeranians to the park after a rough day at the office, fate steps in. An unlikely hero comes to the rescue when one of her dogs gets loose. Short, pale, and kind of cute,

Seth doesn't have a lot of confidence with the ladies, but he hits it off with Patrice. But some things might be too good to be true. While Patrice wonders if Seth could possibly be "the one", fate steps in again with a horrible twist. Will it be a deal breaker or just a storm before bright blue skies?

FORTHCOMING TITLES:

MY MODERN MIDLIFE CRISIS

www.ingramcontent.com/pod-product-compliance
Lightning Source LLC
Chambersburg PA
CBHW021642110726
47902CB00007B/1796